D1112592

Beat Up a Cookie

Other Walker and Company Titles by Denise Dietz

Throw Darts at a Cheesecake

Beat Up a Cookie

An Ellie Bernstein / Lt. Peter Miller Mystery

Denise Dietz

Walker and Company
New York

This book is for my kids
Sandi, Jon, and Glen
and for
Alan Alda

First published in the United States of America in 1994
by Walker Publishing Company, Inc.

Published simultaneously in Canada by Thomas Allen & Son
Canada, Limited, Markham, Ontario

Library of Congress Cataloging-in-Publication Data
Dietz, Denise.
Beat up a cookie: an Ellie Bernstein/Lt. Peter Miller mystery / Denise Dietz.
        p.   cm.
            ISBN 0-8027-3186-4
              I. Title.
         PS3554.I368B4   1994
       813'.54—dc20   93-45646
                                CIP

Printed in the United States of America
2 4 6 8 10 9 7 5 3 1

$\triangledown$

Prologue

March 7, 1983

THE SOLDIERS APPEARED fatigued.

For eleven days straight their unit had been served liver and fish for lunch.

"If I eat one more fish, I'll develop gills," said the tall, handsome captain. "I've had so much liver, I can only make love if I'm smothered in bacon and onions." He began to speculate about the perfect lunch. "There was a place in Chicago, near the Dearborn Street Station, can't even think of its name, but the ribs—the best in the world."

Haunted by his vision, the captain finally discovered that the restaurant was called Adam's Ribs. He managed to phone stateside, then arranged for his order to be delivered by plane.

MPs were told that urgent medical supplies should be routed immediately, and the food was overnighted to Korea. Within twenty-four hours, the officers of the 4077 M*A*S*H unit were feasting on ribs and . . .

Hawkeye forgot to order the coleslaw, thought Eleanor Bernstein, picturing the vivid scene from her favorite TV show. She nearly drove past Charley Aaronson's Dew Drop Inn but caught herself in time and, instead, slowly maneuvered across a couple of entrance tittie-bumps.

Coleslaw. Ribs. Yum!

Parking her Continental between a Chevy pickup and three listing motorcycles, Ellie heard her stomach growl. Even though she'd just finished her own feast of veal saltimbocca, ravioli alla pesto, and chocolate cheesecake.

"When you reach the ripe old age of thirty-three," she murmured, "a slip of the lips is a pound on the hips. Calories and cheating both begin with the letter *C*."

Her husband Tony was cheating at this very moment.

So Ellie had cheated with food. To hell with her diet. She'd start a new one *next* Monday, granted that she always started her diets on Mondays. Sometimes she even lasted (and fasted) until Tuesday.

Now she glanced through her car window at the congested parking lot. The Dew Drop must be stuffed with bodies. What a terrific location for a gangland massacre. Al Pacino and his scarfaced thugs would be sitting ducks, dead ducks, or pressed duck saturated with rosemary-garlic sauce.

On the other hand, *one* person could commit the perfect murder, then disappear into the crowd. How? Why? The only thing Ellie devoured more avidly than food was a scintillating mystery.

Okay, she thought, let's hypothesize the perfect murder. Time of day? Night. The moon was a mere sliver of lemon cake; its glow wouldn't give the perpetrator away.

Victim? Well, she didn't want to ponder that aspect. Perfect crimes were fun; victims were not. Unless the victim was fictitious. Or already dead. Yes, already dead was good. Tennessee Williams had died last month, February 25. Although she admired his work, Ellie didn't know Williams personally. He'd do just fine.

Motive? A psychopathic actor auditions for a role in *Cat on a Hot Tin Roof.* Rejected, he blames it all on Williams, then furtively follows the famous playwright to Colorado Springs, Colorado.

Scene of the crime? The Dew Drop's rectangular gray cement building was sandwiched between a defunct Catholic school and a newly constructed souvenir shop and had once been a family restaurant called Costilla de Adam.

Plot? The killer stalks Williams and knifes him. No, too much blood. Strangles him, disappears into the crowd . . .

then what? Then the police would discover the motive, the perpetrator, and what the hell was Tennessee Williams doing in Colorado Springs anyway?

Okay, enough fictitious mystery. Time for reality.

Ellie pulled the key from her ignition. Reality was husband Tony, a real estate broker who at this very moment was screwing his new client. Ellie had accidentally overheard a phone conversation between Tony and his friend Dave, a journalist. "She's young, slender, and hot to trot," Tony had bragged. "You should see the carpet burns on my ass, Dave."

Hurt and furious, Ellie had baked a batch of chocolate chip cookies, Tony's favorite, then hidden them inside her closet so that Tony couldn't find them.

Tonight her nine-year-old son, Michael, was sleeping over at a schoolmate's house, leaving Ellie free to indulge in her high-calorie, albeit lonely, meal. However, the food-equals-revenge ritual at Uncle Vinnie's Gourmet Italian Restaurant had lasted too long, and she'd never make it home before the start of "M*A*S*H"'s eleventh-season finale. Thus she had decided to detour, visit Charley's lounge. Charley had several televisions suspended from the ceiling, looking, thought Ellie, like black spiders with bloated bellies.

Inside, the Dew Drop resembled a Mobile Army Surgical Hospital unit. Most men and women wore olive-drab T-shirts and matching pants. Ellie felt alien in low-heeled pumps, black A-line skirt, and a silk overblouse one shade brighter than her auburn hair.

Charley Aaronson had advertised a M*A*S*H-Bash party, offering "cash prize money" for the best 4077 look-alikes, and the public had responded enthusiastically. Charley must be breaking every fire law, Ellie thought, then saw that the fire chief was in attendance, along with practically everybody else under the sun. Moon. Except Tony. But Tony had other fish to fry. Or ribs to nibble.

"Hi, Charley," Ellie shouted. "Business is booming."

"Eleanor, can you believe this crowd already? All these meshuga pipples." He swished at his perspiring face with the edge of his apron. "Looks like Yankee Stadium on a doubleheader afternoon."

"An afternoon with two heads? You sound like Casey Stengel."

Ellie smiled fondly at her friend. Charley's bald pate sported an ill-fitting toupee styled after his hero John F. Kennedy's hair. Every night Charley patrolled the Dew Drop, a benevolent vulture, his magnificent hooked nose sniffing out underage invaders. Ellie surmised that Charley's mind was as sharp as the knife he used to slice his fruit garnishes. Yet customers tended to relax in his presence, lulled by his seemingly inane remarks. There was no drug dealing at the Dew Drop; except for the inevitable Sunday football pools, no illegal betting. There had never been one hint of trouble inside Charley's establishment.

"So why ain't you in costume, Eleanor?"

"I didn't have time to change clothes."

"You shoulda come as Hot Mouth." Framed by a shelf of liquor bottles, Charley leaned across the bar's surface. "You know, that fercockteh nurse played by what's-her-name."

"Loretta Swit, and it's Hot *Lips*, Charley."

"So with the right clothes and yellow hair, you'd be a dead ringer."

"Are you kidding? I'd have to lose at least fifty pounds."

"I think you look fine."

"That's because you have to lose weight, too. Maybe we should join one of those groups, Overeaters Anonymous or Weight Winners."

"I tried Weight Winners. It didn't work. So I'm a dropout, so sue me." Charley patted his enormous belly, shouted "More of me to love!" then reached behind his back for a cushioned barstool. "Here's an extra seat. Rest your tush next to the screen. Have a drink on me. Toasted Almonds? White Russian?"

"Holy cow, Charley, you have a memory like a sponge. White Russian, please." Ellie plopped her fortysome-thing-inch tush down on the stool, then reached toward a bowl of pretzels. "Why didn't Weight Winners work?"

"Who wants to give up food because it's fattening?" Charley's eyes widened. "*Mein Gott,* the tables and chairs are pushed together. My waitresses have to schlep on air. S'cuse me, Eleanor." Scooting out from behind the bar, he was immediately surrounded by several new arrivals.

Where on earth will you put them? Ellie sipped her White Russian while she studied the room. Frazzled cocktail servers wore black shorts and yellow halter tops. They resembled bumblebees swarming in confusion. Spilled drinks and popcorn made a slushy snowscape beneath Charley's utilitarian furniture.

An elbow almost dented Ellie's left shoulder.

"Sorr-eee." The young owner of the elbow smiled impishly. Her blond wig had loosened, and she was attempting to secure it with bobby pins. Her motion was off balance, her hazel eyes unfocused.

"Are you all right?" asked Ellie.

"Sure, fine."

"Do you want to sit down?"

"Nope, thanks. My name's Ginny, but t'night I'm Hot Lips Hoo—Hool—Hool'gan." She held up a tall glass with five cherries swimming amid melting ice cubes. "Rum punch. Had myself teensy bit lots to drink. Add cherry to each new glass so's I can keep count." Unbuttoning the top of her shirt, she added, "Warm in here. Hey, I'll confess next week. Catholic, y'know? Nice to meetcha."

Ginny staggered a few steps away until she bumped into a mustached soldier who halted her advance by caressing her breasts. She giggled and leaned forward, molding her body against his hands. "You like gin, mister? Let's trade. Order me a rum punch an' I'll letcha drink Gin."

Embarrassed, Ellie swiveled her stool and glanced toward the nearest ceiling-mounted television. Most of the time Charley's electronic screen screamed forth Denver Bronco football games, NBA play-offs, the World Series. Tonight's presentation was unusual but very shrewd.

As the "M*A*S*H" theme began, she saw Charley approach a man seated at a table close to the bar, heard Charley say, "I'm blocking the screen," and heard the man reply, "Not to worry, Nancy's taping it. Sit down."

"Eleanor," shouted Charley, "when you finish that drink, tell the fercockteh bartender to give you another Russian. Okay? Good. Rest your tush."

Ellie's gaze returned to the TV screen.

Charley slid onto an empty seat. "Thanks, Mr. Trask," he said. "My wife would thank you if she'd stuck around instead of flying the coop. My son at MIT college-school would thank you if he knew how to talk instead of saying everything with a seesaw ruler."

"Slide rule," corrected Trask. "Don't students use calculators nowadays?"

"Slide, seesaw, swings, so the Dew Drop is a crowded playground because of you, Kenneth Trask." Charley peered through cigarette smoke at the man who had proposed tonight's party. Trask had attended costumed as Hawkeye Pierce. Except Trask didn't really resemble Hawkeye. His hair was too tidy, combed into a pompadour, and his Hawaiian shirt and fatigue trousers had been pressed with an iron. "Tonight's profits'll pay my son's intuition."

"*Tuition*, Charley. I knew our M*A*S*H-Bash would be successful," said Trask smugly. "It proves that nobody wants the show to end."

It proves that people will use any excuse for a party, thought Charley. Ordering a seltzer from one of his waitresses, he watched customers parading along the bar's surface, hoping to win his advertised look-alike contest. Too bad Eleanor didn't come as Hot Lips. Even overweight she'd be a dead ringer. But so was that skinny girl stumbling across the bar with her shirt open so that everybody including God could ogle. Charley knew the girl; she'd been at the Dew Drop before. Virginia-something. Usually he cut her off early.

Charley wasn't a "M*A*S*H" fan, had watched maybe

half a dozen shows during the eleven seasons, but he was familiar with the leading characters. Even if he wasn't, recent publicity about the finale had been plastered all over the newspapers. Meshuga!

The contest judges were local celebrities. One was a deejay from a popular radio station. The judges quickly eliminated several contestants, including a couple of men who returned to Trask's table.

"Charley Aaronson, meet Fred Remming and Howie Silverman," said Trask. "Fred's pretending to be Radar and Howie thinks he's Klinger."

Because of the contest, both men wore name tags.

Radar? Klinger? Radar was a device the police used to trap you speeding, thought Charley, but what the hell was a Klinger? Somebody who klung?

In any case, Fred/Radar was short and plump, with clipped poodle curls. One hand clutched a brown teddy bear. Howie/Klinger sported a beard and wore a dress. Excusing himself, he headed for the rest rooms.

Bringing his attention back to the contest, Charley fingered the cash prize money in his trouser pocket, while Trask pointed to a figure standing on top of the bar.

"That's my best friend, Sean McCarthy," said Trask. "Isn't he the spitting image of Father Mulcahy?"

Charley followed Trask's finger and squinted at sterling-silver hair, partially covered by a straw hat. A cross on a chain rested against a black turtleneck, and two tiny crosses decorated the collar of Sean McCarthy's fatigue shirt. Blue eyes twinkled behind wire-rimmed glasses.

Applause was deafening when Sean captured first place.

Trask's table was close enough to the bar so that Charley could hear Virginia-something mutter about screwing one of the judges in vain. The fercockteh radio announcer maybe, thought Charley.

A mustached soldier comforted Virginia with a kiss so deep he almost swallowed her tonsils, and Charley shook his head. In *his* youth, couples kissed privately, under the table. "S'cuse me," he mumbled, rising from his seat.

While paying off the winners, he noticed a man dressed as a cowboy. Must have wandered into the lounge by mistake, thought Charley, admiring the Marshal Dillon hat. Now that was a fine TV show. "Gunsmoke." Good clean fun. Schmucks died and they didn't spill any blood, either.

"Having fun, Eleanor?" Charley maneuvered his belly close to her stool.

"You bet. I don't know why I love this show so much." After glancing at some young lounge patrons, she returned her gaze to the screen. "Maybe it's because I was born during the so-called Korean conflict. Another reason is that 'M*A*S*H' is funny, but it doesn't idealize or poke fun at war like 'Hogan's Heroes,' for instance. Sorry, Charley, my husband claims I have a tendency to soapbox, while my mother says I rationalize everything."

"That's okay, Eleanor, drink another Russian."

"Thanks, but I haven't finished this one."

On the mounted TV screen, the final episode of "M*A*S*H" continued. Inside the familiar operating room, doctors were talking about what they'd eat when they left the 4077 and returned home. Hawkeye wanted a piece of chocolate cake; Colonel Potter, fresh corn on the cob. B.J. sighed over a glass of ice-cold milk.

"I'd like some hot pussy," said a sly male voice.

Ellie heard and glanced down the bar at Ginny's partner. His mustache dripped with foam, and his hand cupped a breast inside the girl's olive-drab shirt.

"Uh-oh." Dropping her glass and staggering backward, Ginny cradled her mouth with one palm, then lurched toward the rest rooms.

Ellie started to rise, but Charley shook his head.

"She's done this before," he muttered. "I'm gonna rip her off."

"Don't you mean *cut* her off?"

"Rip, cut, she's kaput." Catching the bartender's eye,

Charley nodded toward Ginny, then sliced his throat with his first finger.

"I should follow, hold her head," said Ellie.

Charley shrugged. "Why get involved?"

"You're right. Yes. I'm going home."

He patted her red silk shoulder. "Stay, Eleanor, the show's just started."

"No, it's time to stop rationalizing, get *involved*, talk to Tony about . . . things. Thanks for the Russian."

Charley watched Eleanor weave her way through the crowd. Then he filled a pitcher with Bud and carried it to the same table where he'd sat before.

Kenneth Trask smiled his thanks and turned toward Fred/Radar. "Did you write the letters, Freddy?"

"Ran off a hundred copies."

"I specifically told you no copies."

"But I signed different names."

"You idiot! It has to sound as if a hundred people are bitching about the series ending."

"Cost me twenty bucks in postage."

Trask leaned forward in his chair and glowered.

Charley watched Fred/Radar's plump cheeks turn red, like giant maraschino cherries atop a strawberry daiquiri.

Then the man wearing a dress—Howie-something—returned to their table, carrying the limp form of Virginia-something. She nestled against the chest hair that escaped from between the buttons on Howie's bodice. Hefting the girl a few inches toward the ceiling, he drawled, "Lookee what I found while taking a whizz."

"Just because you're wearing a dress, you shouldn't go into the ladies'," admonished Fred.

"Found this sweet li'l bundle near my urinal. She was on her knees, prayin' for some buckaroo to come along and brand her ass with his hot, sizzlin' iron. Watcha say, Freddy? Wanna play cowboy?"

Charley watched Howie-something deposit Virginia-something in Fred/Radar's lap.

"How many letters did you write, Howie?" asked Trask.

"None. The series wasn't canceled by CBS, the stars decided to end it themselves."

"I spent twenty bucks on postage," whined Fred, trying to ignore the girl sprawled across his lap.

Twirling his strand of pearls, Howie leaned forward and nudged the young woman, whose brown hair was slicked back, her wig resting on her shoulders like a dead yellow cat. "What's your name, sweetcakes?"

"M'name's Gin. Lost my punch. Order me 'nother, an' I'll letcha drink Gin."

"Radar's gonna drive you home, darlin'."

"Can't go home. Lost my cherry."

"Jesus, she's blotto." Howie snickered. "She should be worth more than twenty bucks postage, Freddy, if she doesn't pass out first. Or maybe you'd prefer it that way."

Fred gulped his beer, his hand shaking so hard that drops from the mug spattered over Ginny's shirt.

"Ish raining," she slurred, grabbing Fred's teddy and kissing its button nose. "I once had a Poop bear named Winnie. Winnie the Poop. Hey, did I winnie the look'like contest?"

"No, sweetcakes," replied Howie, "you lost."

"Bastard . . . he promised—ohmigod! *I* promised to meet Mommy's boss here tonight."

Her indignation and memory nudge caused her to wriggle deeper into Fred's lap. "Got to visit the men's," he whined, shifting Ginny so that she slumped in his chair. Teddy's ear invaded her mouth like a baby's pacifier.

Charley watched Fred twist through the crowd toward the back of the lounge as the man clothed as a priest—Sean McCarthy—hunkered down next to Trask.

"Thanks for the prize money, Charley; drinks on me, boys," Sean croaked, his voice hoarse from laughter emitted during his victorious march around the Dew Drop tables.

"How many letters did you write, McCarthy?" Trask nodded toward Sean's name tag. "Or should we call you Father Mac?"

"Letters? Christ, I forgot. *Errare humanum est.* To err is human." Sean winked. "How many did *you* write, boy-oh?"

"One hundred and seventy-five." Trask turned toward Fred. "They were all penned by hand, with names culled from the telephone book."

"Jesus," said Sean. "How did you find the time to—"

"My wife took care of it."

"That wasn't fair. Nancy couldn't care less about the show. Ken's wife isn't a 'M*A*S*H' fan, Charley."

Good for her! thought Charley. One less crazy in this world.

"Nancy didn't mind." Trask gestured toward the girl huddled in Fred's chair. "Father Mac, I'd like you to meet Gin. Gin, Father Mac."

Sean bowed gravely.

Ginny's teeth had punctured the teddy's fur ruff, and white stuffing drifted onto her shirt like huge dandelion puffs. "Father Mac?" Her fingers made the sign of the cross. "Forgive me Father, for I have sinned."

Sean leaned over and duplicated Ginny's genuflection, his thumb lingering on each nipple. "*Ego te absolvo.* You are forgiven," he said in the last remnants of his Mulcahy mimic. "*Errare humanum est.*"

"Hey, wait a minute. You just felt me up. You're no priest." Dropping the teddy, Ginny adjusted her blond wig and vacated her chair. "Kiss my ass, Father," she added, then wobbled toward the man with the foamy mustache.

"If you kiss *my* ass," called Sean, waving his prize money, "I'll buy you a drink; the whole damn bottle."

Ginny raised her middle finger. The man with the mustache captured her hand and inserted her finger between his fatigued thighs.

"With that yella wig hidin' her brown hair," drawled Howie, "our Gin looks a lot like Hot Lips."

Trask whistled. "Sure does. She's a real beaut, Howie."

"Glad we didn't waste her on Fred."

"Where the hell *is* Fred? By the way, Howie, did you make a pass at our Gin in the john?"

"Me screw a lady in the men's? You're kidding."

"Haven't you ever done it there before?"

"Not in Charley's tavern." Strumming an imaginary guitar, Howie sang, "Oh there's a tavern in the town, in the town, and there my true love laid me down, laid me down."

"*Did* you get laid in the men's?" Sean asked.

"Nope. If our Gin hadn't been so drunk—"

"A drunk's fun," interrupted Trask. "She'll do things she wouldn't dare try sober. Isn't that true, Charley?"

Charley shrugged, then watched Sean McCarthy slide onto the chair where the girl had sat. Sean's booted foot kicked Fred's teddy bear, and Charley thought the fercockteh bear resembled a corpse, with stuffing instead of blood escaping from its terminal wound.

On "M*A*S*H," there was lots of blood. On "Gunsmoke," Marshal Dillon drew from the hip, shot, and the bad guy fell. No blood. Dillon loved Miss Kitty, who had a heart of gold. *She* never got drunk or wandered into the men's room. You knew Miss Kitty wasn't a virgin, but she did it privately, under the table. Marshal Dillon must have used strong condoms because Miss Kitty didn't get pregnant, not like Charley's wife had the first time they'd done it. She'd lost that baby, but it was too late because they were already married. Come to think of it, Virginia-something was a dead ringer for his goyish wife.

Speaking of which, the fercockteh girl, pressing one hand against her mouth, was lurching toward the rest rooms again.

Trask stood and stretched. "Excuse me, gentlemen," he said, "but nature calls."

Charley watched Sean McCarthy scoop up the teddy and finger a cross across its severed ruff.

"*Ego te absolvo,* bear," said Sean.

The M*A*S*H-Bash turned out to be the most successful night in the history of the Dew Drop Inn. An exhausted

Charley Aaronson didn't even total receipts until the following morning.

While Charley counted profits, Ellie Bernstein sipped from a mug of coffee, munched her third Danish, and read the newspaper. She learned that the final "M*A*S*H" episode, "Goodbye, Farewell and Amen," was viewed by almost 125 million Americans. The show earned CBS a 60.3 ratings and a 77 share, which meant that 77 percent of the people watching TV on March 7, 1983, were tuned in to the program.

Am I a statistic? Do I count? Maybe, she thought, maybe not. Because Tony had arrived home prior to the "Amen." Drunk and furious, he'd charged into the family room, turned off the TV, and insisted—no, *demanded*—that they make love. Maybe the new client wasn't so hot to trot after all.

Eyes blurred by discreet tears, Ellie groped for another Danish, lifted the newspaper, and tried to focus on a high school graduation photo directly above a column that reported a young woman's untimely death.

Holy cow! This wasn't fiction. Chewing her pastry, Ellie recalled their brief conversation:

Are you all right? Sure, fine. Tonight I'm Hot Lips Hoo—Hool—Hool'gan.

The woman, identified as Virginia Whitley, had been found in the Dew Drop's parking lot, victim of a hit-and-run accident. Although her face beneath a blond wig remained unmarked, her body had been crushed. During the autopsy the doctor had determined that Virginia's bloodstream contained .327 percent alcohol, and she had recently had sexual intercourse. The article quoted a soldier from Fort Carson. "I was going to drive Gin home," he said, "but she ran toward the latrines and never came back."

Ellie heard Tony's footsteps. They sounded angry. Maybe she should clean her closet until his temper cooled. Behind a shoebox was her box of chocolate chip cookies so she wouldn't starve.

$\triangledown$

1

ELLIE BERNSTEIN SCRATCHED her fat cat. "Wish I was making love smothered in bacon and onions," she murmured.

Unfortunately, bacon wasn't allowed on her diet.

"When you reach the ripe old age of forty-four," she added, "a slip of the lips is a pound on the hips."

That particular aphorism caused her to remember a certain Monday night eleven years ago, when she had parked her Continental outside the Dew Drop Inn after consuming a high-calorie feast that included chocolate cheesecake. Well, she didn't eat chocolate cheesecake anymore. Even though she was and always would be a chocoholic.

At least she was a divorced chocoholic. Following her divorce from Tony, she'd traded in her Continental for a Honda Civic, joined Weight Winners, lost fifty-five pounds, and become a group leader for the organization.

Whereupon she'd met homicide detective Peter Miller.

Peter would love making love covered by bacon. And ribs. And thighs. And breasts. He could eat *anything*.

Holy cow, she had to stop daydreaming. With a pensive smile, Ellie emptied the contents from a second manila envelope onto her family room floor. Sunlight emerged between the leaves of her plant-curtained window and bounced off walls filled with reproductions of Chagall paintings, finally landing on several shiny Polaroid snapshots and a telephone shaped like a duck decoy. Peter had given her the phone last Christmas because, he claimed, she had begged to play decoy during the diet-club murders.

Ellie shuddered. She didn't care to dwell on those bloody homicides, even though the killer had been caught, tried, and convicted.

Strange how Tony'd always given her sexy nightgowns, while Peter had presented her with a quacking phone. On the other hand, thought Ellie with a blush, she didn't wear nighties when she and Peter shared her water bed.

Sitting cross-legged on the beige carpet, Ellie studied pictures of her Weight Winners members. Her black Persian, Jackie Robinson, wandered amid the piles of stacked photos, searching for a possible kitty tidbit.

Ellie rescued a diet-club member from Jackie Robinson's sharp claws. "Hey, puss, I'll swat your furry rump if I have to start all over again. I'm arranging these by months and dumping the ones that are outdated. Be patient. Peter will come home tonight with a bribe. He spoils you rotten."

The duck quacked, and Ellie answered.

"Hi," said Peter.

"I was just talking about you."

"To whom?"

"Jackie Robinson."

"Sweetheart, you really must stop reprimanding your cat, or you'll have no voice left to lecture dieters."

"What makes you think I was scolding Jackie Robinson?"

"He was begging for food, right?"

"Food junkies run in my family," she muttered.

"I'm not an addict."

"You're not family."

"I could be if you—"

"There's no diet-club meeting tonight," she said quickly, "so I don't have to reprimand. How are you, honey? Tired of grateful heroines and exciting car chases?"

"Just tired."

"Nothing happening?"

"Nope, I should be home in time for Monday night football. Damn, I've just jinxed myself; there goes the other line. Hold on."

Ellie pictured Peter bustling about his office. Dark hair, blue-gray eyes, black-and-silver mustache, slim body. At age forty-six he was sweet as cotton candy, tender as a marinaded T-bone, slightly chauvinistic, and sensational between her water-bed sheets. It was his occasional chauvinism that had kept Ellie from saying yes to his let's-get-hitched, even though she loved him.

Because a hitch was a noose in a line. Because a hitch *temporarily* secured that line to an object. Because—

"Are you still there, sweetheart?"

"Peter, do you realize that I'm talking into a duck's butt? This is the most ridiculous phone—"

"See you later; I now have two calls on hold."

"I love—" she started to say, but Peter had hung up.

Returning to her chore, hoping she could finish quickly and catch a few late-afternoon Indian summer rays, Ellie alphabetized three photographs and placed them inside her file box behind an index card marked "November."

Then she halted to examine a recent Polaroid. The woman in the photo had introduced herself as Mrs. Franklin Harrison Burns. An anachronism who preferred her husband's name to her own, Mrs. Burns—first name Magnolia—looked like the Liberty Bell and sported a boned corset that failed to slim her waist or rib cage. Ellie had sensed the wheels turning inside Magnolia's head while the southern belle mentally determined how she could change diet ingredients to fit her own recipes. Ellie knew all the signs and was determined to work extra hard with this new member. Anybody could lose weight if they stuck to their food program—even Mrs. Franklin Harrison Burns.

Franklin Harrison Burns finally noticed the message taped to the door of his refrigerator.

DEER HARRY, I'M SHOPING AT THE MAUL.
MAYBEE A MOOVEE TO. FOOD IN FRIG. LUV,
MAGGIE.

At least she hadn't misspelled the word "food." Nobody
could. F-O-O-D—just like it sounded. Foo-ood.

Burns opened the right-hand side of his double-doored
"frig" and immediately spotted a casserole dish filled with
spaghetti and Magnolia's own homemade sauce of ketchup,
margarine, and tuna fish. Ignoring the casserole, Burns
twisted a can of Classic Coke free from its plastic holder. He
poured half the can into a glass with a Daffy Duck decal,
filled the remaining space with Chivas, drained his drink,
belched, and placed the newly opened Chivas bottle on the
kitchen table.

"Scotch and water, mud in your eye," he sang off-key,
trying to remember the next line. "Scotch and water . . .
ummm . . . Scotch and water . . . darn it, give up, Frank, I
mean Harry."

Harry had been called Frank until 1973. During the
second season of "M*A*S*H" people began noting his Frank
Burns resemblance, and to avoid the inevitable comments
Frank had switched to using his second name. He looked
even less like a Harrison than a Franklin, so Harry, he
decided, would be his name until the day he died.

Turning away from the table, Burns stared directly into
the cold eyes of Robert E. Lee. Although other Robert
E.s—plus many etched photos of gray-draped soldiers—
dominated every wall, this particular portrait was his wife's
favorite. Thus she kept it close to the refrigerator, her
favorite appliance except for her chest freezer, filled with ice
cream, Sara Lee bakery items, and a side of beef. But the
freezer was in the garage, and the garage was a virtual tomb,
and according to Magnolia General Lee didn't belong inside
a tomb.

When Harry wed Magnolia Smithers, she'd been the
epitome of a twentieth-century Scarlett O'Hara. Little did

he know that her deep accent masked an illiteracy that, over long duration, had turned from amusing faux pas to irritating boredom. Somehow Magnolia had managed to graduate from high school despite her inability to read or spell and had met Burns during an AMA convention.

Representing a medical supply house, Harry, then known as Frank, had extolled the benefits of a new lightweight enema bag. Magnolia, one of several hoop-skirted hostesses at the Atlanta hotel, had lured the dazzled Burns to a deserted room. She'd been a virgin, and he was flattered that she'd chosen him for her initiation ritual. F-O-O-L. Foo-ool.

During twenty-one childless years of marriage, Harry had developed a nervous stomach and a set of ulcers to go along with his thin frame. He could never adjust to his wife's heaping plates of hominy grits. Her grits, and everything else she cooked, tasted like the cotton Magnolia claimed slaves had picked on her Tara-style plantation until the Civil War had stripped her family of wealth and power.

Year by year Harry had grown thinner, perpetual worry lines creating a deep dent between sparse eyebrows. Meanwhile, Magnolia bloomed. Her body swayed as though hoops and crinolines dominated the space beneath the summer dresses she wore during every season. She bought corsets in an effort to slim her waist and plump her small breasts. Recently she had joined a diet club.

But it was too late. Harry had already met Iris Maria of the long dark hair, black eyes, and a melodic Spanish accent that made Magnolia's southern drawl sound obscene. Iris Maria had three children, who, like a litter of friendly puppies, attacked Harry's knees when he came to visit. A fourth offspring was on the way, Iris Maria had confessed from her soft mattress, where Harry never knew if his orgasmic screams were the result of their hot sex or the burritos that burned holes through his ulcerous stomach.

In any case, Harry had taken off early today from his job at the medical supply center in order to confront Magnolia with the bad news. A divorce would have to be negotiated.

Harry squared his chinless face, fidgeted with the buttons on his acrylic sweater-vest, and settled down to read the newspaper.

He scanned the real estate section, trying to assess what his small home was worth. On the west side of Colorado Springs, not far from Colorado College, it had a paid mortgage, was carefully patched and painted, and might bring a fortune adequate to appease his illiterate wife with financial security.

Maggie could use the money to open a southern-style restaurant, thought Burns, chuckling. She could serve ketchup casseroles and her "secret ingredient lemonade."

Early this morning he had called real estate offices to inquire about listing his property. Magnolia had been in the kitchen, cooking their gritty breakfast.

Burns sighed with pleasure. On the few occasions he had come home after the lunch hour, Maggie had been glued to her TV soap operas. Shopping, foo-ood, and soaps; her reasons for living. Harry was delighted that today she had opted to visit the "maul." In the peace and quiet of his living room, he considered and rejected several opening lines. Maybe the best way was simply to say "I want a divorce." On soap operas, people got divorced weekly. Or separated. Or killed. It all depended on the ratings.

Magnolia's ratings had slipped lower than her saggy panty hose. Iris Maria wore a black garter belt and—

The doorbell rang with the first ten notes of "Dixie."

"What can I do for you?" asked Harry, opening the front door.

"I'm from the real estate company. I've come to make an appraisal on your house."

"That was quick. I only called this morning."

"The early bird gets the worm."

Harry's face brightened. "That's what I always say. Come inside. Heck, you look familiar. Have we met before?"

"Possibly. It's a small world. *You* look like Frank Burns. Do you know who I mean?"

"Yes, but I don't see the resemblance myself."

"Could be the spittin' double."

"Yes, well, that's not really important, is it? As you can see, my house is small, but it has three bedrooms and two baths—"

"He's a sanctimonious prick."

All of a sudden, Harry wanted Magnolia. His wife could always get rid of visitors with her confusing, illogical remarks and embarrassing attempts at southern hospitality. Harry had already decided he wouldn't deal with a company whose representative used the word "prick."

"Who's a sanc—what you just said?"

"Frank Burns. Screwing Hot Lips, promising marriage and respectability. Giving her cheap presents, like you've been doing with your trashy Mexican whore."

"Now just a minute," said Harry indignantly.

How did this stranger know about Iris Maria? Harry had made two phone calls, both from the privacy of his home during Maggie's absence. Did his wife have enough smarts to hire a private detective? Harry doubted it. Yet the face of this agent did seem familiar. Was Magnolia having her husband followed?

"I think you'd better leave. I don't want to do business with your company." Harry's angry eyes made up for his lack of chin as he jutted his face forward like a furious turtle snapping from its shell.

The agent strolled over to the fireplace, reached up, and unsheathed a saber from its crossed scabbard.

"What do you think you're doing?" screeched Harry. "That's my wife's Civil War saber. You put that down."

Weapon extended, the agent walked toward Harry. "Show me your garage."

"Sh-sure. You don't need the s-sword. What real estate office did you say you represented?"

"Move!"

Harry decided he'd better humor this nut. He'd pretend to list the house and sign forms. Then, later, he'd call the police. He would report it to the real estate board, too. What reputable office would hire somebody who accumulated listings with threats?

And how the heck did this stranger know about Iris Maria?

"Garage is attached to the house, so you can enter through the kitchen," said Harry, walking in front of his unwelcome guest at saber's length. "Watch out for the steps," he cautioned automatically.

"Nice garage; very few cracks or openings," said the agent, pulling the electric cord that snaked from an outlet to the chest freezer.

"Hey, why did you do that? The food will defrost."

"I want to prove that I mean business. Because I intend to do business with *your* company." The agent laughed, then slashed the freezer's white enamel exterior with Magnolia's saber.

I never realized Maggie's heirloom was so *sharp*, thought Harry, swallowing saliva-seasoned fear that tasted like lemon-pepper.

Yet he tried to maintain his composure. "As you can see, there's plenty of room for a washer, dryer, and two cars. That's mine over there," he added, pointing toward a compact Escort.

"Get in the car, Burns."

"Now just a minute. This has gone far enough—"

"Get inside the goddamn car! Or would you prefer the freezer? You can rot with the other dead meat."

Harry felt the sharp tip of the saber pierce through his sweater all the way to his undershirt. Picturing the scarred freezer, he broke into a cold sweat and quickly slid behind the wheel of his Ford.

Then, thoroughly frightened, Harry gave a nervous giggle. "My car doesn't come with the house."

Surprisingly, the agent laughed again. "That's just what Frank Burns would say. Damn, you've sure collected lots of stuff in the back of your car."

"Medical supplies. I could make you a good deal if—"

"Perfect." The agent reached into a pocket, retrieved a pair of Rubbermaid gloves, tugged them on, and nodded toward the freezer. "If you try to escape, I'll slice your head off, understand?" Rooting among supplies, the agent finally located packages of surgical tape.

Harry felt his wrists and drawn-up knees being secured to the steering wheel. Painfully twisting his neck, he saw the agent place Magnolia's freshly laundered towels along the bottom of the double garage doors. Then, lowering his face, Harry attempted to bite the tape that bound his wrists.

"Oh no you don't!" Swiftly wrapping a towel around the saber's hilt, the agent aimed toward Harry's stomach.

Harry felt the cushioned hilt wallop hard, but not hard enough to bruise or crack a rib. "Oomph," he gasped once, then again as the weapon found its target a second time.

While Harry attempted to regain his breath, the agent scurried into the kitchen and grabbed the Chivas bottle.

Harry felt fingers pry his mouth open and tasted warm Scotch. He tried to close his mouth and couldn't. He vowed not to swallow, but his reflexes failed. The garage blurred. Harry gagged as mucus squirted from his nose. He wanted to vomit, but instead passed out.

The agent wrapped Harry's unstarched fingers around the empty Chivas bottle, then tossed it toward the passenger seat. "Needed a little courage to do it, huh, Burns? That's what they'll say. Oh yes, in case I forgot to mention it before, thanks for leaving your keys in the ignition."

Harry didn't hear his engine roar into life, or the radio deejay announce the leading news story.

But the agent did. "Tomorrow they'll sadly trumpet the untimely suicide of Frank Burns. What a shame. Burns had everything to live for. Nice house, good business, a loyal wife, and a devoted whore."

Strolling inside, the agent wiped fingerprints from Magnolia's saber and replaced it above the fireplace. Still wearing rubber gloves, humming the "Suicide Is Painless" theme from "M*A*S*H," the agent walked over to the telephone, unscrewed the round-holed disk end of its receiver, and collected a tiny bugging device from its nest of wires. Then the agent picked up Harry's Daffy Duck glass and said, "Souvenir." Finally, the agent reentered the garage and carefully removed Harry's surgical tape.

Franklin Harrison Burns slumped forward. On the car radio the Beatles sang "Help, I need somebody" while exhaust fumes thickened the air. Inside Magnolia's chest, beef began to defrost. Soon it would rot.

2

ELLIE SECURED HER plump rump with string. She preferred prime rib to rump roast, but she'd overextended her food budget, and anyway, Peter wouldn't care. Didn't he avidly consume those awful sausage doohickeys?

Speaking of hickeys . . .

Blushing, she fingered her triple-strand pearl choke collar. She wasn't ashamed of Peter's enthusiastic neck nibbles, but the kids would arrive soon, and her son Mick noticed everything.

Maybe I can blame it on vampires, thought Ellie, sprinkling her rump with garlic powder.

Okay, her oven was preheated, her fresh veggies waited to be wokked, and an uncorked bottle of cabernet sauvignon breathed on the countertop. It was time to click her remote and watch the news, followed by "M*A*S*H." According to Ellie's TV listings, her local NBC affiliate was rerunning the first years again. Although she despised those laugh tracks, each show still seemed fresh, original.

Granted, "M*A*S*H" wasn't as popular as "Star Trek" reruns. There were no M*A*S*Hies, like Trekkies—Trekkers?—but the show must be popular, or why would it be televised every night at 6:00 and 10:30?

Entering her family room and walking over to the window, Ellie parted the fronds of a plant and peered outside. Indian summer had given way to a virtual winter wonderland. Should she light her first fire of the season? There was plenty of dry wood stacked near the fireplace. Yes, a cozy blaze would mellow what might be a potentially volatile situation—*if* both men arrived at exactly the same time.

So she lit a fire, took a few moments to bask in its glow, and turned on the TV.

Damn, she'd missed the first fifteen minutes of the newscast, the part where they capsuled world events, then dwelled on local happenstances like murder and mayhem. Oh well, after the weather report came sports.

Sports! Yum! Ellie was a "M*A*S*H" fan, but she was a Denver Bronco fanatic. She could even identify the players by their jersey numbers: quarterback John Elway, lucky number seven; Simon Fletcher, who earned money for charities by sacking the opposing quarterback, seventy-three; etc.

Channel Ten's meteorologist issued a perfidious smile as he aimed a wooden pointer toward snowflake asterisks on a Colorado-shaped map.

Kenneth Trask settled into his comfortable armchair and ran the numbers on his remote control box.

"Why don't you just punch five?" asked Jacques Hansen, his brow creased in its perpetual scowl.

Trask had once heard somebody describe Hansen's face as "donning the hate-mug." Jacques worked at the Office of Special Investigations on the Air Force Academy base, and he loved his job.

"Patience, my friend," said Trask. "Tenacity is a virtue, along with faith and hope. Fuck charity! You of all people should understand the art of anticipation. Don't you lick your chops over the thought of accumulating unsuspecting suspects, then tricking them into signing confessions?"

"I don't trick them, I shame them." Hansen's thin lips stretched into a grin. "And if they give me the identities of their fellow offenders—"

"Isn't that McCarthyism?"

"Joe McCarthy was a saint."

"Joseph McCarthy was an asshole."

"Wait a minute, Ken, he was tenacious."

"Only in the beginning. Then he found fame, lost his cool, and jumped the gun. Success, my friend, is not spur-of-the-moment. One must plan very carefully. Anticipate."

Trask's first finger hovered above the remote control, and Hansen flinched when the static merry-go-round began again. Hansen wanted to look away, but instead he stared, mesmerized, at the screen.

A giant wheel's metal finger quivered on BANKRUPT. Lucy Ricardo pounded at the door of a locked walk-in freezer. Finally the theme music "Suicide Is Painless" clashed with the chime of Trask's front doorbell.

"It's open," he shouted.

An accompanying gust of wind rippled the folds of the American flag mounted above the fireplace mantel as four men bustled inside the living room.

Arriving to greet the men was Nancy Trask. She held a tray containing chocolate cake cut into tiny squares, miniature ears of corn, and shot glasses filled with cold milk—a traditional weekly homage based on the wishes expressed in the final "M*A*S*H" episode.

Standing directly beneath the flag, Nancy narrowly missed completing the image of a girl next door welcoming home her errant soldier. She was a shade too severe, with close-cropped brownish hair, sienna-tinted eyes, and a mouth always on the verge of smiling.

Trask's buddies knew that she was clay molded by her husband. She talked in questions, glancing toward Ken after every sentence for his nod of approval or negation. "I'm going to the bathroom?" she would say, or "I'm answering the phone?" She had borne Trask one son (God forbid she squeeze out a daughter) christened Kenneth Junior—K.J.— who had grown and flown from his parents' art deco–embellished nest.

Nancy placed her ceremonial tray of food on top of a rectilinear coffee table, circa 1930, and drifted silently from the room. Trask surmised that his wife was either preparing a cookie batter, folding laundry, or in the sewing room pinning a new pattern. Nancy had created the blue drapes that covered their living room window, patiently stitching complicated valance, pleats, and an almost invisible hem at the bottom. This evening Nancy's drapes were open, framing the snowy landscape.

It feels warm and cozy inside, thought Trask, even without a fire. A fireplace blaze would initiate intimate conversation and detract from *his* show.

"Sorry we're late," said Gordon Dorack—The Dork, to other group members—"but Fred's car ran out of gas."

"Almost ran out of gas," whined Fred Remming, placing his round buttocks against the meshed fireplace screen.

For a moment Trask wished he *had* built a fire as he visualized flames licking at Fred's ironed Levi's. Tonight Fred's face was bright crimson instead of its usual pink—a result of the icy wind.

"*Almost* ran out of gas?" exclaimed The Dork. "*Almost!* What d'ya call pushing a Jeep three blocks to the Chevron if that's not out of gas?"

Fred blew his nose into a bandanna-style handkerchief. "There was some fuel left. I didn't want to hurt the engine or get stuck in an intersection. Besides, I pushed too. Probably caught my death from that stupid wind. Howie insisted on steering, and he weighs more than my Jeep. Father Mac watched out for other cars. I think he blessed them. It was so embarrassing. People assumed Father Mac wanted to wash their windshields for money. I thought I'd die from humil—"

"How much is *some* fuel?" Jacques Hansen turned his bristly crew cut and wire-rimmed glasses toward Fred's flushed face. "Was the gauge on empty? Below empty? Did the motor sputter and die?"

"I d-don't know. I guess it was b-below em-empty." Fred paused, then whined, "So I ran out of gas. So what? It could happen to anybody."

Howie Silverman guffawed. "Give Hansen the names of

three other people who've run out of gas, Freddie my boy, and he'll probably let you off the hook."

"Oh, I see, Jacques was joking. Interrogating me like he does his homosexual cadets."

"I never joke." Behind his glasses, Hansen's eyes were icy gray, almost colorless.

Trask watched his best friend, Sean McCarthy, smile at the little drama. Sean wore his usual black turtleneck tucked into khaki pants. Slight in appearance, he had a deceptive wiry strength. Trask had arm wrestled with him many times, and always lost.

"*Ego te absolvo*," Sean announced to the group, although he stared directly toward Jacques Hansen. "You are forgiven."

"Up yours, Father Mac," said Howie, shedding a wool topcoat. Melting snow clung to its brown fur collar. Under the coat Howie wore a plaid shirt, western-style pants cinched by an enormous turquoise-and-silver belt buckle, and Tony Lama lizard-skin boots. Just an old cowhand from the Rio Jersey. Trenton, New Jersey.

"*Ego te absolvo*," repeated Sean.

"You always say that." Fred sniffed, then sneezed. "Ever since the Dew Drop's M*A*S*H-Bash. You'd think you were a real priest instead of a telephone repairman."

"How could you run out, Fred?" Dorack was unable to relinquish a conversation until it reached its conclusion. "I gas up when the needle hits half."

"Half full," asked Sean, "or half empty?"

Trask watched The Dork peel off earflap hat, scarf, mackinaw jacket, and heavy cardigan, leaving a "M*A*SH" sweatshirt over a turtleneck tunic. At six feet tall, fully clothed, Dorack resembled the Oz scarecrow—if he only had a brain.

Weaving fingers through his straw-yellow hair, Dorack replied, "Well, I guess I buy gas when it's half—"

"Shut up, the commercial's ending," warned Trask.

"Ken, we must have seen this episode a million times," whined Fred. "They're rerunning the first years again."

"If you don't like it, go home."

Fred automatically glanced toward the window, whose panes reflected swirling snow.

Silently, all four men piled their outer clothing on top of a corner table. Howie Silverman appropriated a bentwood rocker. Gordon Dorack and Fred Remming deflated the poofy cushions of a sectional couch. Sean McCarthy sat cross-legged, crushing orange strands of shag carpeting. Jacques Hansen, already seated, kept his body ramrod straight, inches away from the slats of a ladder-back chair. Each man, including Trask, munched cake and corn, then downed the milk. Dorack took a token bite from his wedge of chocolate cake.

On the TV screen, Hawkeye was greeting a friend he had known since the fifth grade—Tommy Gillis—who was writing a book called *You Never Hear the Bullet*. "There was a young blond kid in my outfit," says Tommy. "I looked at him one day and half of him was gone, and you know what he said? He said, 'I never heard no bullet.' "

The doorbell chimed.

"Let it ring," said Trask. "Nobody interrupts my show." Nobody would dare!

"Gosh-darn it," sniveled Fred.

"Shut up!"

"But Ken, it's Melody."

"Who the hell's Melody?"

"My cousin. She's meeting me here tonight."

The bell chimed again.

Sean unfolded his body from the carpet and swiftly opened the front door.

With a sigh, Trask turned away from the screen and focused on a bulky, snow-shrouded figure.

"Come in, my child," said Sean in his Father Mulcahy voice.

Melody Remming entered the room. She was the female duplicate of cousin Fred; her brown poodle curls were scissored just below her ears, her balloon cheeks flashed bright red, and her lips were tinged with blue. Melting snow covered a thick blue quilted jacket and dripped onto white ski pants. Knotted around her throat was a red silk scarf.

I pledge allegiance to the flag, thought Trask.

"What were you doing standing outside in the snow?" Dorack rose to his feet, removed Melody's jacket, tossed it on top of the table, and steered her toward the couch.

"Freddie said to meet him around six. To wait outside and not come in." She plopped down between Dorack and her cousin. "You said you had to check with Mr. Trask, Freddie, and see if it was okay for me to join his group."

Melody's inflection was the antithesis of her name—high and squeaky, like fingernails across a chalkboard. Instinctively, she snuggled her shivering body closer to Dorack's thin frame.

An aspirin commercial interrupted the action on the TV screen. Rising from his chair, Trask shook Melody's frozen fingers. "Welcome to my home, young lady."

Not my type, he thought, noting the small bumps beneath her blue sweater. Anyway, I prefer blonds.

Melody smiled timidly. "We've been introduced before, Mr. Trask, but you wouldn't remember me."

"My wife Nancy's probably in the kitchen."

"I need aspirin, Ken," whined Fred, his eyes riveted to the TV advertisement. "I've caught a gosh-darn cold."

"There's medicine in the kitchen cabinet. If Melanie would be so kind—"

"Melody," corrected the girl in her high, scratchy voice, still sitting on the couch like some patriotic sculpture. She glanced longingly toward Dorack's leftover cake. "Do you mind if—"

"Yes! That's for group members only, young lady." Trask returned his gaze to the screen as the "M*A*S*H" rerun reran.

"Hey, I'm sorry I told you to wait and forgot, Mel," whispered Fred.

"*Ego te absolvo,*" said Sean.

The show reached its conclusion. "I'd give you a kiss, Hawk, but I can't lift my head," murmurs a mortally wounded Tommy Gillis.

"You'd just get my mask icky," replies Hawkeye.

"I heard the bullet," says Tommy, dying.

Credits were superimposed over Hawkeye, Hot Lips, Trapper, and—

The doorbell chimed again. This time a young man handed Trask three pizza boxes.

Trask paid the delivery boy, turned off the TV, and led the way into his tidy kitchen. Seated at the head of a butcher-block table, he surveyed his guests and saw Melody surreptitiously spit pieces of limp green pepper into her cupped palm.

"I understand you've been meeting like this for years," she said, reaching toward a white linen napkin.

"Most of us watch the reruns every day, but we get together on Mondays," replied Sean. He smiled at Nancy as she removed a Moosehead from the refrigerator.

Melody's face scrunched, and her freckles merged. "Why Mondays?"

"Because that was when they used to televise the actual show?" said Nancy, handing the Moosehead to Sean while, at the same time, she glanced toward her husband.

Trask nodded.

Nancy looks nice tonight, he thought. She's working out at the health club like I told her to, changing some of that flab into muscle again. If she could only grow tits.

Trask felt an erection begin to build, a spur-of-the-moment hard-on. He glanced toward the wall phone.

I'll call later, after the 10:30 rerun, he thought.

"Ken started the group so we could get our weekly 'M*A*S*H'-at-six-fix," stated Sean.

"Otherwise we'd break out in a 'M*A*S*H'-rash," said Howie.

"Our weekly fix of Hawkeye, Hot Lips, Radar, Klinger, and Frank Burns," concluded Dorack.

"And Father Mulcahy," added Sean.

"If you say 'a-go-tay-absolvo' again, I'll tape your mouth shut," threatened Fred.

"I just love Alan Alda," sighed Melody. "He reminds me of Abraham Lincoln."

"He does not."

"He does too, Freddie. Not so much in appearance. Hawkeye's better looking. I meant his personality. I'd vote for Alan Alda for president. I like tall men."

Trask grinned when Melody glanced up at Dorack from beneath lowered lashes.

She's not my type, but she's perfect for The Dork.

"I understand Alda's queer; Abe Lincoln was, too," stated Jacques Hansen. Those were the first words he had uttered since his accusatory exchange with Fred.

"What did you say?" asked Melody.

She glared at the OSI officer, thought Trask, as though Hansen were a giant green pepper risen from the cardboard pizza box.

"Jacques thinks anybody who ain't a Republican's a closet homosexual," drawled Howie, accepting a bottle of Bud from Nancy.

"But Lincoln was a Republican—Lincoln was—Jacques's crazy," sputtered Melody. "Alan Alda has a wife and daughters and he's ever so . . . so *virile* . . . and, well, if he was gay, he'd admit it."

"He'd appear on Geraldo," added Dorack.

"He isn't gay, is he, dear?" said Nancy.

"Not to my knowledge," replied Trask mildly, counting silently to ten. It wouldn't do to exhibit anger in front of his guests, although he felt like removing one of Nancy's heavy frying pans from its peg on the wall and bashing Hansen's head in. Alan Alda, as Hawkeye Pierce, was Trask's personal hero.

"He's a fruit," yelled Hansen. "The family thing is a cover. You can tell by all his *feminist* activities."

Howie guffawed. "Jacques, you're an asshole. Feminism

is an ideology. I don't buy everything those radical bra-burn-ing broads have to say, but feminists advocate political and economic equality. It's not a state of being feminine."

Hansen's face flushed red to the roots of his bristly crew cut. "Give me ten minutes alone with Hawkeye and I'd make him admit it. He's a traitor, too."

"A traitor?" Trask eyed Nancy's frying pan again.

"He's always putting down the war, the army, U.S. involvement in foreign affairs—"

"Why do you watch the show?" interrupted Melody. "And why did you join Mr. Trask's club if you're so gung ho about war?"

"I like war movies. Duke Wayne and Robert Ryan. Cliff whatchamacallit, you know, the long-distance guy who starred in that movie about the Green Ber—"

"You honestly believe 'M*A*S*H' is a war show?" asked Melody incredulously.

"Damn straight!"

Voices rose in an indignant chorus. When there was a pause, Trask saw Dorack smile at Melody, then turn toward Hansen. " 'M*A*S*H' is antiwar, you jerk."

"It is not! Some of the stories . . . the characters . . . Margaret and Frank are very patriotic."

"If you ask me, Frank's queer," drawled Howie.

"Now who's the asshole? Frank's married, and he's always chasing Margaret Hou—"

"That's just a cover," said Howie, grinning.

"If there was an election, the American people would choose Frank Burns for president." Hansen's voice was as cold and gray as his eyes.

Melody's pug nose scrunched. "I don't like Frank, and no woman would vote for him. Would you, Mrs. Trask?"

"I don't think so. Would I, dear?" Nancy glanced toward her husband.

"No."

"Frank reminds me of Richard Nixon," said Melody.

"Would you buy a used car from Frank Burns?" Howie

grinned at Dorack, who sold used cars. "Besides, Burns has no chin. Americans love chins." Howie shifted his gaze to Sean. "You haven't said anything, Father Mac."

"He's forgiving us," muttered Fred.

"For what?" asked Melody.

"I don't know. Hey, if there was an election and all the 'M*A*S*H' people were on the ballot, who'd you vote for? I'd choose Radar. He's good and kind and—"

"A virgin," teased Melody. "I'd vote for Alan Alda, of course. Maybe Margaret Houlihan for vice."

"Hot Lips would never make it; she'd be nailed for morals," said Sean, finally entering the discussion.

Fred sneezed. "You'd vote for Father Mulcahy, right?"

"No, a priest couldn't win, and I don't like losers. I'd vote for Colonel Potter—the Eisenhower image."

"Who would I vote for, dear?" asked Nancy, glancing toward her husband.

"Hawkeye."

"Who would you choose, Mr. Trask?" asked Melody.

"I haven't voted since Johnson whipped Goldwater."

"Frank Burns," shouted Hansen, "would win in a walk."

"Frank doesn't walk, he slinks," said Melody with disgust. "Burns is a sanctimonious A-hole. Hawkeye is worth ten Franks. Hawkeye's my hero."

For the first time, Trask smiled sincerely at Fred's cousin. "Nancy," he said, "next Monday when you phone in the order for our pizzas, kill the green peppers."

Outside Kenneth Trask's house the temperature continued to drop, and the falling snow stuck to lawns and pavements like Elmer's glue.

Franklin Harrison Burns was cold, too. However, his ulcers no longer complained, and he would never have to eat hominy grits or spicy burritos again.

Outside Harry's garage, a man furtively backpedaled toward the sidewalk. Parked curbside was a silver BMW with the name of his real estate company tastefully stenciled on each door.

Should he drive away? But what if somebody had seen his car? It would be easy to identify, dammit. Should he call the police? But then he'd become involved. So what? He was merely an innocent bystander, wasn't he?

Jesus, that would be a first. Nobody had ever called him innocent before.

$\triangledown$

3

I HEARD THE bullet.

Tears trickled down Ellie's cheeks.

Beneath faded jeans her knees flattened the family room's carpet, while her thirtysomething-inch tush rested comfortably upon bare heels. Her gaze had been riveted on the TV screen, yet she was delightfully aware that Sandra Connors, Ellie's favorite Weight Winners protégée, had moved farther down the couch toward Michael "Mick" Bernstein, Ellie's favorite and only son. From the corner of her eye, she saw a small boot nudge an oversize Reebok.

Sandra, with her wheat-colored hair and blue eyes, resembled Lewis Carroll's original Alice, except Sandra's rabbit hole was nearby Colorado College.

Mick was a conglomeration of his parents' genes. He had inherited his father's tall, slender frame, thank goodness, and the thick mop of Robert Redford hair was also Tony's. But Mick's blue-green eyes were Ellie's. The diamond stud in his ear was hers, too, "borrowed" from her jewelry box.

Due to his homogenized pedigree, Mick sometimes displayed both Jewish and Catholic guilt—an endearing quality. That same trait could be attractive in Tony, but it wasn't. Because Tony's contrition made Ellie feel defensive. Take the M*A*S*H-Bash, for example. Eleven years had elapsed since then, but she'd never forget Tony's actions that night, or the morning after, when he'd awakened with a humongous hangover, pulled her from the closet, tearfully apologized, and then insisted that his infidelity was the result of her weight problem. Thus *she* had comforted *him*, promising to diet, a promise she'd kept, broken, kept, broken, until she realized that manipulative Tony always blamed his sins on her. It was always her fault. Fortunately, she had risen from the ashes only slightly singed. "Phoenix" and "penitence" both began with the letter *P.* So did (will) "power."

With a sigh, Ellie rose from the floor, turned off the television, and headed toward the kitchen, planning to baste her roasting rump with pan drippings.

"I could watch 'M*A*S*H' reruns over and over," said Sandra. "It makes all those macho clone movies look like comic books. Tommy Gillis. Every time that episode is resurrected, I can't help crying."

"You cry at everything," teased Mick, even though a suspicious moisture had gathered at the corners of his own eyes during the show's conclusion. Pointing toward the snow-crusted window, he recited, " 'Lay him low, lay him low. In the clover or the snow! What cares he? He cannot know. Lay him low!' "

"Are those the lyrics for a new folk-rock song?"

Closing his eyes, Mick said, " 'Dirge for a Soldier.' G. H. Boker. Born 1823, died 1890. English Lit."

"You sound like your mother."

Mick's eyes blinked open. "Is that a compliment?"

"You bet. Ellie has more quotes than Keebler has chips."

"Okay, here's another chip. Kipling, Rudyard, born 1865—"

"I've heard of Kipling!"

"Died 1936. 'For it's Tommy this, an' Tommy that, an' Chuck 'im out, the brute! But it's Saviour of 'is country when the guns begin to shoot.' "

"Tommy—Tommy Gillis—oh Mick."

"See? You cry at everything, even an obscure poem."

"I do not!" She sniffed, then punched Mick's muscled arm with her middle knuckle. "I weep buckets when I hear your band play. The music's so loud."

"You're just pissed because you haven't been invited to sing with my group."

"You promised—"

"I know, but Belinda's really *hot.*"

"Miss Belly," scoffed Sandra, picturing the beautiful entertainer, who had a low, throaty voice and a slender body, all legs. "Belly-up, if you ask me. Anyway, I prefer to sing with John Russell at the Dew Drop Inn, right here in Colorado Springs."

"Fine, that's fine," replied Mick. Lead guitarist of his own band, Rocky Mountain High, he attended the University of Colorado in Boulder and constantly pressured Sandra, a music major, to transfer her credits there. "Sing anywhere you like, but you're pissed just the same."

That truthful remark silenced Sandra, but not a small child in a playpen who had awakened when electronic TV voices changed to live conversation. The little girl had been asleep on her stomach, her Pamper-ed rump pointed toward the ceiling. Now she sat up and wailed.

Mick's eyes narrowed as his mother returned, carrying a plastic bottle shaped like a clown. "I don't know how you can babysit Annie for Dad."

"It's not li'l pumpkin's fault." Ellie placed the bottle on an end table next to an authentic reproduction Tiffany lamp, scooped up the child, stripped her diaper, then clothed Annie in training pants and orange pajamas with a bunny appliquéd on what would one day become a breast.

Annie settled herself trustingly in Ellie's lap and reached for the bottle. "Gimme, Errie," she said. Twenty months old, she had trouble pronouncing the letter *L.*

Mick tried to hide an exasperated sigh. After his divorce, Tony had married an ex–Dallas Cowboys cheerleader. Sixteen months later, Ann Marie arrived. Recently the cheerleader had abandoned mate and maternal instincts to seek stardom in Hollywood. Tony sold his Denver house, moved back to Colorado Springs, sublet a condo, and rejoined his real estate firm. He had hired a housekeeper who doubled as babysitter, but the woman was susceptible to mysterious illnesses, so Annie often ended up on Ellie's doorstep.

A bright, inquisitive little girl, Annie responded with a shrug to life's unexpected roller-coaster loops, accepting "Errie's" bountiful affection as her due. Mick hated himself for feeling the way he did, but he was unable to deal with Dad and Annie, even though his stepsister adored him, even called him "Mymick."

Settled back inside the playpen, Annie was content with cloth building blocks, clown bottle, and a frozen bagel.

"Why do you give Annie frozen bagels?" asked Sandra.

"It's better than a teething ring. She can gum it to death, and at the same time it tastes good."

Mick burst out laughing. Ellie blushed. Embarrassed by the innuendo, Sandra stretched a denim-clad leg toward the three-globed ceiling light fixture.

Mick watched admiringly, then turned toward his mom again. She wore pearls and a yellow cardigan sweater that zipped to her, well, cleavage. There was no other word for it. A guy couldn't say "breasts" or "boobs" when talking about his own mom. On the other hand, a mom didn't talk about gumming, well, things.

"When's Peter due?" he asked.

"About the same time as your father. They both called. Tony's planning to appraise a house. Peter's checking out a bank robbery that he says is county rather than city; his department shouldn't be involved. I expect both men will ring my chimes around seven-thirtyish."

Disturbed by his mother's casual acceptance of an awkward situation, Mick decided to change the subject. "You know what, Mom? If your hair was blond instead of red, you'd look a lot like Margaret Houlihan on 'M*A*S*H.' "

Mick's compliment was no exaggeration, thought Sandra. Only a light web of smile lines radiating from the corners of her blue-green eyes indicated that Ellie could have produced an offspring who was pushing twenty-one. Ellie had a tapered nose, a generous mouth, and a determined chin. If her hair had been platinum, she really could double for Hot Lips.

"They say that everyone looks like somebody else," exclaimed Sandra, "and you could be Margaret's twin sister."

"I'm perfectly happy to be me," said Ellie.

Unless I could be Norrie Charles, novelist. Ellie's lips turned up in a self-mocking grin. During her separation from Tony, she'd tried to write a mystery about a cheerleader who murders members of a football team and is exposed by an average housewife.

Never finished that epic, she thought. Steven Spielberg once said, "People have forgotten how to tell a story. Stories don't have a middle or an end anymore. They usually have a beginning that never stops beginning." Her creative endeavor had a beginning that never stopped, so she'd hidden the unfinished manuscript (and her pseudonym) on the shelf that held her childhood Nancy Drew mysteries.

Yes, life was exciting and fulfilling, despite Mick's attitude toward his stepsister, Tony's return, and—

There was a loud knock on the front door.

"Peter? Tony? Come in," she shouted, "it's unlocked."

Tony entered. He appeared tired and visibly shaken, even though he greeted his tall son with a sugary smile. The sugar dissolved quickly as he said, "What's with the earring, Michael?"

"Everybody wears 'em, Dad, even famous athletes. Several Denver Bronco stars—"

"Have you suddenly decided to play football? If I recall, you struck out in Little League."

"Sign *Annie* up for Little League. Her mother can lead the cheering at home games if she comes back home."

"Mick! Tony! Stop it!" Ellie stepped between them.

"Sorry, Mom." After retrieving jackets from the hall closet and returning to the family room, Mick mumbled something about escorting Sandra to the dorm before the snow became impossible to navigate.

"Don't be ridiculous," said Ellie. "Muffin doesn't live that far away, and you haven't had dinner yet."

"See you later, Mom. C'mon, Muffin."

Sandra grinned at the pet name, then leaned over the playpen and gave Annie several kisses. Her waist-length hair swept forward, tickling the little girl's chin.

Ignoring Sandra, Annie scrunched up her face and wailed, "Mymick, Mymick."

He responded with a quick hug, and the child seemed satisfied, although her lower lip quivered as she waved her tiny fingers bye-bye.

"Would you care to join us for breakfast, Sandra?" asked Ellie. "I could serve leftover rump."

"Sure. Thanks. Sorry. Mick—wait—rats!"

"Sit down, Tony," said Ellie after the front door slammed shut. Jackie Robinson had slipped through the brief opening and sauntered somewhat furtively toward the fireplace. Tongue-toweling snow from his black fur, the cat, who didn't like Tony, hissed loudly in between licks. His sibilant sound matched the sizzle of flames consuming pine. "Just for the record, Tony, your Little League remark was totally uncalled for. Mick skis like an Olympic champ."

"It was his damn earring," grumbled Tony, removing his camel-hair coat and London-tailored suit jacket. Carefully folding both garments across the playpen, he bent forward, pinched Annie's cheek, straightened, and said, "Didn't I give you that earring for our tenth wedding anniversary?"

"Nope, my fortieth birthday. You handed me a hundred-dollar bill and told me to 'buy something nice.' "

"Jesus, that would make Michael's earlobe worth fifty bucks. I hope he doesn't pawn it."

"His earlobe?"

"No, the diamond."

"You've lost your sense of humor, Tony. Sit down."

Despite their bumpy past and potholed present, Ellie took a moment to admire her ex-husband. Half Italian mafia, half Jewish prince, Tony was tall and lean. His blond hair, dark eyes, Semitic nose, and wicked, wolfish grin assured financial success. Women, he had often explained, made the final decision on purchasing a home.

"Do you want something to drink?" she asked. "You look unglued."

"Would you make me a whisper martini?"

"Sure." She walked into the kitchen, poured gin over ice cubes, and whispered the word "vermouth," thinking about the many times she had done this during their marriage.

Tony followed, eyed the wine, sniffed the roast, then said, "When does Michael return to school?"

"Tomorrow morning."

"Is he on vacation?"

"No, his band was booked into the Springs Saturday night, and he has only one class on Monday, English Lit, solid A-plus, so he decided to stretch the weekend. Besides, he's crazy about Sandra Connors. You can tell because they argue all the time."

"We never argued, Eleanor."

"That's right, Tony. I used to say 'sorry' before I discovered what it was I'd done wrong. Let's go back into the family room. I'll stoke the fire."

"You look great," he said, sinking onto the couch and gulping his drink down. "I like what you're wearing, even though you should zip—"

"This old yellow sweater?" Ellie scooped up the cat and sat across from her ex-husband on a plump love seat. "Funny, you never noticed it before."

"You look different. Maybe it's because you've lost so much weight. I do think you should zip—"

"Okay, Tony, tell me what's bothering you."

"How do you know something's bothering me?"

"We were married for more years than I care to count. Is it your wife? Annie? The hypochondriac housekeeper?"

"I finally fired the housekeeper. My mother has offered to board Ann Marie, at least temporarily."

"Oh," said Ellie, glancing toward the happy child who was making faces at the cat. "I had hoped—well, never mind, I guess that's best."

"Eleanor, you won't believe what happened tonight," Tony finally blurted. "This man named Franklin H. Burns phoned my office early this morning, asking for an appraisal on his house. I tried to call back around four. No answer. I was driving here to pick up Ann Marie and the Burns home was on my way—he lives only a couple miles from you—so I figured I'd take a chance and stop. I knocked and rang the bell. No one came to the door, but I decided to look around and appraise the property."

"What happened? A dog attacked?" Or, Ellie thought, an irate husband?

"Dog? No. I was circling the garage when I heard something. Car engine. I smelled exhaust fumes and called the police from a neighbor's phone. Can you believe it? That stupid man killed himself in his car, an *American* car, for Christ's sake."

Holy cow, thought Ellie, if that stupid man killed himself inside a Toyota, would it be okay? Tony's voice gave every indication of honest indignation, but it also had the earmarks of honest angst. Well, after all, he *had* lost a potential client.

"Wait a minute," she said. "Burns called for an appraisal, then committed suicide? How did he sound?"

"What do you mean how did he sound? He was *dead*."

"Not tonight, Tony, this morning. Did he sound resigned? Upset?"

"My secretary took the call."

"Maybe he didn't want to sell his house. Maybe he had financial difficulties and couldn't see a way out. That happens. Was he old?"

"How the hell do I know? I didn't go inside the garage. The motor was running and the man was *dead*. By the way, a Ford Escort sure gets good mileage. The needle was on half."

"I thought you didn't go inside the garage."

"The police mentioned it."

"My Honda gets great mileage."

Tony scowled. "The next time you trade in a car, Eleanor, a Lincoln Continental no less, think American."

"Good grief, Tony, you drive a German—" She paused, then said, "I wonder why he called *your* office."

"Who?"

"Burns."

"There you go again, breaking everything down and analyzing. I imagine he called my office because it has the biggest Yellow Pages ad. What's your theory? Do you believe Harry Burns called early this morning, trusting I'd arrive in time to abort his suicide attempt?"

"I thought his name was Franklin."

"Tom, Dick, Harry, what's the difference?"

"How do you know his name's Harry?"

"Why are you interrogating me?"

"I'm not. I'm curious."

"Curiosity killed the cat," said Tony, glancing toward Jackie Robinson.

"Satisfaction brought it back."

"You're impossible, Eleanor. Why aren't you more compassionate? Burns is dead. He can't feel anything, but I've had a shock. If you don't mind, I'd like to use the bathroom."

"Of course. It's the second door on the—"

"I know where the bathroom is." For the first time, Tony's mouth quirked at the corners. "I used to live here, remember?"

As her ex-husband strolled toward the hallway, Ellie recalled a conversation with Peter. She had offered to play decoy during the diet-club murders and he had responded with anger. "You'd be dead," Peter had shouted. "You wouldn't feel anything at all. It's always the one who has to go on living who suffers."

But Tony made himself the victim in any unpleasant situation. It was hard to feel compassion. Besides, something didn't ring true. Could she have imagined his reaction? Way out of proportion, since Tony didn't actually know

Burns. Why was Tony so scared? Was Burns's death a reminder that mortality was inevitable? Or was Tony simply annoyed over the loss of a listing?

"When did you get the water bed?" he asked, reentering the room, sitting on the couch.

"After our divor—"

"I can understand your concern for a stupid suicide," he interrupted, "but can't you spare some sympathy for me? *I* found the dead body."

"You didn't find the body. You smelled exhaust fumes."

"Same thing. I was involved."

"How were you involved?"

"Are you being dense on purpose? I was there. I was grilled by the cops."

"Peter says police officers don't grill people like cheese sandwiches. They merely question—"

"Dammit, Eleanor, I was grilled royally."

Maybe Tony *was* messing around with the wife, thought Ellie. Maybe Burns found them together and . . . and what? Could Tony kill somebody and make it look like a suicide?

No way! In any case, what would be Tony's motive? If he was screwing the wife, he'd just tuck in his million-dollar penis, pull up his five-hundred-dollar suit pants, flash his wolfish grin, and hightail it out of there.

"Okay, I'm sorry for my lack of sensitivity," she said, "but I've seen dead bodies, too."

"That's different. You've always been into murder."

"Really, Tony, *into?* How sixties. It's the nineties; you're supposed to say 'let's do murder.' "

"Very funny! You're *into* a detective, aren't you? Or is it the other way around?"

"Another martini?" she asked, her voice icy.

"I don't want to drink and drive with Ann Marie. Besides, isn't *he* coming for dinner? I smelled a roast."

"I smell a rat."

"Is your detective planning to marry you?"

"Sorry, but that's none of your business."

"Okay, you're right."

"Do you know what Mick said?" asked Ellie, hoping to change the subject and lighten the atmosphere. "Your son thinks I resemble Hot Lips."

"Who?"

"Loretta Swit, the 'M*A*S*H' star."

"I suppose so, if you changed the color of your hair. Does *he* like hot lips?"

"*He* has a name. I just remembered, Tony, you hardly ever watched 'M*A*S*H.' You didn't care for the show."

"I didn't care for it because you were obsessed by it. Just for the record, Eleanor, you sound bitter."

"If I'm bitter, it's because—never mind. Oh, to hell with it. I *am* bitter. Don't forget, Tony, it was *you* who brought about our divorce. *You* broke our vows. *You* had your cheerleader on the side, turning cartwheels and spreading her legs into convenient splits. Come to think of it, she resembles Hot Lips more than I do."

"*You* never used to be so crude, Eleanor. Or vindictive. Jesus, my wife's gone. Probably forever."

"Sorry," said Ellie automatically, thinking how Tony could still push buttons. Was that her second, third, or fourth sorry?

"Guess I'd better get myself gone, too," he said. "Where's Ann Marie's snowsuit?"

"Hanging in the closet. I'll get it."

He grinned wolfishly. "First door on the—"

"Shut up, Tony."

After Annie and Tony had departed, Ellie entered the kitchen and turned down the oven. Peter would be late if he got called in on the death of Franklin "Harry" Burns.

Have I ever met him? She wondered. His name sure sounds familiar.

Holy cow! Mrs. Franklin Harrison Burns. Magnolia. The

new Weight Winners member whose photo she had filed earlier today.

Wait a minute. Hold the phone—hold the duck. There was another reason why the name sounded so familiar. Yes. The character on "M*A*S*H."

What a strange coincidence that the "stupid suicide" her ex-husband had discovered was also named Frank Burns.

$\triangledown$

4

ON ABC, THE Raiders were getting their butts kicked.

Jackie Robinson bristled his thick Persian tail and stalked across the carpet. His whiskers quivered. Then his measled muzzle turned up in the semblance of a cat smirk as he weaved his black fur between a man's long legs.

Lieutenant Peter Miller removed a cellophane-wrapped cookie from the pocket of his wet London Fog.

"It's a bit soggy, J.R.," he said, bending forward to offer his bribe. The cat was addicted to Oreos, but they had been removed from his world when Ellie got serious about dieting. Peter had wisely wooed and won the haughty animal's affection with Nabisco kickback.

"I have another cookie for Annie," said Peter, "unless Tony has picked her up already."

"Gone," replied Ellen sadly. "It's nine o'clock. I have good news and bad news. Which do you want first?"

"Bad, I guess."

"Tony's going to board Annie with Grandma Bernstein."

"That's bad?"

"Not really, but he could have consulted me."

"She's not your child," Peter said, softly.

"Would you have minded? I mean, would you object if Tony decided to board Annie here?"

"Of course not. This is your house, and I love kids. Just for the record, Annie's smarter than most kids. I think she gets it from me," he added boastfully.

"She's not your child."

"Right. What's the good news?"

"It's the third quarter and your Raiders are getting slaughtered. If they lose tonight, my Broncos will lead the AFC West." Ellie hung Peter's trench coat inside the closet that also contained Annie's portable playpen. Returning to the family room, she inhaled baby powder, warm milk, and crackling pine. "How was your day, honey?"

"Did you see that tackle? *Holy cow!*" He grinned, aware that Ellie had attended a Catholic school where nuns didn't allow cussing. It was okay, however, to desecrate a cow. Although Peter had no great love for cows, he usually profaned a bull during his verbal explosions.

Seating her lieutenant on the couch, Ellie removed his wet Hushpuppies and massaged his frozen toes. She unfastened the knot of a necktie that waved in the same direction as a nose once broken, then reset incorrectly. Finally, she brought him coffee and a thick sandwich whose hot gravy disguised carbonized roast.

"Okay, okay," said Peter. "Is this leftover Annie syndrome or what?"

"I'm glad to see you, and it's nasty outside, and you deserve some TLC. Tender loving—"

"Care? How come yesterday, during the Bronco game, you wouldn't leave the room to get me another beer? 'Dammit, Loot, fetch it yourself,' was the delicate way you phrased your refusal."

"I didn't want to miss John Elway's next pass."

"Hey, wait a minute. Do you think you're the only detective in this relationship who recalls things in perfect detail? 'I'm not your slave,' you growled."

"The score was close," muttered Ellie as she kneaded the tight muscles in Peter's neck and practically lifted the sandwich to his lips.

"Bullshit. Your Denver Donkeys were way ahead." He glanced toward the TV, then back at Ellie. "This attention couldn't be for information about the bank rob—"

"How much did they steal? Was anybody hurt? Was it a

full-fledged robbery like . . . oh, say Bonnie and Clyde? Or
was it more like Wood—"

"James Wood? Grant Wood? Bob Woodward?"

"Cute, Peter. No, I meant Woody Allen."

"Woody Allen?"

"His movie with that hilarious bank robbery. The handwritten note bit." She took a deep breath. "Speaking of
notes, did you find one inside his house or car? Was it written
by hand? Was it typed? Or does the average self-executioner
use a word processor nowadays?"

"What the hell are you talking about?"

"Suicide notes."

"Shit! How did you hear about Burns? When I arrived at
the scene, newshounds were just beginning to sniff. *Tony.*
Tony was the real estate agent who called the police, right?"

"You didn't see him?"

"Nope."

"But he said he was grilled by cops. And he knew stuff,
Peter. For instance, Tony knew that the victim was called
Harry and the gas gauge was on half."

"Take it easy. I didn't get there first. Tony gave his
statement to a uniform and said his name was Anton R.
Bernstein, so I didn't—"

"Tell me about his statement."

"What does the *R* stand for?"

"Rat-fink. The statement, Peter."

"Tony smelled exhaust fumes and called nine-one-one.
Please, I'd rather not discuss this."

"What did the garage look like?"

"It has double doors and it's painted white."

"I meant *inside.*"

"Forget it, Norrie, dead bodies aren't exactly dinner
conversation."

She could tell from his use of her nickname that Peter
wasn't really angry—only resigned to the inevitable. He had
once dubbed her Norrie, derived from Eleanor, because she
tended to *ignore* his advice.

"A singed beef sandwich and dill pickle is not my idea of dinner," she replied. "Anyway, I don't want a description of the body. I've never met Burns, but I've met his wife, so I feel close to the case."

"It isn't a case yet. How do you know the wife?"

"She just joined Weight Winners."

"Okay, tell *me* about *her.*" Peter glanced up from his sandwich, gravy dripping from the ends of his mustache.

"Wait a sec." Ellie left the room and retrieved a Diet Slice from the refrigerator. Then, wriggling next to Peter, she said, "It wasn't a suicide, was it?"

"Why do you say that?"

"Vibes. What did you find?"

"Nothing. It's none of your business, Ellie."

Uh-oh, he called me Ellie. He's getting angry. I'd better shut up.

"What did you find, Lieutenant?"

"I told you, nothing. Besides, there could be a logical explanation—"

"What did you find?"

Peter scowled. "You won't give me any peace until I confess, will you? All right, it was a perfect suicide scene, if any death can be called perfect. Towels along the garage doors, Burns slumped over the dash of his car. It all fit, like pieces of a jigsaw puzzle. An empty bottle of Chivas on the front seat; he probably drank himself insensible. No glass. He drank straight from the bottle, but it was too neat. If he had consumed the whole bottle, he should have drunkenly missed his mouth and spilled Scotch on his clothes. We'll check that. Of course, we don't know how much was in the bottle or how much alcohol's in his system. We're not even sure about the cause of death. He could have choked on his own vomit. That's not fun to think about, is it? He urinated, soiled—"

"Okay, Peter, that's enough."

"Didn't you ask for details? Don't you know what happens when the sphincter muscles relax in death? Or would

you prefer a description of a movie murder? Nice red blood.
Sterile wound."

"Good grief, was there *blood*?"

"Of course not. He supposedly asphyxiated."

"*Supposedly*?"

Peter's tense shoulders slumped. "Norrie, I'm sorry I went
into analeptic details. It was unfair. I'm tired and baffled. I
don't know. Call it instinct. I feel something's wrong. An
autopsy will tell us more, but—"

"But what?"

"Burns didn't exhibit a hell of a lot of body hair, Norrie,
but he had these patches on his wrists."

"Patches?"

"Hairless, as though he had been tied up inside the car
with sticky tape, maybe surgical tape. There were cartons of
medical supplies in the back of the vehicle. If Burns kept an
inventory, we'll find out what's missing."

"I'll bet he was killed for his drugs. Some crazed junkie. That
happens all the time. Peter? Honey, stop watching the damn
Raiders and look at me. Couldn't it have been a junkie?"

"No, it was too thoughtful. A crazed junkie would have
hit Burns over the head or knifed him or shot him, then
grabbed his supplies. Why bother staging a suicide? A person
high on drugs wouldn't have the smarts to do that. Somebody needing a fix would be too jumpy. If this thing is
murder, and I'm not saying it is, it was probably committed
by a professional amateur."

"Professional amateur?"

"You collect authentic reproductions, don't you?"

"Damn." Ellie turned off the TV, then offhandedly prod-
ded fireplace logs with a poker. "Maybe it was a supplier and
Burns reneged," she said, not wanting to relinquish her
theory. "Have you ever heard Woody Allen's line about
organized crime? 'It's no secret that organized crime takes
in over forty billion dollars a year. This is quite a profitable
sum, especially when one considers that the Mafia spends
very little for office supplies.' "

She waited for Peter to smile. He didn't. "Maybe Burns needed money," she said slowly. "He was planning to sell his house, called Tony for an appraisal. I'll bet he was in financial trouble, desperate."

"No, Norrie, apparently he was doing very well. Of course, he could have a hidden chalet, gambling debts, a mistress. We won't find out until we investigate."

"How do you know he was doing well?"

"His coworker lives next door, came running to the scene with the rest of the neighborhood. By the time we finished, the voyeurs looked like bizarre snowpeople. There was even a man with a red-orange nose and an upside-down pipe. Frosty. Gene Autry?"

"Burl Ives, although I think Autry sang it first. What did the coworker say?"

"That Harry Burns was really happy lately, for the first time in years. 'On top of the world.' Harry's sales were up, and he had a huge commission check due. He left the office around lunchtime, humming."

"Doesn't sound suicidal to me. What would be his motive?"

Peter finally smiled. "You've met his wife."

"Right. Where was she when—"

"Chapel Hills Shopping Mall. She shopped, watched a movie, then returned home carrying three rope-handled bags filled to the brim with junk jewelry, undergarments, nonprescription diet pills, and knickkacks."

"Diet pills? Weight Winners doesn't allow pills. Damn! What kind of knickknacks?"

"Civil War stuff. A poster of Rhett and Scarlett. A planter shaped like a Confederate flag. A small sculpture of a man on horseback. General—"

"Lee? Robert E.?"

"Jackson. Stonewall. Ms. Burns was spending her husband's commission check ahead of time. Or else she was pissed about something and charging stuff to punish him."

"What movie did she see?"

"An oldie. The original *M*A*S*H* with what's-his-name—Elliott Gold?"

"Gould. Barbra's ex."

"Stanwyck?"

"No, Streisand."

"Why did you ask about the movie, Norrie?"

"It might have been a fake alibi, Peter. Magnolia could have stashed all those purchases and waited for the right moment to—"

"Dammit, *I'm* not a professional amateur. We checked her theater stub and the dates on her receipts."

"Sorry, honey. How did Magnolia react when she heard about her husband's murder?"

"We haven't established it *was* a murder."

"You should have been a lawyer. I meant his death."

Peter grimaced. "Ms. Burns swooned. I'm not talking faint here. Wrist to forehead, hand crumpling tiny hankie. She staggered backward and—"

"You caught her?"

"Uh-uh, she weighs more than I do. Ms. Burns landed on her fanny and lost her breath. We unfastened a tight, uh, whatchamacallit."

"Girdle?"

"No, corset. I almost had to perform mouth-to-mouth resuscitation. By the way, Ms. Burns had some of those same patches as her husband."

"She did? Where?"

"When she landed, her skirt fell up, and her panty hose fell down. She had strips of hair missing from her thighs."

"Peter, she probably waxed her legs."

"She what?"

"You poor innocent. Shaved her legs with hot wax. I'd guess she didn't use a beautician and left some hairy spots. Hey, Magnolia could have used the same goop on her husband. Maybe they were into kinky sex."

"Speaking of sex." Rising from the couch, Peter leered à la Groucho and gestured with an imaginary cigar. Then, crossing the room, unzipping her sweater, he nuzzled the mounds of her breasts.

"If I swooned," she gasped, "would you catch me?"

"Are you planning to swoon?"

"Only if you promise to give me mouth-to-mouth."

Peter scooped Ellie up, carried her easily into the bedroom, and placed her on top of the water bed.

"Earlier tonight," she murmured, "I told Mick about gumming it to death because it tasted good."

"Gumming what?"

"A frozen bagel."

"*What!*"

"Nothing. Never mind. Peter, you promised mouth-to-mouth resus—"

As always, their coupling was first gentle, then fierce. When they'd finished, she rested her flushed cheek against Peter's chest.

"Do you want me to wax your body?" she asked softly.

"No, thanks." He glanced toward the snow-shrouded window. "I need an extra layer of fur for protection against the elements, like Jackie Robinson."

The heavy cat, accustomed to frequent mattress swells, unwilling to relinquish the comfort generated by controlled water temperature, sprawled across Ellie's ankles, holding her prisoner as Peter again stroked her body.

A little later, Ellie murmured, "You know what Mick and Sandra said tonight? They said I looked like Hot Lips."

"Hot Lips who?"

"Houlihan. Loretta Swit."

"Oh, *that* Hot Lips. I thought you were talking about a hooker I once arrested for soliciting at a convention."

"Before or after?"

"After. I had to secure the evidence."

"That's entrapment."

"I know," Peter said smugly. "I couldn't get the charges to stick, and she was ever so grateful."

"You rat. Do you think I look like her?"

"The hooker?"

"No, Loretta Swit."

"I've never seen Loretta naked, so I can't really make a comparison." Peter yawned.

"Holy cow, I just thought of something. Years ago, during the 'M*A*S*H' finale, a girl costumed and wigged as Hot Lips died outside the Dew Drop Inn. Are you listening to me?"

"Died outside the insie." Peter traced her belly button with a warm finger. "You have an insie."

"It was *supposedly* a hit-and-run accident. Her name was Ginny—Virginia-something."

"How do you remember things like that?"

"Well, it started when Tony refused to let me work and imaginary crime-solving was my main occupation. If we were married, would you let me work full-time instead of part-time?"

"Sure, you could support me."

"Honest?"

"Cross my heart. I wouldn't want you pissed off, charging stuff at the mall."

"Peter, what did Burns look like?"

"Norrie, please, forget Burns."

"Answer my last question and I'll leave you alone."

"He was thin all over. Thinning hair, nose, mouth. No chin. A photo showed him in service uniform. He looked like that 'M*A*S*H' character. Thin-blooded. Probably got drunk real fast . . . breathed fumes . . . died quickly."

"That's strange. Virginia—*Whitley*, that was her name—anyway, she was trying to look like Hot Lips Houlihan and the suicide tonight resembled Frank Burns. Isn't that a strange coincidence, Peter? Peter?"

Ellie glanced down at the pillow, but her detective, sound asleep, didn't answer.

Three long streets from Ellie's heated home and water bed, the student dorm extended one entire block. Snow disguised the dorm's unimposing industrial-painted facade. Vanilla icicles twisted from its flat roof, looking like Dairy Queen swirls, and Sandra was aware that she'd missed Ellie's supper feast. Mick had consumed hamburgers, fries, and hot chocolate at a stand near campus, but Sandra insisted on sticking to her diet, having successfully maintained her original loss of thirty pounds. Inside her dorm room, on her desk, sat Bumblebees. Tuna cans.

Now she buried her wet face against Mick's equally damp jacket and hugged him. Beneath his jeans, she could feel an active bulge.

"Come on, Muffin," he pleaded into her dripping hair.

Sandra shivered with delight at Mick's use of the nickname Ellie had bestowed upon her.

"Cold?" He drew her closer.

"I just realized that your mom nicknames everybody she loves with food."

"What do you mean?" Mick sighed in exasperation. He had been trying to convince Sandra to spend the night with him, but she kept changing the subject.

"Ellie calls me Muffin and Annie Pumpkin. I'm surprised she doesn't have a food name for you."

"She used to call me Pizza Face."

"You're kidding."

"Nope. When I was fourteen, fifteen, I had the most classic case of zits you ever saw. Mom was always trying to get me to wash my face. Boy, was I a mess."

"Me, too," admitted Sandra, her freckled nose wrinkling in disgust. Three years ago, oh so overweight, she'd been riddled with pimples—pestiferous spots that had festered inside and outside. Ellie had helped transform Sandra into a respectable butterfly, but her emotional scars hadn't disappeared like the acne, and sometimes they lay very close to the surface.

I'm afraid to make love with Mick, she thought. What if I'm no good? On the other hand, I'm probably the only virgin left in Colorado. Maybe Kansas, too.

"Come on, Muffin," pleaded Mick, "let's go inside. I'm frozen solid."

"Ellie expects you home soon."

"Hey, what's your problem?"

"I guess I don't want to seem too easy."

"Too easy?" Mick groaned and stepped away. "It's John Russell, isn't it? You've been sleeping with that damn piano player while I'm in Boulder, right?"

"Have you slept with Belly?"

"Of course. The whole band has. Is it Russell?"

Sandra hid a grin with one mitten. John treated her like a kid sister. "I don't kiss and tell, Mick."

"If that's what you're worried about, neither do I."

"You just did."

"What do you mean? Belinda? Belly doesn't count. I wouldn't say anything about *us*."

"Because I'm your personal property?"

"Yes!"

"Good grief, Ellie told me there'd be days like this."

"What does that mean? Next you'll probably insist I'm just like my dad."

"Sometimes you are like him. That remark about your stepmother wasn't very nice."

"Jesus, I wasn't trying to be nice."

"Don't get mad."

"I'm not mad."

"Okay, you're grumpy."

"I'm *not* grumpy." All of a sudden he grinned. "Sorry, Muffin, call me Dopey. In a few minutes I'll be Sneezy. Then we'll have to find Doc. Please let me inside your dorm."

"I can't. I'm Bashful." Sandra saw Mick shudder and sensed that, this time, it was from the cold rather than desire. The bulge in his jeans had disappeared, hibernating. "All right, you can sleep in my room tonight, but we don't mess around unless I say so."

"Deal. C'mon, Bashful."

Together, clothed in underwear, they huddled beneath the

covers of Sandra's chaste twin-sized bed. The sheets were icy. Mick's tall athletic form dominated the space, and Sandra cuddled against his length as they waited for body heat to generate warmth to the lumpy mattress.

"Muffin?"

"You know, it's funny how much your mom looks like Hot Lips. I never noticed it before."

Mick sighed, defeated. "Remember the fairy tale about Rose White and Rose Red?" He felt Sandra's head nod. "When I was a kid, I thought Mom was Rose Red, beautiful and mysterious. Yup, Rose Red, the Virgin Mary—"

"That's normal. I imagine every small boy—"

"And Virgil."

"Virgil?"

"Mom's fluent in Latin. French, too. I picked up a few words and phrases by osmosis, but she can read, speak, and understand the stuff."

"No kidding. I'm lucky if I can remember the lyrics to John Russell's rock songs, especially if they don't rhyme."

Mick scowled at the mention of Russell, then said, "When I was small, Mom used to drop these homilies into my lap. Began every sentence with *Dei gratia*."

"Which means?"

"By the grace of God. Hey, we even had a cat named Advocatus Diaboli. Devil's Advocate."

"Oh, I love that. What else?"

Mick yawned. "Sorry, I'm wiped out. We played until dawn Saturday, then I helped the others get ready to leave on Sunday. Today, Mom had chores that she claims Peter always forgets."

"Good night, sleep tight, don't let the bedbugs—"

"Aw, Muffin, you really want me to talk Latin?" Mick drew Sandra into the curve of his body and reached for her bra snaps.

"Stop it, Dopey, I'm not ready yet."

"Sorry." He removed her bra.

"You know who else looks like Loretta Swit? My dorm-mate, Natalie. She's in the next room. Nat's a dancer like me, only better. Can't sing though. She has blond hair and a sexy mouth—"

"Maybe I should go next door to *her* room."

"I suppose any girl with platinum hair and a sexy mouth could look like Hot Lips. I wish I resembled somebody beautiful and famous."

"You do, Muffin. You look a lot like Sissy Spacek."

"Do I really?" she asked, delighted, thinking that he couldn't have said anything more flattering. Relaxing, she cuddled closer to his warm body. "Mick? I think I'm ready now."

Silence.

"Dopey?"

More silence.

Sandra glanced down at the pillow. Mick's face was turned sideways. Long lashes shaded his cheeks. His diamond earring glittered, and she remembered the argument he'd had with his dad. *Natalie's* boyfriend was old enough to be her father. Sandra had never met him, but Nat called him "Daddy Longlegs" and had said something about him financing her dancing career. They were sleeping together, or at least he was screwing her, because Nat said sex made her legs weak, and . . .

I'm probably the only college-age virgin left in Colorado, she thought. Kansas, too. Maybe the whole world. A satanic cult could sacrifice my virginal body to . . .

With that last unfinished thought, Sandra fell asleep.

$\triangledown$

5

THE SMELL OF bacon grease permeated the room. Jackie Robinson dogged Ellie's footsteps, meowing for something more substantial than an elusive aroma.

Peter sat at the kitchen table, reading the newspaper, and Ellie could see sports headlines. His Raiders had lost. Badly. Two days ago, the Dolphins had devoured the Seahawks. That made her Broncos first in their division.

Sandra and Mick had called earlier and were due for breakfast any moment, so Ellie restrained herself from probing any further about the Burns suicide.

She heard sounds from the front hallway. "Hell—" she began to shout, then swallowed the rest of her salutation. Oh. Damn. The kids are arguing. Not wanting to snoop, Ellie turned up the volume on her portable radio. Sinatra sang about love and marriage.

"But you fell asleep," Sandra said.

"That was last night. This morning I was awake, and your exercise bit was a definite turn-on."

"Give me a break, Dopey. The deal was that *I* decide when. It can't always be your way."

"My way?" Mick nodded toward the kitchen. "You sound like Sinatra. I'll bet nobody ever drove Old Blue Eyes bananas, then reneged."

"I didn't renege, and I don't eat bananas; too many calories." She blushed, then added, "Look, Mick, I want it to be perfect. Romantic. If you can't control your urges, sleep with Belinda."

"Okay."

"While you're at it, take her to the Gala."

"What's a gala?"

"I thought you understood French. My dance recital. Saturday night. I can get you another ticket, and Natalie's dancing, too. Then you'll have a choice. Belly's room, wherever she shacks up, or Natalie's bed."

"Right, fine," said Mick, hanging his jacket inside the hall closet.

"Right, fine," echoed Sandra, hanging her jacket on the opposite side.

Then they entered the kitchen and sat next to each other.

While the men shoveled pancakes and bacon into their mouths, Ellie and Sandra breakfasted on poached eggs, wheat toast, and four ounces of freshly squeezed orange juice. Although the atmosphere was strained, Ellie kept the hot coffee flowing.

"You should have called your mother, Mick," chided Peter, assuming the unfamiliar role of Dad. "It was really nasty out, and she worries."

"Come on, Pete, Mom can't check up on me in Boulder."

"I didn't want to check up on you," said Ellie, turning off the radio. "Maybe a brief phone call next time, okay?"

"Okay. I'm sorry, Mom. *Errare humanum est.*"

"To err is human." Ellie laughed. "What made you think of that, Mick? It's been years."

"Muffin and I spent most of last night talking," said Mick. "You. Latin. The Seven Dwarfs, especially Bashful." When Sandra nudged him in the ribs with an angry elbow, he added, "Hey, Mom, remember Diaboli?"

"Advocatus Diaboli. He was the family puss when Mick was—what?—ten? Eleven? I should have saved the name for Jackie Robinson here, at least the Diaboli part." Ellie watched her Persian lick syrup from a pancake that Peter had slipped under the table.

"I'm sorry I didn't call, Mom. I'll do better next weekend," said Mick.

"Are you planing to visit again, honey?"

"Yup. The band is booked Friday, and I've been invited to Muffin's dance thing on Saturday."

"Be sure to bring Belly," whispered Sandra, then, louder, asked, "What happened to Advocatus Diaboli?"

"Chased a squirrel up a tree, fell, and broke his neck," replied Ellie. "Don't ever believe that myth about cats always landing on their feet or having nine lives."

"Can I help with the dishes, Ellie?"

"No, Muffin, the *men* will wash them."

Mick and Peter both glanced at their watches.

"Duty calls," said Peter.

"Have to run," said Mick. "It's a long drive, Mom."

Jackie Robinson sauntered toward his litter box.

Ellie stacked dishes as Peter left for his precinct, Sandra for class, and Mick for Boulder. With their departure, the silence seemed magnified. Even Jackie Robinson slipped outside to join his neutered buddies and indulge in whatever sexless activities eunuch felines found stimulating.

The sun shined, melting snow. Earlier, during what Peter called her "crack-of-dawn jog," Ellie had passed the Burns house. Now she flipped the pages of her trusty U.S. West directory and reached for her duck.

A harsh southern-accented woman's voice shouted, "If you don't stop, I'll call the police."

"Magnolia?"

"No. I'm Miz Smithers, Magnolia's mama. Who's this?"

"Eleanor Bernstein. I'm a friend of your daughter's."

"Just a minute. Hang on, you hear?"

A younger voice murmured, "Miz Bernstein? How nice of you to telephone." Then Magnolia burst into tears.

"I'll come over right away," Ellie said into her duck's butt.

Beneath a limited-edition plate, "Mammy Lacing Scarlett," Ellie's Union-blue corduroy slacks rested on an overstuffed chair. Crossed sabers hung above the fireplace. Confederate flags and framed prints of gray-clad soldiers dominated every wall. Cut-glass bowls overflowed with essence of lavender. The potpourri clogged Ellie's nose, and she could almost swear that she felt a light film of perfumed pollution settle upon her orange sweater.

After sneezing twice she attempted to keep her expression sober, which was difficult, especially since she kept honking into a tissue.

Standing by the fireplace, directly under the sabers, Mrs. Smithers was short, plump, and corseted. She wore her hair in tight silver-brown ringlets. Her tiny button eyes snapped like pieces of sizzling charcoal. A black shawl shrouded a black taffeta dress, while a white cameo brooch appeared threatened by an abundant double chin.

Clutching a soggy lace handkerchief, Magnolia made her entrance from the stairwell. Her nose was red. She had tried to curl her brownish hair like Mama. The left side kinked, but straight strands fell to her right shoulder. Magnolia's eyes were rimmed pink, like an albino rabbit, and duplicated the color of her dress.

Mrs. Smithers aborted Ellie's greeting by loudly whispering, "I told you to wear somethin' black, Magnolia."

"Mama, I don't have nothin' black."

"A closet full of gowns," said Smithers to "Mammy Lacing Scarlett" then glared at her daughter again.

"Nothin' black, Mama, I swear to God." Magnolia's bottom lip quivered.

"Well, missy, we can't go shoppin'. It wouldn't be fittin' on this tragic day. I have another black garment in my suitcase." Smithers swiveled her face toward Ellie. "I got in so late last night, I didn't have time to unpack. The airplane almost crashed, an' they didn't have any teensy bottles of cookin' sherry, just vodka an' such, so I had to drink Bloody Marys with toe-mah-toe juice an' everybody knows they spray toe-mah-toes with poison. Thought I'd end up *dead*, like Magnolia's husband. Then this mornin' the phone kept ringin'. Ring! Ring! Tragedy! Tragedy!"

"But Mama, I can't fit your dress," wailed Magnolia.

Mama waved away her daughter's objection with several ringed fingers. "We can do alterations, or maybe Miz Bernstein here would be kind enough to purchase a bottle of Rit Fabric Dye."

"Of course, Mrs. Smithers," replied Ellie, watching Magnolia's pink ruffled dress sway across the room until the naturally hooped body perched on top of a horsehair sofa. "Or you can call a store and ask them to deliver. I have a friend, Hannah Taylor, who's the assistant manager of a lovely clothing—"

"How nice of you to visit, Miz Bernstein," said Magnolia politely, as though hosting a tea party.

Ellie pointed toward the blue-scripted pastry box resting on a scroll-legged table, a traditional food donation she had purchased on her way to the Burns house. "Mrs. Smithers, I would love a cup of coffee, maybe one of those little pastries. I—I didn't have time for breakfast this morning." Picturing her kitchen table, Ellie felt the words stick in her throat, but she wanted Mama to leave the room.

"We don't have coffee," said Magnolia.

"No caffeine," amended Mama, "although I understand the late Mr. Burns drank Coca-Cola and that's full of caffeine. Fizz and bugs. Bugs breed in fizz, y'know. If I wanted to poison somebody, I'd give 'em Coca-Cola. I once saw a toothbrush dissolve in Coke. All the bristles disappeared."

"Maybe," suggested Ellie, "you could make me a nice hot cup of tea." Orange pekoe and bugs.

Mrs. Smithers hesitated, her body ramrod straight. With amusement, Ellie viewed the woman's inner struggle, until southern hospitality won over curiosity.

"Lemonade," said Mama. "I make it from scratch. Magnolia does, too. Real lemons, sugar, and my own secret ingredient. A recipe handed down from plantation days. Cost more, but it's worth the price."

"Use Equal packets instead of sugar, Mama."

"That would be wonderful, Mrs. Smithers," said Ellie. "Thank you so much. I can't wait to taste your original lemonade."

As Mama's taffeta dress rustled toward the kitchen Magnolia said, "How nice of you to visit, Miz Bernstein."

"Please call me Ellie."

"You can call me Mag . . . Mag . . . Maggie." Magnolia's corseted bosom heaved, and she began to cry.

Ellie maneuvered to the sofa, thinking how the horsehair must scratch legs not protected by corduroy. She patted Magnolia's hankie-clad hand. "I'm so sorry."

"I don't know what I'll do without Mr. Burns. He was my whole life."

"Life goes on, Maggie."

"That's what Mama says. But Mr. Burns was so kind an' he wouldn't deny me when I wanted to go shoppin'. I can't think what I'll do now."

"Didn't your husband have any life insurance?"

"Oh yes, yes he did. The Silver and Gold Insurance Company. Two policies. Fifty thousand dollars term and— oh, I don't know. Mr. Burns took care of that. I can't balance a checkbook."

"When your claim's settled, you can go shopping."

Am I nuts? thought Ellie. Why did I mention shopping when she's just lost her husband? Potpourri dregs must have traveled from my nose to my brain.

"I can't go shoppin', Miz Bern—Ellie. Mama says I have to fly home to Atlanta. She says the insurance company might not pay because of the su—because he killed himself. And if they do pay, I'll have to donate my money for reconstruction of Civil War landmarks. Life's a you-know-what, rhymes with witch, an' then you die."

"How about a cherry Danish, sweetie?" Desperate, Ellie couldn't think of anything else consoling.

Magnolia glanced toward the pastry box. "I shouldn't. I

have too much collateral in my blood. That's what killed Mr. Burns."

"He had too much collat—cholesterol?"

"No, ulcers."

Ellie heard Mrs. Smithers bustling about inside the kitchen.

So did Magnolia. "I can't go in there," she whimpered. "The kitchen's attached to the garage where Mr. Burns . . . Mama says I'm bein' silly, but I don't care if I never eat again. I'll fade away to skin an' bones an' join Mr. Burns in heaven. Well, maybe one Danish."

Swaying to her feet, she retrieved a pastry, then returned to the sofa.

"Why do you think he did it?" said Ellie softly.

"I can't imagine. We were so happy." Magnolia lowered her voice. "I think Harry had somebody else . . . another woman on the side. She . . . somebody kept callin' this mornin'. Over and over. That's why Mama sounded so rude when you phoned earlier. I'm sure Harry had a you-know-what, rhymes with bore."

"Do you know who the, uh, woman is, Maggie?"

"I don't think so. She wears perfume. Mr. Burns sometimes stunk."

Ellie wondered how any odor could overpower the lavender essence. "Do you think Mr. Burns was"—she hesitated, searching for an adequate word—"was in *trouble* with the other woman?"

" 'Course not." Magnolia finished her pastry in three bites. "I'll tell you a big secret. Mr. Burns pulled the cord to our freezer an' the food melted. I think he was gonna leave me, Ellie. That's why I joined up with your diet club." For the first time her pink-rimmed eyes turned mean and squinty. "That cheap smelly whore can't have him now, can she?"

"Why on earth would he pull the freezer cord?"

"He didn't want me to eat."

"But if the food spoiled, he couldn't eat it either."

"Mr. Burns drank strong spirits for lunch. It made him crazy. He slashed the top of the freezer, too. Now if that's not the act of a crazy person, I don't know what."

"He slashed the freezer? That doesn't make any sense. Did Mr. Burns have enemies?"

"You sound like the police." Magnolia swayed to her feet, rushed toward the pastry box, chewed up another Danish, then returned to the sofa. "People loved Harry."

How, thought Ellie, could she bring the conversation around to "M*A*S*H" and Frank Burns?

"Maggie dear, did Harry ever attend a party—well, actually it was called a M*A*S*H-Bash—over at the Dew Drop Inn? About eleven years ago?" Ellie mentally kicked herself. Magnolia Smithers Burns was a tad simple, but she'd certainly note the abrupt change of subject.

She didn't. "What's a mashbash? Is that like a chili cookoff?"

"No, sweetie, it was a party to celebrate the 'M*A*S*H' finale. They had a look-alike contest, and I understand your husband resemb—"

"Harry stayed home nights unless he had business appointments." Again her eyes slitted. "Eleven years ago, he didn't do his fuckin' business at night."

Ellie wondered what "fuckin' " rhymed with. Mentally, she traveled down the alphabet, rejected "buckin' " and "duckin'," then gave up at the letter *K*.

"Maggie," she said, "I wonder if you could you give me a list of Harry's friends and customers."

"Whatever for?" she asked as Mrs. Smithers returned, balancing a lacquered tray.

The lemonade's secret ingredient was a gummy molasses that turned the beverage from its usual yellow to a murky brown color. Ellie took a polite sip and almost gagged.

"Mama, she wants a list of Harry's friends," said Magnolia, gulping down the lemonade.

"Whatever for, Miz Bernstein?"

"I thought I could help y'all out," improvised Ellie,

subconsciously mimicking the southern cadence of her hostess. "Call, tell people 'bout the funeral, y'know?"

Mama sniffed. "The late Mr. Burns will be on display at his church. I placed the announcement this mornin' in the newspaper. They sounded nice over the telephone. Very nice. For Yankees."

Rising to her feet, Ellie looked directly at Magnolia. "I've heard that your husband resembled Frank Burns. Do you know who I mean?"

Magnolia's eyes darted toward the television, to her mother, then back to Ellie. "I don't watch TV. Mama says it's all trash, made up, 'cept 'Dallas,' which is truthful. But they took 'Dallas' off the air, an' sometimes it seems like a dream that it was ever on, y'know? Anyway, Mama says 'lectricity from the TV makes you, uh, sterile. But lots of people thought Harry looked like that 'M*A*S*H' man. Once we went shoppin' for groceries an' some people made a fuss. It was so embarrassin'."

"Was Harry embarrassed, too?"

"At first. The people said they belonged to a club that watched 'M*A*S*H' reruns. There was a lady with short brown hair, an' some men, and I think one of them was a priest 'cause they called him Father. They made a real fuss, and even wanted to take a camera pitcher of Harry, but they didn't have a camera. The priest wrote Harry's name down and our address, too, I think. Harry laughed, since they could be customers one day, y'know? Harry was like that. Always sellin' and makin' a good livin'. He was so smart."

Magnolia sobbed audibly, lifting her hankie to a nose that now guarded a sticky lemonade mustache.

"If he was so smart, why'd he kill himself?" Mrs. Smithers sniffed.

"He didn't, Mama, it was an accident."

"Hah! Sorry, Magnolia, but you've gotta face facts. Your husband was Yankee trash, and a drunkard to boot."

"Oh no, he had a li'l lunch snort, Mama. Harry was gettin' in the car to drive back to work—"

"Snort? If you lit a match and shoved it down Mr. Burns's throat, he'd regurgitate flames."

"Please," said Ellie uncomfortably. "We really don't know yet how—"

"Magnolia must nap now, Miz Bernstein," interrupted Mama, smoothing a fold in her taffeta. "Will we see you at the funeral service?"

Ellie nodded as the first ten notes of "Dixie" sounded.

On her way outside, she passed Lieutenant Peter Miller.

"What the fuck do you mean by a condolence call? You're full of shit, Ellie."

Uh-oh, her detective was *furious.* When Peter turned angry, he dropped "Norrie." When furious, he swore like Al Pacino—desecrating both bulls and the act of lovemaking.

"I would do the same for any member of my club," she replied. "The poor woman was distraught—"

"Not as distraught as I am right this minute. Keep out of my case, Ellie."

"Case? Aha, so you *do* think it's a homicide. Why? The freezer, right? You don't believe for one moment that Harry—"

"How do you know about the freezer?"

"Magnolia just happened to mention it."

"Just happened? Bullshit!"

"What's the motive, Peter?"

"I have no idea, dammit! The only person who had a motive is the wife, and she couldn't possibly get back and forth from the mall in time to murder—"

"Maggie would never kill her husband. Harry was nice to her. Besides, she has to donate his insurance money to a bunch of Civil War fanatics. No way! Unless—"

"Unless what?"

"Maggie just happened to mention that Harry had a woman on the side."

"Magnolia Burns was at the fucking mall!"

"Peter, knock off the swearing. I won't apologize for acting neighborly, and I wasn't in any danger. Okay, Maggie went shopping, but what if the mistress killed Burns?"

"Not unless she brought her three kids along to watch; she was stuck with them for the day. Besides, she has no motive, either. Burns planned to divorce Magnolia and marry Iris Maria. She's pregnant—the mistress, not the wife."

"Iris Maria? You've been busy, Peter."

"I've been doing my job, Ellie, *my job*, not yours."

"What's *my* job? Washing the breakfast dishes?"

"That's right. They're still stacked on top of the sink. Just for the record, Ellie, stale bacon grease is not an aphrodisiac."

"Well, I'm not in the mood for sex, Lieutenant. And you might as well know right now that Miz Smithers invited me to Harry's funeral."

Ellie didn't attend the funeral after all. Those rites were performed Friday morning. The time conflicted with her lecturing duties at the Good Shepherd church, and she couldn't find a substitute. Surely Peter would attend, survey the mournful assemblage. Somehow she'd wheedle the information out of him later.

> *Wheedle:* to entice by soft words or flattery.
> *Weed:* to get rid of something harmful.
> *Weed:* a dress worn as a sign of mourning (as by a
>   widow, i.e. Magnolia).

The widow wasn't at the Weight Winners meeting, of course, but a new member, Melody Remming, took her place. Ellie found herself talking to the young woman, who was as friendly as the poodle puppy she resembled. Melody was gregarious. She confided that she had fallen madly in love at first sight with a man "ten feet tall, who weighs less than I do." So she'd decided to join Weight Winners and shrink to the skinniness of her adored one.

After the meeting, Ellie found Melody thumbtacking a piece of paper to the church bulletin board. The paper included Melody's phone number and suggested that anybody interested in joining a "M*A*S*H" fan club should call. Above the handwritten message was a truly remarkable sketch of Hawkeye, Hot Lips, and a few other cast members.

"Star Trek addicts have clubs," Melody explained. "They even hold annual conventions. So I got this idea, I mean, well, we could start in Colorado, maybe even go national, call ourselves 'M*A*S*Hies' or something. Remember that old movie with Gary Cooper? They started John Doe clubs to help each other." Her cheeks flamed. "We could donate to medical causes, Ellie, like Jerry's kids, AIDS, whatever. It would be a way to help and have fun at the same time."

"That's a wonderful idea," said Ellie doubtfully.

"I know it sounds crazy, and it probably won't fly, but I started thinking about it when I attended this 'M*A*S*H' thing last Monday night. That's where I met Gordon."

Gazing at the notice, Ellie wondered if she'd ever been that optimistic. Idealistic. *Obsessed.* Tony said she was obsessed with the show, and certainly it was better to donate one's hard-earned money to medical causes than space travel, but deep down inside Ellie had the feeling that "M*A*S*H" fans didn't want to help. They wanted to laugh.

"I'm an addict myself," Ellie admitted, trying to erase with words the blush that had extended to the roots of Melody's curls.

"Are you really? Maybe you could come with me to next Monday night's get-together. You'd meet Gordon."

Ellie smelled lavender potpourri as a thought clicked into place. "Is one of the 'M*A*S*H' club members a priest?"

"No. Oh, you must mean Father Mac. His real name's Sean McCarthy, but he looks a lot like Father Mulcahy, and he once won first prize at a M*A*S*H-Bash party."

"Holy cow! The Dew Drop Inn."

"That's right. How did you know?"

"I was there."

"I was, too. My cousin Fred came as Radar, but he said to leave him alone because he wanted to sit with 'the men.' The only guy who even said hello to me was drunk, sloshing down one martini after another. He wore cowboy clothes. I don't usually drink, but the cowboy bought me a double martini. Then I felt sick and left."

"Melody, do you recall a girl who died in the parking lot? Virginia Whitley? I believe most people called her Ginny or Gin."

"Nope. How did she die?"

"Hit-and-run."

"Oh, what a shame. Please join me Monday night, Ellie. The president of the club doesn't seem to like women, and I'm the only one there. Well, he has a wife, Nancy, but she's a real wimp."

"Tomorrow night I'm attending a ballet performance, and Sunday I watch football," said Ellie, thinking out loud. "Monday afternoon I'm supposed to substitute-lecture, but I should be finished around four-thirtyish."

"Please come with me," begged Melody. "Please?"

Ellie's mind raced. Cold as frozen yogurt, Peter had refused to discuss the Burns suicide, even though she'd tried to propose her theory that the deaths of Virginia Whitley and Harry Burns were related. Over the past eleven years, how many unsolved crimes had involved victims who resembled "M*A*S*H" characters? Peter could punch buttons on his damn computer and find out. Or he could peruse his files. Or he could—

Wash the breakfast dishes. Translation: Mind your own business.

But it *was* her business, thought Ellie. Magnolia had joined Weight Winners. Tony had discovered the body. And, according to some folks, Ellie looked like Hot Lips.

She pictured Peter's reaction to Melody's invitation; could imagine his warning: "Say no, Norrie. I don't give a shit if Burns is a suicide or a homicide, stay away from my goddamn case. Say no!"

She said yes.

$\triangledown$

6

Proceeds from Sandra's Gala were to aid an association called The Organization for the Evolution of Students for Ballet—TOES for short.

Inside the recital hall Kenneth and Nancy Trask, Jacques and Victoria Hansen, Gordon Dorack, Fred and Melody Remming, and Sean McCarthy occupied one row.

Ellie, Peter, Mick, and Belinda lingered in the lobby so that Mick's date could finish her cigarette. Anger over Ellie's condolence call and Mick's unresolved argument with Sandra contributed to a cool, stilted atmosphere.

"I'm not crazy about ballet," said Belinda, drawing deeply from her filtered cigarette, then blowing smoke rings toward the balcony steps. "It's pretty, but it's so slow."

"Not all ballet movements are slow. Like music—the word 'allegro' means lively and fast dancing, compared to 'adagio,' which is slower. There should be a real mix."

Recognizing Ellie's use of familiar musical terms, the singer lost her sophisticated pose. "I've never been to a ballet," she confessed. "It's a lot different from a rock concert. I hope I'm dressed right. I borrowed a long skirt."

Belinda Wood ("Call me Belly, everybody else does.") was tall and leggy, always in motion. A fidgety-budget, Ellie thought, who constantly patted her brownish permed hair and picked imaginary pieces of lint from Mick's suit jacket. Belinda kept straightening her tight skirt and adjusting the strap of her lacy camisole when it slipped off one shoulder. She wore tons of makeup, but Ellie had to admit that it was applied professionally, from the slant of her Cleopatra eye-liner to the carefully brushed lipstick in two different reddish-purple shades. A dark blusher gave Belinda's olive-tinted complexion an exotic overcast.

Nervously lighting another cigarette, Belinda quickly squashed it out when lobby lights winked.

The program was indeed a mix, starting with a chorus production from *Oklahoma*. Agnes DeMille's original cho-reography had been incorporated, and colorful crinolines flashed as the performers combined a lively square dance with sensuous lifts. A microphone rose from the stage apron. Sandra, wearing gingham dress and cowboy boots, ap-proached the mike. She sang, "People Will Say We're in Love," while, behind her, two figures separated from the chorus for an original pas de deux.

"Oh look, Peter, how delicious," said Ellie softly. "There was no entrée, but for the coda they're using a series of fouettés, with momentum increasing every revolution."

"How do you know so much about ballet?"

"Maria Tallchief was my role model when I was a kid. My mother used to call me Ellie Small-Indian. A misnomer. I looked more like what's-his-name."

"Tonto?"

"No, Sitting Bull."

"Holy cow!" Mesmerized, Peter watched a graceful blond dancer rise on her toes with each turn.

The audience jumped from their seats, applauding and shouting "Brava!" as Sandra's soprano voice carried the last note of her song into Barbra Streisand territory.

"She didn't tell me," Ellie whispered into Peter's ear. "Muffin didn't say anything about a solo."

"I guess she wanted to surprise us. You said she sang beautifully, but I never realized how talented she is. Who's the blond ballerina?"

"Her roommate, Natalie. Sandra says Nat's a bitch and the *best* dancer in the world. That's a slight exaggeration, but she performed flawlessly just now."

The stage curtains opened to reveal a simplified set for Tchaikovsky's *Swan Lake*. This time the ballerina was short-statured, her oversized breasts throwing her off balance. Her partner tried valiantly in the lifts, but both dancers lacked grace. The audience applauded politely.

Curtains closed. Curtains opened. Ellie squinted as black-leotarded figures competed with a black backdrop. A jazz selection composed by John Russell pounded from mounted speakers. Suddenly, several white-clad bodies leaped across the stage in a spotlighted blur while the audience gasped at the effect. Sandra was one of the white leotards, hanging effortlessly in the air during her elevations, pushing off from the stage floor, then landing on the other foot.

Once more Ellie whispered, "Muffin is fine, having fun, but Natalie's jetés are cleaner, crisper. I'm impressed."

Intermission. Mick seemed dazed as Peter waited in line to buy wine served in plastic cups.

"Lieutenant Miller should save his money," said Belinda. "I know a cop doesn't make all that much, and I have booze." She reached into a large beaded purse and retrieved a silver flask. "Whiskey. I always carry it, especially when I sing. It clears a path through the smoke in my throat."

Peter returned to their small group, distributed the Chablis, and gave Ellie a hug. "Sorry about that wash-the-dishes remark, sweetheart," he said. "I'll wash them for a week, starting tomorrow."

"No way. You'll bring home greasy burgers or take-out Chinese and dump the containers."

"Unfair, Norrie, I can wok. Dance, too." Improvising some simple tap steps, he sang, "Wokking my baby back home."

Peter's finally mellowed, Ellie thought happily, smoothing a fold in her simple black sheath. Later she'd ask him who attended the Burns funeral. Later, when Peter was relaxed, *very* relaxed, she'd wheedle and weed. This was going to be a fine evening after all.

The second half of the recital began with a Paris nightclub

scene à la Gene Kelly and Cyd Charisse. Then a chorus line of jocks from the college football team, costumed in wigs and netted tutus, kicked like stoned Radio City Music Hall Rockettes.

The finale was an original vignette starring Sandra and Natalie. John Russell played piano. A deep-dimpled girl named Marion Bloch executed plaintive flute notes that brought childhood dreams to mind. Music had been composed by Chris Gagnon, a creative genius who waited tables at Uncle Vinnie's Gourmet Italian Restaurant.

The simple set featured a dressing table with an enormous mirror attached to its surface. Sandra and Natalie sat on either side of the missing glass, their movements coordinated. Sandra had pinned her hair into a bun to accommodate Natalie's shorter, shoulder-length style. From the audience, the dancers looked like carbon copies. Ellie checked her program and noted that the sequence was titled "Reflections."

Every arm movement, every finger flutter, every arabesque was performed in duplicate until the conclusion, when Sandra assumed the male role, raising her left hand above her partner's head. Natalie grasped Sandra's index finger with her right hand and spun in a series of pirouettes. Then Sandra slipped behind Natalie so that it appeared as though only one figure stood center stage, holding a gracefully sustained pose. The music faded away.

There was a moment of stunned silence before the audience erupted into a jubilant roar. When the crescendo slowed Sandra stepped from behind Natalie, and the girls dipped together into a duplicate dancer's curtsy. Whistles and shouts of "*Brava!*" rose to an ear-splitting level.

"Let's go backstage and congratulate Muffin," Ellie said when the din had finally subsided.

"Of course," said Peter. "Mick?"

"Later."

"Come on, Mick, Muffin won't still be angry over your little spat."

"I said later, Mom."

Mick and Belinda remained seated as Ellie and Peter joined the throng of well-wishers heading for the back of the theater. The other half of the audience wended their way down the aisles toward exits.

"You ready, Mick?" asked Belinda, already fishing for a cigarette from the crumpled pack inside her purse.

"Not yet. Let's wait until the crowd thins."

Instead of a cigarette, Belinda pulled out the silver flask and tipped it to her lips.

"Don't do that," yelled Mick.

"Why not?"

"This isn't one of our gigs. This is a ballet, for Christ's sake."

"Well, la-di-da. Screw you, Mickey Mouse."

"Okay. Let's get out of here."

"I wanna go backstage."

"No."

"Yes. I wanna congratulate that virgin friend of yours. Sandra Dee?"

"Leave Sandra alone. She has more talent in her little finger than you have—"

"In my whole body?" Belinda smiled. "I don't think so." She gave a shrug with her right shoulder and the camisole strap fell down her arm, exposing a bare breast.

Mick yanked the strap up.

"C'mon, I wanna go backstage," said Belinda. "I'll perform a striptease in the friggin' lobby if we don't."

"Okay, okay, you win."

As they rose from their seats, Belinda staggered.

Damn, thought Mick, drinks before the performance, wine during intermission, nips from her flask. She was sloshed and primed like a pump. A drunk Belly usually led to an amorous Belly. What a mess!

The stage curtains had remained open, exposing the dressing-table set. Mick steered Belinda around the flats and behind the fire wall. There was a large No Smoking sign, which Belinda ignored. She extended the flask toward Mick.

"No, thanks. Hey, Belly, I really think you've had enough," he said, then watched her defiantly gulp down every remaining drop.

She clutched Mick's arm, leading him farther into the recesses of the cavernous area, where sawhorses stood guarding stacks of wood. It was dim, gloomy, and vacant.

Dropping her cigarette, she pulled both camisole straps down to the waistband of her skirt. "Wanna fuck, Mick?"

"Not here," he said, crushing her filter with his boot.

"Why not? It's perfect." Her camisole and skirt lay in a crumpled heap on the floor while Belinda posed in a black garter belt, white hose, and heeled sandals.

Nervously, Mick studied the dusty area. Did a sawhorse just move? Was that a woman hiding behind the flats? Jesus, it could be a dancer, a prop person, even a curious member of the audience. Fortunately, nobody popped into sight. However, indistinct conversation filtered onstage from the wings. This was insane!

"Come on, Mick," urged Belinda, "come on, come on—"

"Shut up, Belly, I think I hear something."

"Look, there's a trapdoor. We can have privacy."

Mick glanced down. The trapdoor, covered with sawdust and wispy scraps of unswept powdery dust, also showed footprints leading toward the wings, as though somebody had removed shoes, then shuffled through the sawdust. Mick pulled the roped handle, lifted the wooden hatch, and peered into complete darkness.

"Ick, I changed my mind," squealed Belinda, kicking the door shut. "It's dark down there, prob'bly has big ol' rats. Don't care for rats, but I adore mouses like you, Mickey." She breathed whiskey fumes into Mick's face as she again chanted her litany. "Come on, Mick, come on, come on." Clumsily, Belinda spread a piece of paint-spattered sailcloth across the trapdoor. "Now. Right here on top." She unzipped his fly. "You ready?"

"I don't have a condom."

"Big deal. I have 'em. All colors. All sizes."

"I know you'll find this hard to believe, Belly, but I can't."

"Can't or won't? You're really a shit, Mickey Rat. Why don't you find your dancer friend, Minnie? Fuck her!"

Mick slapped Belinda across the face and felt instant guilt.

"Ssscat, mouse," she hissed, caressing the angry red mark with her hand.

"Belly, I'm sorry."

"Don't care," she screamed. "Go 'way."

"Hush."

"Don't tell me to hush, you rat. Go find your pure Minnie Mouse. *Go!* I mean it."

Positive her shouts would bring the whole world running, including his mother, Mick tried to placate his singer.

"I'm really sorry, Belly," he said. "I shouldn't have hit you. You're drunk and—"

"I'm always drunk. When I sleep with you or the other boys in the band, I get totally zonked so I can pretend it doesn't matter."

"Why?"

"You are such a jerk." Belinda lit a cigarette with shaky fingers. "Don't you know that I was the original girl from the wrong side of the tracks?" Her voice dripped with sarcasm. "I used to pretend I was Natalie Wood. That's how I picked my last name. I got sick when she died, puked for three days straight. I've been making it with somebody since I was eleven years old. First for food. *Food*, Mick. Then clothes. To get ahead in this shitty world. I had to fuck your drummer, the one who thinks he's Ringo; had to sleep with the son-of-a-bitch before I could get an audition for your band."

"Belly, I didn't know."

"Would you have invited me to this la-di-da ballet if you didn't have plans for later?"

"Sure, Belly, I wanted you to come."

"Right." She laughed harshly. "Go 'way, Mick."

"Let me take you home."

"Get out of here," she shouted. "Leave me alone!"

Like a chastised puppy, Mick scurried toward the wings.

Slowly Belinda replaced her skirt and top. Her enormous capacity for liquor hadn't been reinforced, and she'd begun to sober. Mick's slap still stung, but she shouldn't have been so nasty about his little dancer.

I really fucked up, she thought. Mick is nicer than any other kid I've ever met. And he did invite me to this recital thing. Someday, when I'm a big star, I'll attend every premiere, ballet, opera, draped in mink, diamonds, and fancy gowns. Mick's band is a beginning. I'm being seen and heard. Mick even promised that his group'll back me on a demo tape.

Hey, maybe she could use Mick's guilt about hitting her and still get the demo. She wished she could begin the whole evening over, act more ladylike, take back the stupid words yelled earlier.

She could start by being nice to his friend. Mick would see that she was sorry, maybe even think she'd been kidding. She'd compliment Sandra's performance. Sincere. That was the ticket. She'd be sincere to Sandra Dee, or die trying.

Belinda instinctively peered into the "mirror" that still decorated the deserted stage. She saw sets on the other side. Reflections, hell! It was all an illusion. Her world included illusions, too, onstage and off.

After wandering through a maze of discarded props and costumes, she found the dressing rooms. A huge mass of people surrounded performers at the end of the hallway. She didn't see the girlfriend or Mick.

One door had a cardboard star with hand-printed letters: SANDRA AND NATALIE. Making an instant decision, Belinda ducked inside to wait.

Christ, what luck. The blond-bunned girl sat at the dressing table before a real mirror, her face buried in crossed arms. Her back was toward Belinda.

The first line of a message, scribbled with lipstick, marred the real mirror—words Belly had never seen before.

Must be French ballet words, she thought. The rest of the message was hidden by Sandra's head.

Belinda shut the door with sweaty palms and opened her mouth. Christ, it was hard to apologize, to sound sincere. If she didn't need that fuckin' demo—

"Hi, I'm Belinda Wood," she announced in her friendliest tone, "but you can call me Belly. Everybody else does. We've never met, but I'm sure you've heard me sing with Mick's band."

Shit! A bad beginning. Hadn't Mick once said something about Sandra wanting to sing with his band?

"You were wonderful tonight, Sandra. Are you crying over Mick? He couldn't stop talking about you. How beautiful you are, how good you danced and sang. He thought you were the best. Me, too."

Well, that's better, but still no response. What the fuck does she want from me?

"I don't mean anything to Mick, Sandra, honest. His mom said you had a fight, but Mick doesn't hold grudges."

I hope, thought Belinda. She walked toward the dressing table. "I have a boyfriend, and we're engaged," she lied, placing her hand tentatively on Sandra's shoulder.

With astonishment, Belinda watched Sandra crumple from her chair to the floor. Both blue eyes in the dancer's pale face were open, staring, and a spreading pool of blood dripped from her chest.

That's not Mick's Sandra, thought Belly. That's the other dancer. I can see the difference up close. Her hair is more platinum than blond. I think I'm going to be sick.

Turning away from the body, Belinda vomited into a wastepaper basket. Then she screamed. "Help! Murder!"

Stupid, really stupid; they might blame *me*, she thought, and tried to swallow her second scream. But it was too late. Faces were already peeking around the doorway.

One girl shoved her way through, and Belly watched the real Sandra collapse on the floor, right next to the other Sandra. Who was, for the record, smiling.

That smile, thought Ellie, bending down to check Natalie's pulse, meant that Natalie had known her killer.

A shiny dog tag, engraved with the name Margaret Houlihan, lay across Natalie's leotard. Lipstick-printed words appeared on the mirror's surface:

ADVOCATUS DIABOLI.
WHORE. GOD WILL PUNISH YOU FOR YOUR SINS.

Several hours later, a body was found in downtown Colorado Springs, not far from the courthouse, a few blocks from the police station. The dead man's expired driver's license identified him as Leo Krafchek. A lined piece of paper was pinned to his shirt; on it, pasted letters painstakingly scissored from *TV Guide* spelled out:

ADVOCATUS DIABOLI.
SCUM. GOD WILL PUNISH YOU FOR YOUR SINS.

▽

7

MICK ADMITTED THAT he and Belinda had wandered backstage. Belly had placed a tarp over a trapdoor, but first Mick had seen footprints. What size footprints? Well, they didn't belong to the abominable snowman. Or Dopey. Dopey who? Dopey Dwarf.

One of the cops muttered "Smart-ass kid" and Ellie wanted to smack him. Because her son looked exactly the same as he had at age eleven when their beloved cat Diaboli had fallen from a tree and broken his neck.

"*Advocatus Diaboli.*" Devil's advocate. What exactly was a devil's advocate? One who pleads a less-accepted cause for the sake of argument? Or some nut who hears a demon's voice and responds by murdering "M*A*S*H" look-alikes?

"Whore." Was Natalie promiscuous?

Ellie watched several dancers point out an underground passageway that led to the hidden trapdoor, allowing performers to travel backstage without being seen or heard by the audience. Every dressing room had its own entry, but nobody had used it for this recital. In fact, the catacomb lights hadn't even been turned on.

There was too much chaos after the curtain call, claimed the cast, so they hadn't noticed anything or anybody unusual. The busty ballerina remembered that Natalie had entered her dressing room to remove her heavy greasepaint.

"Nat was allergic to stage makeup; she broke out in pimples."

Still dizzy, on the verge of hysteria, Sandra blamed herself for letting Natalie enter the dressing room alone.

"It's not your fault," said Ellie. "You couldn't possibly have known. *It's not your fault.*"

"I can't go back to the dorm. I want my room changed. I'll never dance again. I'm quitting school."

"Tonight you'll sleep over at my house, but first you'll call your folks. Take a short vacation. You're not quitting school, okay?"

"Where's Mick? I want Mick."

Watching her tall son press Sandra's tearstained face against his suit jacket, Ellie thought, it could have been Muffin. No, she doesn't look like Hot Lips. We buried Diaboli in the backyard, and Mick cried even though Tony said big boys don't cry. Mick swore he didn't want another cat, but we adopted Agatha Christie, who mysteriously disappeared, then Jackie Robinson, and it was all right. Muffin will dance again. Everything will be all right.

Where's Peter? I want Peter.

But Peter was asking questions, and Ellie was a big girl. A big girl who retreated to the theater's rest room so that she could lock herself inside a stall and cry alone.

Almost subconsciously, she read the stall's graffiti. One notation stated: "MELODY LOVES GORDON."

Melody *Remming?*

No, Tommy *Tune.* What was Melody doing at the recital? Watching the ballet, of course. Very good, Norrie, advance to the head of the class. And while you're there, ponder this. If Melody had anything to do with Natalie's murder, why would she leave her signature on the bathroom wall?

Sunday. Football. While Broncos reared up and trampled Jets, Ellie greeted Dr. and Mrs. Connors, who had driven from Hygiene, Colorado, to collect their daughter. Ellie sensed that the Connorses—had they dared—would have entered her home adorned with garlic cloves, a huge cross, sterling silver bullets, and pointy wooden stakes.

Watching Mrs. Connors scowl, Ellie could practically hear the woman's thoughts. After all, Ellie had encouraged Sandy to lose weight and indulge in this ridiculous performing thing. Sandy had been menaced during the diet-club murders. Danger seemed to follow Ellie Bernstein around. The man who wore faded jeans and a black-and-silver Raiders sweatshirt had introduced himself as *Lieutenant* Miller, and Mrs. Connors knew darn well he wasn't a soldier. Their daughter's attachment to Ellie was detrimental to her health. Mrs. Connors sniffed audibly, then lit a cigarette.

Under her mother's disapproving eye, Sandra gave Ellie a hug and whispered that she'd be back to school soon, even if she had to thumb a ride all the way from Hygiene.

Mick overheard. "Give me a call and I'll come get you," he said, extending his arms.

Ignoring the adults, Sandra stood on tiptoe to press her cheek against his lips.

Mrs. Connors yanked her daughter away.

Dr. Connors muttered, "Couldn't we just stay and see how the game turns out?" while the family exited.

Following Sandra's departure, Mick collected his freshly laundered clothes, then joined other band members in a Day-Glo-painted van. Students all, they had to return to Boulder. Belinda wasn't a student. Basking in the publicity of having found Natalie's body, she would bus back at a later date.

"Bye, Mom," said Mick. "Bye, Pete. Sorry."

"For what?" asked Ellie.

"Everything."

Was guilt hereditary? Or environmental? Could it be recycled like aluminum cans? With that last thought, Ellie retreated to the bedroom and brushed her hair into shiny flames. Mata Hari she wasn't, but Small-Indian could wheedle with finesse.

Halftime. A sports analyst sketched diagrammatic maps while Ellie filled icy beer mugs.

"Here we go again," said Peter. "First you get stalked by a madman who's killing your diet-club members, now this.

Hell, I can't blame—I guess it's not your fault that you're the victim type."

"Victim type? That's a put-down."

"I didn't mean it the way it sounded. It's just that you look like Hot Lips, too, remember? C'mere, you gorgeous thing."

Ellie snuggled on top of Peter's lap. "Are there many unsolved cases in your files, honey?"

"Why do you ask?"

"Small talk."

"You're not very subtle, Norrie."

"I really want to know."

"Why?"

"Self-preservation?"

"Since when are you concerned with—damn, your Broncos just blocked a field goal."

"Well, that's exactly what I mean, Peter," she said, glancing toward the TV. "The best offense is a good defense, right?"

"Wrong! The best defense is keeping your nose out of my business."

"Look, my mother always told me to ask a boy about *his* hobbies, *his* work, *his* favorite sport. Mom said that would make me popular. So I'm asking."

"I'm not sure I have a hobby. Does sex count?"

"Peter—"

"I like to read, especially T. S. Eliot."

"You like *poetry*?"

"No, cats. I've read 'Old Possum's Book of Practical Cats' from cover to cover."

"You're changing the subject, Peter."

"We were talking hobbies."

"We were talking unresolved homicides."

"That's *your* hobby, Norrie. Anyway, the other cases in our files could be unrelated—"

"What other cases?" Ellie snuggled closer.

"Dammit, there are always unsolved cases inside police files. Big cities like New York, L.A., Houston could number hundreds. Here in the Springs we might average two, three a year, or none at all. Most of the crimes are bar brawls, jealous spats, drug-related stabbings, and the perps are usually at the scene."

"Tell me about your other cases."

"No."

"More beer, Peter? Here, finish mine."

"No way! Well, all right, it's dumb to waste it. I hate waste. What are you doing?"

"Giving you a massage. Earlier, after brunch, you said you were tired and stressed."

"Hey, a masseuse doesn't give rubdowns down there. Norrie, watch your hands."

"Holy cow! At least one portion of your anatomy doesn't seem all that tired. Finish your beer."

Peter belched, then grinned. "S'cuse me. Damn, I feel a buzz coming on, and I have to work tonight. Shame on you, prying for information with booze and sex."

"You don't have to work tonight, Peter, it's Sunday. Who attended the funeral?"

"Which funeral?"

"Frank Burns. Natalie's parents are from Chicago. Her body will be flown there. Unless the perp travels long distance, he won't show up for her b-b-burial."

"Are you crying, Norrie?"

"Yes. Who attended Frank's funeral?"

"Not Frank, sweetheart, Harry."

"Please tell me. It'll take my mind off Natalie, and I swear I'll stop bawling."

Peter's eyebrow quirked. "His wife was there, of course. Also Mrs. Smithers, plus a few coworkers."

"What about his mistress?"

"Missing."

"I wonder why."

"Norrie, the girlfriend didn't kill Burns. Neither did his wife. Or his coworkers. Nobody had a motive except the mother-in-law who hates Yankees."

"Ohmigod, Peter—J.R."

"Your cat?"

"Magnolia said Mama Smithers watched 'Dallas' because it was truthful. Why couldn't she turn fantasy into reality? Remember that cliffhanger when J.R. was shot?"

"Norrie, Mrs. Smithers was in Atlanta when—"

"Have another beer, Peter. What unsolved cases?"

"Are you crazy? Look, halftime's almost over."

"You said before that there were files of unsolved cases. You said New York has plenty, but Colorado Springs might average two, maybe three a year."

"Sweetheart, you're talking gibberish. How'd we get from Dallas to Atlanta to New York? Put your hands back, Norrie. Ahhhh, that's nice. Hey, where're you going?"

"To fetch another beer. I'll be your slave, Loot, I'll even wax your body."

"You little devil. You took off your underwear after the Connorses left."

"How do you know that?"

"I'm a good detective. No bra dents. No panty line."

"What unsolved cases?" asked Ellie, returning to his lap, unzipping his jeans.

"Leave me alone. Don't leave me alone."

"Make up your mind. What cases?"

"Okay, okay, off the top of my head, I can recall a policeman shot in his car and a woman kidnapped from the Safeway shopping center, later found dead in a cemetery. There was an unmarried couple living together who were killed and discovered in the trash Dumpster at an apartment complex. Is that enough?"

"Did any of those victims resemble 'M*A*S*H' characters?"

"I have no idea."

"What about Virginia Whitley?"

"Who?"

"Come on, Peter, the Dew Drop Inn. March 7, 1983."

"Technically, that was a hit-and-run. Since we never

found the driver, it's filed as an unsolved vehicular homicide. Take off your blouse."

"Could I peruse the files?"

"You're pushing your luck, Norrie. Absolutely not. There's something else . . . something . . . oh yes, your last name. Bernstein. My fault. Should have changed it to Miller."

"I don't understand. Wait, I see. Holy cow! My name sounds like Burns, right? Change the E to a U and—"

"Correct. Two strikes, Norrie. Help me unzip your fly. My fingers·are numb. Christ, did you see John Elway's touchdown pass? It must have soared sixty yards."

"Peter, take off that damn Raiders sweatshirt."

"I've told you everything I know," he groaned. "Will you really be my slave, Norrie?"

"Sure, but only if you wash the breakfast dishes."

"Okay, after the game."

"What game?" she asked, pushing him onto the couch cushions and molding her body to his. "Ohmigod, your fingers aren't numb, Peter, I'm soaring sixty yards."

Monday evening. Ellie was home alone, trying to decide what to wear. Casual or dressy? Comfort along with honesty, she decided, was almost always the best policy.

Her duck quacked.

"Hi," said Peter, "I'm glad you're home. I thought you mentioned something about a Weight Winners meeting."

"That was earlier. What's happening?"

"Well, it seems as though we have a serial killer on our hands."

"Did you find another dead body?"

"Lots of dead bodies."

"How many?"

"Twelve, thirteen, maybe more."

"Holy cow, Peter, didn't you *count* them?"

"Detective McCoy's counting them now."

"Wait a minute. Where are you calling from?"

"The precinct."

"You carted dead bodies to the precinct?"

"McCoy helped. We tossed them into my trunk. It wasn't easy, Norrie. Have you ever seen the inside of my trunk? There's a spare tire and—"

"Okay, Peter, what's really going on?"

"I told you, dead—"

"Bodies. Yeah, right. How big *are* your stiffs?"

"Very good, Norrie. Did you ever play with Barbie and Ken when you were a kid?"

"Thanks for the compliment. I think Barbie came along a few years after my first period. I played with a doll called Betsy-Wetsy. She peed. Ohmigod, you found murdered *dolls?*"

"Yes, ma'am. One of the Barbies was hanging from a tree. She had this noose tied around her—wait a sec, Norrie. Okay, Will McCoy says it was Skipper, not Barbie."

"Are you laughing? You are! I don't think it's funny, Peter."

"Neither do I, not really. Our killer's got one hell of a sick mind, sweetheart."

"*Our* killer. What makes you think—"

"The dolls were dressed in G.I. Joe clothes."

"Even Barbie and Skipper?"

"Yup."

"Hot Lips," gasped Ellie.

"Some of the bigger dolls, like Raggedy Ann and Andy, wore hand-stitched fatigues and infant-size T-shirts dyed olive-green."

"Rit fabric dye."

"What did you say?"

"Nothing. Stupid idea. Go on."

"There was also soldier paraphernalia. For instance, miniature guns and knives and grenades. Plus a miniature doctor's kit, not to mention helicopters, the kind you build from scratch."

"Where did you find all this?"

"Memorial Park. A guy was walking his dog, saw the mass murder scene, then called us. Thank God we collected all

that stuff before the newspapers and TV stations got wind
of it. We'll check for prints after McCoy finishes counting
body bags."

"Body bags?"

"Grocery sacks."

Ellie felt slightly sick to her stomach. Yet she also felt a
certain satisfaction. This proved that her "M*A*S*H"
theory was correct.

"Of course," added Peter, "a kid could have set up that
scene and left it there."

"No way, Lieutenant. My son did a head count every night
before he went to sleep. If somebody was missing, Mick
would go nuts and search until he found him or her."

"Her? Mick played with doll dolls?"

"Yes. At first his macho father objected rather strenu-
ously. But then Tony decided that Mick could use his doll
dolls for corpses. Mick even crushed one Barbie with a tank
and poured my red nail polish over her body."

"In any case, our computer's down and we're trying to
run a check for similar MOs. What are your plans?"

"I'm meeting Melody Remming, that new Weight Winners
member I told you about."

"Be careful, Norrie. Make sure you're around other people."

"You be careful, too."

"Why? I don't resemble any of the 'M*A*S*H' characters."

"Yes, you do. Slightly. Alan Alda with a mustache."

"Nobody would kill Hawkeye except Frank Burns, and
he's already been eliminated."

"Peter, you're laughing again!"

"If we don't laugh, we cry. McCoy says hello. Oops, he lost
his place and has to count over."

This time Ellie laughed, then said, "What time do you
suppose you'll be home?"

"Probably slip under the sheets while you're taking your
crack-of-dawn jog. No sex. No interrogation."

"If you gave out information freely, I wouldn't have to initiate sex."

"It's more fun the other way. Bye."

Ellie hung up her duck.

I'll be surrounded by other people, Peter. All those "M*A*S*H" club members.

Excited, curious, a bit apprehensive, she locked her front door and left to pick up Melody.

Her new friend lived in a furnished studio apartment at the center of a huge complex. Ellie rang the bell. When the door opened, she immediately inhaled paint, linseed oil, and turpentine.

Melody plied her secretarial skills on a day-to-day basis, but eventually hoped to become established as a freelance artist. Huge canvases dominated every inch of wall space. Blobs of bright abstract colors were thickly applied with a palette knife.

"Hi, Ellie," said Melody in her high, scratchy voice. "Soon you'll meet the whole motley crew. I called and told Nancy that you were planning to join our group tonight."

"Thanks, sweetpea, I'm primed for fun, especially after Saturday's ballet murder. I was there."

"Me, too. The girl danced like an angel. She was so beautiful . . ." Melody paused, then said, "Nancy Trask gave the entire 'M*A*S*H' club tickets."

"Did you—did they—I—" Just in time, Ellie kept herself from probing about the dog tag clue. Peter had withheld that bit of evidence from sniffing newshounds. "I need to visit your bathroom. Is there enough time?"

"Relax, we have plenty of time."

More canvases covered the bathroom walls. They appeared nonobjective, but Ellie had a few minutes to study them from her commode perch. Buried in the swirling primary colors were tiny figures. Nuns marching, their hands folded into pie wedges. A priest offering communion to gaping mouths. A crucified Jesus blessing disciples. The blobs in the background were really birds of all sizes, gliding with outspread wings. Ellie shivered as she pulled down her white CSPD sweatshirt and zipped up her black corduroy slacks. Melody's paintings were brilliant, but disturbing.

Returning to the main studio-room, Ellie noted oil paint applied in darker hues. Priests, nuns, and birds again dominated the motifs.

Observing Ellie's interest, Melody laughed somewhat bitterly. "I had a very religious upbringing," she said. "Catholic schools, the whole bit. My mother attended mass every day of her life until she died. She wanted ten kids, but could only conceive me. She blamed Daddy because he didn't go to church often enough. Isn't that stupid? I mean, well, God doesn't control sperm, does he?"

"Melody, your paintings don't seem very religious, uh, complimentary to the church."

What an understatement, thought Ellie. A nun in the bathroom canvas had been marching sedately—totally naked. One of the gaping communion mouths had displayed vampire fangs. Christ's disciples included Henry the Eighth making love to a headless wife, Lizzie Borden hacking with an axe, and a figure meant to represent Jack the Ripper. In this room, on a handbuilt easel, the work in progress showed nuns as ballerinas, their habits shortened into black tutus. The tiny dancers leaped across the canvas in jetés, suspended in their elevations. Under the tutus, their butts were bare.

Ellie felt like a voyeur. Propped against the corner wall, a painted priest had a sly ecstatic grin on his face. Was he actually masturbating? Melody's artwork was flawless, technically brilliant religious pornography.

"Complimentary to the church?" Melody's brow knitted. "Ellie, I believed in the church all through my childhood, even when there were unanswered questions. I studied history in college because it was so absolute. I mean, the people really existed. I know every president's astrological sign. Go on, test me."

"Sweetpea, that's not really nec—"

"Come on, give me a President's name."

"Okay. Roosevelt."

"Teddy was a Scorpio. Franklin—Aquarius."

Franklin. Franklin Harrison Burns.

"Melody, did your 'M*A*S*H' club members mention a man named Franklin Harrison Burns? Nicknamed Harry?"

"No. Why?"

"He, uh, died last week. Suicide. It happened shortly before your club's get-together. Do you remember anybody showing up late?"

"Yes. Me."

"Was anybody agitated? Stimulated?"

"Not really. They were pissed because my cousin Fred ran out of gas, and they had to push his Jeep. There was this guy named Jacques Hansen who became agitated later. He admires Frank Burns, but the others don't. Hansen's an A-hole; I wouldn't want to meet him in a dark alley. Why do you ask, Ellie?"

"Harry's wife, Magnolia, recently joined Weight Winners. I paid a condolence call, and she claimed Harry had met your friends in the supermarket."

"So?"

"So nothing. I just wondered if your 'M*A*S*H' club members knew him well enough to notice if Harry was depressed." Ellie decided to change the subject. "When did you become religiously disillusioned?" she asked, thinking how her background paralleled Melody's, with a Catholic-oriented lifestyle and parochial schools. Lots of praying. Lots of Latin. No cussing. No sex. During her junior year she'd transferred to a public school, studied French instead of Latin. The students cussed all the time. Sex was available on a daily basis. An overweight overachiever, Ellie wasn't very popular, so she didn't get screwed.

"In my last year of high school," said Melody, "I became pregnant. The boy was a real stud. He looked like Stallone, and had laid half the girls in my graduating class. I found out later that he'd notch his motorcycle after every conquest.

I didn't know anything about contraceptives. The stud disappeared when I confessed his pending Daddy role. I was so naive. He was Catholic. I really believed he'd marry me."

"Then what happened?"

"I wanted to have my . . . the baby. Mother arranged an abortion. I don't know how she justified the sin. Talk about hypocrisy."

"I'm sorry, Melody."

"I had very long hair. The guy used to tie it around his neck in a noose. Mother sheared it all off, like a sheep, so close to my scalp that there were bald splotches. Then I tried to kill myself by cutting my throat. Obviously I didn't succeed, but that's why my voice sounds so scratchy, why I wear scarves."

"Melody, this is really none of my business."

"Mother grounded me for the rest of the school year. I spent hours kneeling and praying inside our church while the priest gave me pitying looks and more penance. You see, Ellie, my sin was the attempted suicide, not the abortion. I went away to college and became an atheist."

"I can understand that."

"Wait until you meet Gordon. I told him what I just told you, and he cried. We haven't done it yet, made love, but I will when he asks me."

Ellie didn't know what to say. Like most people, she had plenty of emotional scars, but they were minimal compared to those of this friendly, gregarious artist.

The two women walked silently through the complex parking lot, past a drained swimming pool, the sagging nets of a small tennis court, and several trash Dumpsters. Ellie had left her car near a large wooden sign proclaiming the name of the complex, a name that sounded familiar.

Holy cow! Yesterday Peter had mentioned an unsolved murder case about a couple killed and thrown into a Dumpster. Ellie suddenly recalled reading about it—when?— two years ago. The murders had occurred in this very same development.

"How long have you lived here, Melody?"

"Almost three years."

"Do you remember the Dumpster murders? The couple found in the, uh, trash?"

"Sure. Police crawled all over the place for days, then it slacked off. At the time, I thought about painting a priest blessing a Dumpster, but it seemed too ghoulish, too macabre. Isn't this your Honda?"

"That's it; hop inside."

Melody gave the directions to Trask's house while she chatted about the "M*A*S*H" club members.

Ellie concentrated on driving, a sharp wind making it difficult to control her fishtailing rear end. It almost seemed as though a mischievous deity was blowing leaves and debris toward her atheist passenger.

That same wind swept the two women up a bricked path and into the Trask house. Swirling through the open door, it whipped an American flag into a patriotic frenzy.

Ellie's eyes were immediately drawn to the television, where a local newscast replayed Saturday night's murders. With relish, the camera zoomed in on Natalie's shrouded figure as she was carried from the recital hall toward a waiting ambulance. Then they showed an army photo of the murdered man, Leo Krafchek.

"Detective Miller's working on several possible leads," announced the pretty CBS reporter.

"Bullshit," said a slight man wearing a black turtleneck shirt and khaki pants, seated on the floor in front of Trask's TV. "*Aegri somnia vana. Aegri somnia vana.*"

$\triangledown$

8

"A SICK MAN'S empty dreams," translated Ellie. "Are you talking about Detective Miller or the murderer?"

Twinkly eyes traveled from her sneakers to the oversize white sweatshirt with blue felt letters that spelled out "CSPD Softball Team." Then a sweet priestly voice said, "Welcome, my child. *Dies faustus.*"

"Why is it a lucky day?"

"Because I have finally found somebody who understands my flummery twaddle."

"There's nothing flummery about Latin. And doesn't twaddle mean silly idle talk? I've got a feeling you're neither silly nor idle."

"And you're very perceptive. My name's Sean McCarthy, but my friends call me Father Mac."

"I'm Ellie—Ellie—" She hesitated, recalling Peter's comment about her last name.

"Pleased to meetcha, Ellie-Ellie. My *aegri somnia vana* referred to the reporter."

"The reporter's a woman," she chided.

"A sick *woman's* empty dreams?" He grimaced, almost as if he'd bit into a sour lemon or a sour memory. "That doesn't sound very comprehensive, Ellie-Ellie."

"Why *empty* dreams, Father Mac?"

"Whatever happened to the old adage 'No news is good news'? If there's no news, those mike-sucking reporters have to pretend something's happening."

"How do you know something isn't happening?"

"Elementary, my dear. Our local TV keeps presenting the same pictures over and over. 'Several possible leads' is police-speak for 'We don't have a clue.' In other words, know-it-all news is no news at all."

"What the heck are you talking about?" whined a short, prissy man.

From his appearance, Ellie recognized Melody's cousin Fred, clothed in new blue Levi's and a starched white shirt.

"You're monopolizing this pretty lady, Father Mac," added Fred. While introducing himself he shook her hand, but seemed to recoil at the contact. His palm was moist and felt like most people believe a snake might feel before they actually touch one.

"This is Gordon Dorack," said Melody shyly, leading a tall man by the hand. "Gordie, this is my friend, Ellie. She's also my diet-club leader, so I'll have to watch what I eat tonight."

Ellie glanced straight up at a tousled towhead with droopy-lidded eyes and a charming smile. Dorack probably purchased all his clothing at Large & Tall Fashions For Less. Could he be a murderer?

A man clothed in gray flannel slacks and a charcoal cashmere sweater introduced himself. Kenneth Trask could sell diet pills to sumo wrestlers, thought Ellie. Wait a sec, the name sounded familiar.

"Are you the architect?"

"Yes," he replied, preening. "You've heard of me?"

"Well, for one thing, you designed my house."

"He builds homes, I insure them," announced a huge man with a dark Santa Claus beard and Santa's jelly-belly stuffed inside a cowboy shirt. "I'm Howie Silverman. Silver and Gold Insurance, if you're ever in the market."

"Gold—Barry Goldman?"

"My partner."

"Then I'm already covered by your company, Mr. Silverman. Barry's my ex-husband's colleague."

"Call me Howie, sweetcakes."

The last member of the club rose from his chair. "I'm Jacques Hansen, OSI," he stated formally. Then, nodding toward the TV, he added, "I could solve those murders if it was military instead of civilian."

Ellie stifled her impulse to salute. "You could?"

"Yes, ma'am, I'd discover what the deceased had in common, find reasons—"

"*Cui bono*," interrupted Sean.

"Stop doing that," shrieked Fred.

"Who will profit by it," translated Ellie.

"It's another way of saying, What's the motive," said a woman with short-cropped brown hair. Nancy Trask had silently entered the room. She held a tray filled with cake, corn, and milk. "Isn't it, dear?"

Kenneth nodded as Ellie admired Nancy's flowered caftan. "Did you sew that dress yourself, Mrs. Trask?"

"Yes, I did. Please call me Nancy. I understand you and Melody are both on diets and can't eat cake or corn. But the milk is skim, so you can join the others in a toast." She placed the tray on the art deco coffee table. "I bought skim milk?" she added, glancing toward Trask.

"I know who killed those people," said Hansen, obviously peeved at the reaction to his original statement. "I figured it out yesterday morning at church."

"Who?" "Who?" "Who?" "Who?" Voices rose in a chorus, like overstimulated owls.

"I don't want to say," Jacques replied slyly. "I never make an accusation until my facts are indisputable."

Ellie stared toward porcupine-quilled hair and wire-rimmed glasses. Was Hansen bluffing? Or was he throwing the scent away from his own trail? What would be *his* motive? Melody said he loved war movies, but that didn't mean he'd go around town murdering people. Although he wasn't physically imposing, Hansen looked like he could slash and stalk. It was the expression in his eyes.

"And I never make mistakes," added Jacques as club members wandered toward the food.

"*Aliquando bonus dormitat Homerus,*" Ellie whispered to Sean. "Even the great make mistakes."

"Do you consider Jacques Hansen great?"

"No, but I think he does."

"Don't underestimate Hansen." Sean grabbed two shot glasses and nodded toward the carpet. Ellie sat, folding her legs Indian-style.

"Jacques has the highest percentage rate of confessions on the base," continued Sean immediately after the "M*A*S*H" toast. "He may look harmless and sound like a dullard, but he's very sharp."

"How did he get to be a member of this group? He doesn't seem to fit."

"None of us really fit, Ellie-Ellie. I'm not exactly sure how Hansen became a member. He and his wife edit a religious newsletter. Ken met him at a city council meeting. Next thing we knew, Hansen started showing up Monday nights. Ken seems to surround himself with nuts and dolts." Sean genuflected. "Be careful, Ellie-Ellie, insanity's contagious."

"What does that mean, Father Mac? Are you warning me to keep away from the group?"

"Not at all, my child, not at all."

"What are you two whispering about?" Melody flashed Ellie a grin. "I'm so glad you came. Ken hasn't suggested that 'the girls' leave the room and keep Nancy company."

"M*A*S*H" club members took their usual stations. Fred, Gordon, and Melody deflated sofa cushions. Howie's bentwood rocker groaned. Hansen sat upright on his ladder-back chair. Trask crouched in his comfortable armchair. Sean and Ellie remained seated on the shag carpeting.

As the show began, Ellie soon discovered that she'd never seen it before. Attentively, she watched Hawkeye offer to buy the seventeen-year-old mistress and slave of a Sergeant Baker. Baker wants two thousand dollars. Hawkeye devises Operation Poker, where Radar uses a telescope to spy on Baker's cards. Winning both the game and the girl, Hawkeye realizes that if he simply sets her free, she'll be sold again by her own family. But when her brother comes to collect her for another sale, she defies tradition. "I tell brother most important words I learn from you," she says to Hawkeye. "Shove off!"

At the kitchen table, all discussion revolved around the episode. Trask saw nothing wrong with the practice of buying *musame*, or in American slang, "moose," during the Korean conflict.

"After all, there were no wives available," said Trask, playfully patting Nancy's behind.

The immaculate woman almost smiled, yet Ellie thought she detected a glint of annoyance in those deep brown eyes.

Jacques Hansen said how there were plenty of servants and slaves mentioned in the Bible.

"Where do you think you'd be today if the slave Jochebed had not given birth to Moses?" asked Melody.

Fred Remming said he'd love to have his own moose and would beat the girl with a stick if she didn't obey.

Howie Silverman said the moose would beat Fred.

Gordon Dorack thought a relationship should be shared equally by two partners. Melody rewarded him with a smile as Howie muttered, "Dork!"

"What do you think, Ellie?" asked Melody.

"Well, I appreciate Hawkeye's desire to help, even though he cheated, and I can't condone cheating." She blushed, then added, "Yes I can, if it's for a good reason."

Glancing around the table, she tried to imagine "M*A*S*H" club members as cold-blooded killers. Later she'd write a list, probing personality traits and motives.

The discussion switched to the Monday night football game. Giants versus Patriots.

"Speaking of patriots," said Hansen, "did you know that Frank Burns won a Purple Heart? The other club members insist that Frank's an asshole," he added, teeth clenched.

Jacques stared at her accusingly, and Ellie felt almost compelled to respond. "Frank doesn't have many admirable qualities," she said slowly, "but I think the show's writers used him as a buffoon. Like Shakespeare does."

"I remember that Purple Heart episode," said Melody. "It was a joke, a mistake." She shook her curls. "Never mind. Discussing Frank Burns with you, Jacques, is like arguing religion with a Jehovah's Witness."

"I'm not a Jehovah's Witness, but sometimes they make sense. They believe in the sinfulness of governments and— look, I don't want to shock you, but there used to be a homosexual right in our own government. His last name begins with the letter Q. Q for queer."

"Shut up, Hansen!" Howie turned toward Ellie. "Don't pay any attention to Jacques. He's got a sick mind."

Soon Melody left with Dorack, who had brought his own car, a Chevy pickup with dealer's plates.

Ellie walked to the curb with them, said good-bye to Gordon, and hugged Melody. "I had a wonderful time. See you Friday at the Weight Winners meeting."

Wandering back inside, she thanked Nancy for her generous hospitality. The men around the table were discussing moose again.

Sean tossed his empty Moosehead toward a trash can, then escorted Ellie down the brick path.

"Where did you learn Latin, Father Mac? Parochial school? College?"

"Neither, Ellie-Ellie. I'm self-taught. Can't really string sentences together or even read the stuff in its original form. I carry a notepad, jot down phrases."

"Why?"

"Why not?"

"That's no answer."

"When I was in school I started losing my hair. Bald runs in my family."

"So you learned Latin phrases?"

"I played the priest in a school production of *Romeo and Juliet*. They cast me because I was baldish and looked ultramontane. Soon I began acting like a priest all the time, blessing everybody. It got me noticed, made me popular. I was trying to impress—you see, I worshiped the girl who played Juliet. Her name was Juliet, too."

In the wispy glow from a streetlamp, Ellie could discern the bleak expression on his face.

"I'm sorry," she murmured, then wondered why she'd said it. Habit? Except she'd really meant it. Had Juliet scorned Sean? Did Juliet die? Did Juliet resemble Hot Lips? Ellie couldn't ask. It was none of her business.

Sean extended an invitation to join the group next week, and she replied, "*Dei gratia.*"

"By the grace of God. You betcha, Ellie-Ellie." Leaning forward, he gave her a quick kiss on the forehead, then battled capricious winds toward Trask's front door.

Reaching inside her purse for ignition keys, Ellie sensed she wasn't alone, and her heart skipped a beat. Holy cow, was she about to be murdered immediately following her first "M*A*S*H" club meeting? Peter would be furious.

She took a deep breath and turned around, fervently wishing she had a weapon, even a baseball bat.

Two strikes, Norrie.

The looming shadowy shape—Howie Silverman—gave a mock bow. "Would you care to join me for a drink at the Dew Drop Inn, darlin'? The owner's my bud."

"How do you know Charley Aaronson?" Ellie's heart resumed its normal rhythm.

"Insurance policy. How do *you* know Charley?"

"My husband sold him his lounge."

"Ex-husband. Earlier this evening, you said that my partner was your ex-husband's colleague." Howie's voice dripped with molasses. "You're just a li'l bitty divorced lady who could use some cuddling, poor thang."

The streetlamp's yellowish light bounced off Howie's shiny shirt snaps, and his grin was very white, outlined by the dark beard.

"I have a boyfriend," said Ellie, feeling dumb. Did one say man-friend after age forty?

"Is he a cop?"

"How did you—oh, my sweatshirt. Colorado Springs Police Department Softball Team. Yes, he's a detective."

"The one on the news? Miller?"

"Yes. How did you know?"

"He's tall and if you unfolded your shirt, it would probably fall way below your knees."

"Wow! You're a pretty good detective yourself."

"Yup. Look, I'll tell you my theory about Saturday night's homicides, and you can relay the information to your cop. He'd probably appreciate your help."

Appreciate my help? Not on your life, bud.

"What theory?" she asked.

"If you really want to know, join me at the Dew Drop."

Placing his palms on the Honda, he pinned her against the door. His beer belly pressed her rib cage, and she felt a shirt snap painfully indent her breast. His breath smelled like garlic-flavored beer.

"Shove off!"

Howie's hand reached between her back and the car door. He cupped her rump and drew her closer. She struggled as he lowered his head. The streetlamp exposed his open mouth. Ellie had a sudden image of Dracula.

"You heard the lady, shove off," ordered Kenneth Trask. The wind had whipped his salt-and-pepper hair from its carefully styled pompadour. In the light's glow his eyes looked flinty. On the end of a choke-collared leash stood a growling Airedale.

Ellie felt Howie give her rump a painful pinch. Then he stepped back and grinned at Trask. "Hi there, Ken. Taking the dog for a walk? Has the game started?"

What game? The football game? Or is he talking about his performance with me? Ellie hunkered down, patted the Airedale's Brillo hair, then scratched its long nose with her fingertips.

"Fred wants to go home," said Trask. "He has a cold."

"Fred always has a cold. I suppose Hansen has an early

interrogation tomorrow morning, and Father Mac wants to attend evening prayers. Fudge carpooling." Howie gave Ellie a wink, turned, then retreated up the path.

"*Fudge* carpooling?"

Trask laughed. "Howie won't swear in front of a lady."

Ellie rose to her feet. The Airedale followed all the way, kneading her chest with his front paws.

"Down, Klinger," commanded Trask, and the dog obeyed.

"Klinger?"

"As a puppy, he was all nose. And my son used to dress him up in doll clothes, so we christened him Klinger."

The dog barked at the sound of his name.

"But Klinger wears women's clothing, Ken. Did your son—" Ellie paused as a thought clicked into place. "Did your son play with doll dolls?"

The streetlight revealed Ken's scowl, then his sudden grin. "Doll dolls, I like that. Yup, K.J. had a few, actually preferred them to *dick* dolls, but he outgrew it. By the time he was sixteen, he was dating and *fudging* and all that good stuff."

"Yes, well, thanks for coming to my rescue, Ken. Howie was getting a little too, er, persuasive."

"No problem, Ellie. Silverman's like Klinger here; all bark and no bite."

Ellie again pictured Dracula. No bite?

"Anyway, I wanted to give you this before you left." Trask handed her a business card with raised lettering. "You said you'd condone cheating if it was for a good reason. Call me, and I'll show you my—renovations." Leering, he cloned Howie's wink. "I'll show you mine, and you show me yours, right?"

Ellie decided to ignore his crudeness. "Thanks for coming to my rescue," she said again, sliding onto the driver's seat. "Say goodnight to your lovely wife for me," she added, slamming the door.

Trask made a circular motion with his hand, and she rolled down the window.

"That's what men are for, pretty Ellie," he replied seriously. "Men were created to protect women."

Maneuvering his head and upper body through the open space, he pinioned her neck with one hand and kissed her. She felt his tongue probe.

Klinger barked and tugged on his leash, pulling Trask away from the car.

Too furious for words, Ellie revved her engine. Three blocks away, she let the wind snatch Trask's business card from her fingers. Then she spat into the street.

She wished she could brush her teeth, but there was no toothbrush inside her Honda, just an unopened can of Diet Coke. According to Mama Smithers, Coke dissolved toothbrush bristles. Would it dissolve the taste of Trask's tongue?

You betcha, Ellie-Ellie.

So she drank every drop. Including fizz. And bugs.

Home again. Home at last. Home sweet home.

Ellie locked the front door, turned on the overhead three-globed light fixture, and surveyed her family room. Technically Peter wasn't living with her—he had his own small apartment not far from the precinct—but Peter's constant visits filled the room.

A woolly cardigan sweater was draped over the stereo. Grateful Dead cassettes anchored Peter's Raiders cap. A pair of dilapidated tennis shoes lay under the coffee table. Jackie Robinson slept on top of one, his furry face buried in the laces. Three days' worth of newspapers were stacked haphazardly near the fireplace, and a coffee mug with black-ringed remnants hid behind a windowsill plant.

The room even smelled male, thought Ellie. Lingering traces of Peter's after-shave mingled with the odor of his pungent sneaker beneath her cat's happy nose.

Ignoring the debris, she collected a pad of yellow lined paper and her trusty Magic Marker and plopped down onto the carpet. Before she could begin to write, the duck quacked.

"I'm at my place," said Peter's sleepy voice. "I need to catch a few zees before I drive back to the precinct."

"Okay. *Requiescat in pace*, honey."

"What?"

"Rest in peace. My rusty Latin's getting oiled."

"You sound like Vince what's his name."

"Lombardi? Van Gogh?"

"No, Price. Vincent Price. I thought they put that *requiescat* thing on tombstones."

"You're right. Sorry. Get some sleep, Peter."

"Love you, Norrie."

"Me too, you," she purred. As she replaced the receiver, the phone quacked again. This time it was Melody.

Her voice was filled with excitement. "Can we meet for lunch, Ellie? I have something important to tell you."

"Tell me now."

"Can't talk now. Tomorrow at noon? Uncle Vinnie's?"

Ellie agreed, and hung up the receiver. Returning to her position on the floor, she printed names:

GORDON DORACK
KENNETH TRASK
HOWIE SILVERMAN
FRED REMMING
SEAN MCCARTHY (FATHER MAC)

She paused, pen hovering, then wrote "MELODY REMMING." Only Melody's disturbing paintings and her "M*A*S*H" club membership made her a candidate. She had attended the M*A*S*H-Bash. She'd been at the ballet.

Am I nuts? Ellie thought. Melody didn't have any motive. The young woman was delirious with Dorack's attention, not jealous of sexy blonds. The stud who deserted the pregnant teenager had resembled macho Stallone, not wimpy Frank Burns. Ellie crossed off Melody's name with a broad stroke of her marker.

Dorack didn't seem the killer type, either. He worked for a Chevy dealership in their used-car division. Had he been at Charley's M*A*S*H-Bash party when Virginia Whitley was the victim of a vehicular homicide? Had he sold cars to any of the victims? Ellie wrote down her questions, thinking how Peter would scoff. Laugh? Appreciate her help? Drawing an arrow, she moved Gordon Dorack to the bottom of her suspect list.

Then she bracketed Kenneth Trask and Howie Silverman together. They were cut from the same cloth, although Trask seemed to have more class. She remembered his kiss. No, he didn't. What would be their motives? Could rejection trigger an explosive response? She'd felt that with Silverman. *Fudge.* Okay, he didn't cuss in front of ladies, but he sure tried to put the moves on them; her rump still throbbed from his pinch. Melody said that Howie had an ex-wife and family somewhere. Did his ex look like Hot Lips? Had she remarried a Frank Burns? Oh, brother.

Trask's motive? Ellie drew a large question mark next to his name and decided to return to him later.

She didn't care for Fred Remming. He was a neutered snake-in-the-grass. His asexuality didn't bother her, but he kvetched like a reptile who'd swallowed a mouse, then cramped from indigestion. Melody said her cousin worked in the utilities building downtown, processing applications and receiving payments through a caged window. He had access to personal information, including addresses. Fred was a definite maybe.

Jacques Hansen. Military rat. He had served in peacetime Germany and was no cliché psychotic war veteran on the loose. He edited a religious newsletter. Could his motive be some vague moral vindication?

Religion. Father Mac. Sean McCarthy.

Ellie liked him a lot. Sean was a duplicate Father Mulcahy with a razor-sharp intellect; a Latin cohort who stimulated *her* intellect. Funny, she could picture Sean as a priest, attorney, or college professor, but Melody said he worked for the telephone company. Had any of the victims' phones been bugged?

Then there was the most damaging evidence of all—the Latin-phrased messages left at Natalie and Krafchek's murder scenes. Sean had learned Latin because he "worshiped Juliet." Had *she* looked like Hot Lips? Farfetched!

Ellie shook her head. Then, under her list of so-called suspects, she wrote "GET A LIFE!"

Because these people all seemed to be preoccupied with the show. On the other hand, Ellie had met "Star Trek" addicts whose whole world—galaxy?—seemed to revolve around Captain Kirk and Spock and "beam me up, Scottie." "Star Trek" addicts were even more preoccupied than "M*A*S*H" junkies, she thought, returning to her pad and notes.

Okay, what about the victims?

Franklin Harrison Burns. According to Magnolia, her husband had met the "M*A*S*H" group while grocery shopping.

The priest wrote Harry's name down and our address, too, I think.

Natalie. How did the lovely ballerina fit?

None of us really fit, Ellie-Ellie.

Did Natalie own a car? It would be easy to find out if the girl had recently bought a new used Chevy from Dorack. The student dorm paid the utility tab, so Natalie would have no reason to come in contact with Fred. How had the killer selected Natalie? How did he know she resembled Hot Lips? Could that murder be an impulse? A "M*A*S*H" club member who attended the ballet and noted a resemblance?

Ellie snapped her fingers, then attacked the pile of newspapers, scattering pages across the carpet until she came to last Saturday's "Leisure Time" foldout. It listed cultural events. On page three a story about TOES was headed with a photo of Sandra, Natalie, and the busty swan. The swan seemed embarrassed, and Muffin looked young and vulnerable, but Natalie stood out, a professional smile on those Loretta Swit lips. Even the grainy picture couldn't hide Natalie's glossy platinum hair.

Ellie's lined paper now had several notations, arrows, and scribbles, including Silverman's rump-pinch, Hansen's religious fanaticism, Natalie's newspaper photo, and Harry Burns's tête-à-tête at the supermarket.

Jackie Robinson's slitted eyes looked accusatory; he seemed to say, "Mee-ow. Number one amateur sleuth should tell Miller-Chan about Father Mac's Latin."

"But then I'd have to confess that I attended tonight's get-together," muttered Ellie, "and Peter might get a teensy-weensy teed off. Forget it, puss."

She'd forgotten Nancy Trask. Holy cow, thought Ellie, now she was really reaching for straws. Why would Nancy kill "M*A*S*H" look-alikes? Because she was jealous of Ken's obsession with the show? Great theory. Hadn't Tony said that Ellie was obsessed? That would put Tony in the same league as Nancy. Except Tony hadn't really cared if his wife was concerned with M*A*S*Hers, masochism, or massacres. Speaking of massacres—that doll thing. Kenneth Trask's son had played with dolls. So had Mick. Not to mention Annie. Inside Ellie's closet, there was a box filled with Annie's dolls, including G.I. Joe. Tony was adamant. If Michael could play with dolls as a kid, Ann Marie should be allowed to play with war toys. And Ellie would be willing to bet that Tony kept a duplicate box at his mother's house.

Barbie for Joe—tit for tat, she thought, then heard distinct footsteps from the front hallway. Peter?

But Peter had called from his apartment, and by now he was sound asleep. Anyway, Peter's soft-soled Hushpuppies wouldn't make that heel-toe click sound.

Ellie crawled toward the fireplace. Jackie Robinson followed, weaving his furry body through her bent legs.

"Some watchcat you are," she whispered.

The Persian hissed in his throat and waved his bristly tail under her nose. She sneezed.

"Get away from me, you dumb puss. If you want to be helpful, call the cops."

Ellie stifled the urge to giggle as she pictured her cat talking into a duck. Then, grasping the fireplace shovel, she staggered to her feet. Her legs tingled with pins and needles.

Extending the shovel behind her shoulder like a baseball bat, she froze.

Whoever it was, the damn perpetrator made no attempt to disguise movement. The closet door even creaked shut.

Ellie could imagine the dialogue when police discovered her dead body. She could see herself as a ghost. The female version of Patrick Swayze.

Cop:	No forced entry, Lieutenant Miller.
Peter:	Ms. Bernstein had a tendency to leave her door unlatched. Can't tell you how many times I warned her about that.
Ellie:	But Peter, I locked the front door. Oh dear, you can't hear me. I'm a ghost.
Cop:	Understand she lost fifty pounds.
Ellie:	Fifty-*five* pounds, numb-nuts.
Peter:	Yeah, she dumped her Oreo cookies, pissing off her cat, so he didn't warn her when the perp unexpectedly entered the premises.
Cop:	What a beautiful skinny corpse. Sorry, Lieutenant, I forgot she was your main squeeze.
Peter:	That's okay. Norrie was always investigating my cases, sticking her nose into places where it didn't belong. It was only a matter of time.
Ellie:	This time I locked the damn door, cross my heart and hope to die!

Ashes fell from her shovel, dotting the air like smog. Ellie sneezed again. Her eyes teared. She felt perspiration prickle under her armpits, between her breasts, and around the shovel's handle. Her eyes were still blurry, so she tried to focus on Peter's Grateful Dead cassettes.

Then, holding her breath, she waited.

$\triangledown$

9

A MAN ENTERED the family room.

Ellie's slippery grasp on her shovel loosened, and it fell with a clang.

Jackie Robinson meowed indignantly, then sauntered toward his litter box. The cat didn't appreciate sudden noises, and he didn't like Tony.

"Eleanor, what the hell?"

Tony looked puzzled, annoyed, concerned, all of the above, thought Ellie. Letting out her breath, she said, "Holy cow, *hic*, how did you get inside?"

"I have keys."

"But you returned your keys during the, *hic*, divorce."

"A real estate agent always keeps an extra set of keys handy. You have the hiccups, Eleanor."

"Yes, *hic*, you're so sensitive, Tony. I get hiccups when I've had a bad, *hic*, scare. Dammit, *hic*, why didn't you knock or ring the, *hic*, bell?"

"I don't know. Habit, I guess. What's the matter?"

"Oh, nothing," replied Ellie, so angry that she felt her hiccups evaporate. "Just a bunch of recent murders, and the kids claim I look like Loretta Swit, and—"

"Loretta Swit?"

" 'M*A*S*H,' you idiot. We discussed it last week. I seem to spend my whole life explaining who Hot Lips is and—"

"Hey, wait. I know who Hot Lips is, and don't call me an idiot. What's the connection?"

"Am I talking a foreign language?"

"You have before."

"What do you want? Why did you come here tonight?"

"Your nerves are shot," he said, plopping down on the couch and glancing around the room.

He was staring at her mess, thought Ellie. Peter's sweater and sneakers and cap and mug—well, maybe not the mug, hidden behind plants. As Mrs. Anton Bernstein, she had been the Happy Homemaker, everything spick-and-span, cookies inside the oven, soup simmering on top of the stove. Erma Bombeck once said, "There are four things that are overrated in this country: hot chicken soup, sex, the FBI, and parking your car in your garage."

Garage! Franklin Harrison Burns!

"If my nerves are shot, it's because you just scared me to death, dammit," she shouted, then watched Tony frown. He didn't approve of cussing females. She should have uttered her usual holy cow. Fudge that! Fudge Tony!

"You wouldn't be frightened if you used some logic," he said calmly. "Why would a killer stomp through the hallway, then hang his coat inside the closet?"

"Okay, I'm sorry. No, I'm not sorry. Why didn't you shout hello or something? You don't own this house anymore, and you had no right to keep the keys."

Tony altered his expression to one of contrition. "Look, I didn't drive here to make you angry, quite the opposite. Would you fix me a whisper martini?"

"Fix it yourself, Tony."

He strolled down the hallway, and Ellie realized that he would pass her bedroom with its unmade bed and scattered clothes—her robe, jeans, and panties, Peter's shorts and shirt. Guilt-ridden, she straightened the family room, neatly stacking newspapers, pushing the coffee mug farther behind a rhododendron. She folded Peter's cardigan, then placed both sweater and cap on the bookshelf, atop a copy of Diane Mott Davidson's latest mystery novel.

Tony returned, carrying a pitcher and glasses. After pouring, he handed one glass to Ellie. She silently counted calories, shrugged, then felt the fiery liquid untie stomach knots. "Why didn't you call first, Tony?"

"I called earlier, and nobody answered. You really should buy a machine, Eleanor. Later the line was busy. I decided to take a chance and drive by. Your lights were on and your car was parked outside."

"So you chose to walk in unannounced," she said, sinking onto the love seat.

Tony flashed his wolfish grin. "I'll hand over the house keys before I leave, okay? Another martini?"

"Are you trying to get me drunk, Tony?"

"No. Just less hostile, more relaxed."

Ellie gulped down the remaining gin and extended her glass. She realized that she was drinking on a practically empty stomach, having skipped dinner. Nancy's veggie platter seemed hours ago, and she'd been so busy nibbling—*studying*—suspects around Trask's table that she'd merely studied—*nibbled*—one carrot and a couple of radishes.

"I have a favor to ask," said Tony, returning to the couch. He kicked off his leather Gucci loafers, and they lay like a rebuke next to Peter's smelly sneakers.

"What flavor?"

"Not flavor, *favor.*"

The whisper martini tasted great. Ellie sucked a gin-favored—*flavored*—ice cube. "I'm not a Girl Scout, Tony. What kind of good deed are we talking about?"

"Would you babysit Ann Marie tomorrow?"

"I—you said Grandma Bernstein . . ."

"Mother has a doctor's appointment, and it's such a hassle to drag a baby along. If it's okay with you, I'll drop Ann Marie off first thing in the morning."

"Why didn't you bring Annie along with you tonight? I have that portable crib."

Tony refilled her glass while eyeing her CSPD sweatshirt. "I wasn't sure you'd be alone. I wouldn't have intruded if *his* car had been here."

"Peter? Why would Peter make a diff—oh, I see. You don't

want me to corrupt Annie's morals. Jesus, Tony, she's not even two years old."

"My mother says kids are impressionable at that age."

"You're kidding. Do you mean to tell me, pure untainted one, that you never screwed your young cheerleader before you married her? You never tumbled that vest full of bouncing titties? Never shouted 'rah rah' during orgasm?"

"Eleanor, please, I never did that in front of Michael."

"I don't make love in front of Annie, you bastard!"

"Your cop spends the night when Michael's here, doesn't he?"

"That's none of your business!"

"Eleanor, we're arguing."

"Arguing? We're having a goddamn fight."

"You said we didn't fight when we were married. You said that arguing was a sign of love. Could it be that you don't hate me anymore?"

"I never hated you," she murmured, thinking hate was too strong an emotion. Hostility? Disgust? Animosity? Jesus, face it, she'd hated him with all her heart.

Tony placed his glass on the coffee table and walked over to the love seat. Leaning forward, he gave her a professional kiss.

"Shove off," she said, wiping her mouth with the back of her hand.

"I want you, Eleanor."

"Bastard! Screw you!"

"I love it when you talk dirty."

"Since when?"

Amazed, she watched him remove his slacks, shirt, undershirt, and shorts. Then he stretched out on the floor, arms and penis extended.

"Let Tony entertain you," she sang. "He will do a few tricks, some old and then some new tricks."

"What the fuck are you singing, Eleanor?"

"The stripper's song from 'Gypsy,' slightly altered. Get up, Tony, or you might get carpet burns on your ass."

He looked angry enough to strangle her, thought Ellie. But he merely grabbed his clothes and left the room.

She heard bathroom noises.

Bet dollars to doughnuts he left the seat up.

"I understand." Tony stood just inside the family room entrance. He had splashed water on his flushed face and combed his hair. "I moved too fast, caught you by surprise. You can't possibly know how much I love you."

"Love me?"

"The last few years were a mistake, a big mistake. We never should have divorced, Eleanor. I want you, and you want me. I felt that before when you kissed me."

"Dammit, you kissed *me.*"

"Then you decided to get even. I deserved it. We're even now, okay?"

Dumb dialogue, she thought, glancing toward the blank TV screen. She needed another drink. No, that was the last thing she needed. In fact, her stomach lurched like a Ferris wheel. If Tony approached the love seat again, she'd spew all over his Gucci loafers. No, he'd taken them off. Okay, she'd spew all over his socks.

"I realize this is sudden," he said, "but I had to deal with your cop. I suppose I have no right to judge—"

"*Facias ipse quod faciamus suades.*" Anger could dissolve nausea as well as hiccups, she discovered.

Tony's brow puckered. "What does that mean?"

"Practice what you preach."

"Must you give me Latin at a time like this?"

"No, I can give you a limerick. 'A wonderful bird is the pelican. His mouth holds more than his bellican. He takes in his beak enough food for a week. But I'm damned if I see how the hellican.' Christ, Tony, you're not even divorced from your cheerleader. Your mouth holds more—"

"Look, I'm big enough to forgive and forget. I forgive you, Eleanor. Can you forgive me?"

I can't believe this, thought Ellie, watching Tony slip to one knee in the classic suitor's pose.

"I want you to marry me," he said, "after my divorce is final. I want us to be a family again. You, me, Michael, and Ann Marie. Remember how I asked you to marry me the first time?"

"How could I forget?"

Again Ellie gazed at the TV screen, replaying the scene. Let's see, she thought, Redford stars as Tony. My part is performed by an overweight Loretta Swit, what the hell! Setting's an Italian restaurant. Instead of martinis, Tony plies me with wine, then presents a rolled piece of paper that looks like a thick diploma. A tiny diamond ring is nestled inside. A gaggle of waiters clap their hands and sing "I hope you will remember this fun event forever" while I try to put the ring on, but it doesn't fit. Embarrassed, I study the blueprints.

Ellie's eyes moved away from the TV as she glanced around her family room, once lines on thin tissue paper. She could picture the blueprints with the name of the architect slashed across the corner: KENNETH TRASK.

When Trask designed her house, he'd just begun his career. Soon he became Trask, Inc., responsible for many community structures. In fact, Ken had designed the recital hall where poor Natalie—

Ellie jumped to her feet, ran to the kitchen wall phone, then quickly Touch-Toned Peter's number.

Trask knew that building inside and out, she thought. He created the blueprints, designed the hall. He knew about the trapdoor, could easily have made his way into the dressing room, then escaped unnoticed. Melody said the whole "M*A*S*H" group attended the performance. Trask is their leader. It's so obvious.

Peter's phone rang and rang. Ellie heard the loud clunk of a receiver dropped against a wooden table, then Peter's sleepy "hello."

"I've solved the case," said Ellie. "Holy cow! I'll bet that bastard was at the M*A*S*H-Bash. Melody said he wanted to sit with the men."

"He, who?"

"Radar."

"Norrie, please, you're talking gibberish."

"He said that his son played with dolls."

"Who?"

"Kenneth Trask. He's our M*A*S*Her."

Hanging up the phone, Ellie remembered an old high school basketball cheer. "Kenneth Trask," she chanted, "he's our man. If he can't do it, nobody can."

"Christ, you have no proof," said Peter. "You make an emphatic statement, then hang up. I trudge here in the middle of the night, and you have no damn proof."

"It's not the middle of the night. What do you mean, no proof? Kenneth Trask was the architect. Self-employed, so he could have killed Burns on a Monday afternoon. Did you think about that, Peter? The M*A*S*Her would have to be somebody self-employed or unemployed."

"Norrie, it was around lunchtime. Anybody could have killed Burns on that particular Mon—"

"Trask attended the recital. He slipped away from the group, killed Natalie, then returned through the trapdoor. He didn't even need a flashlight because he knew the theater's layout like the back of his hand."

"So do most of the actors in this city. Dancers, too."

Ellie added a log to the fire, then fiddled with the buttons on her blue shirt—Peter's shirt. Scalloped tails fell below her bare knees, and she recalled Howie's comment about her tall detective. Howie and Tony and Trask were cut from the same cloth. Fortunately, Tony had left during her phone call.

"Are you suggesting that a dancer killed Natalie for the hell of it," she said, "then printed those Latin words on the mirror? Afterward, just for grins, the dancing perp knifed Leo Krafchek?"

"Of course not, but you can't prove Trask did it. What's his motive?"

"I don't know. Yes I do. He was upset because the network killed his favorite show. Melody said so."

"CBS didn't kill 'M*A*S*H.' The cast decided to end it while it was still a hit."

"Sure, but Melody told me that Ken was upset and wanted all his friends to write complaint letters. Maybe he's murdering for revenge."

"Revenge?"

"I hate it when you sound like that, Peter, so calm, so repetitive. Yes, revenge, because they canceled his favorite TV show."

"Why knock off Hot Lips? Why not Hawkeye? B.J.? Klinger? Radar?"

"I don't know! Dammit, leave me alone!"

Peter placed his arm around her shaking shoulders. "Easy, Norrie. I should be angry about your visit to that 'M*A*S*H' club tonight, but from what you've just told me, they all sound like harmless nuts."

"Except Kenneth Trask!" she shouted. Then her blue-green eyes filled with tears and her mouth quivered.

"Aw, don't cry. You should leave Colorado Springs, sweetheart, take a vacation. This case is getting to you."

"Your suggestion wouldn't have anything to do with the fact that I look a little like Hot Lips and have Burns as part of my last name, would it?"

"Absolutely." Sitting on the couch, Peter patted the knees of his faded denims.

Ellie shifted to his lap. "Okay, maybe I overreacted. I thought I'd found the missing piece of a puzzle, but I forgot that there were other pieces in the box."

"That's my logical Norrie." Peter kissed away her tears and massaged her back.

"All of a sudden, everybody wants me to be logical."

"Everybody? What do you mean?"

"Nothing. Never mind. Peter, what if Trask was the architect for Harry and Magnolia Burns?"

"Norrie, their house was built around 1940. How old is this Trask?"

"Well, restored then. Ken said he restored old homes."

"There's no secret passage into the Burns house."

"If there's no secret passage, why didn't a neighbor see the killer entering or leaving? You checked, didn't you? Even if it did look like a suicide?"

"Burns could still be a suicide. His body was saturated with alcohol. Christ, Ellie, his mistress was pregnant. He could have been in over his head."

She ignored the exasperation in his voice, the loss of her nickname. "Did you question the neighbors?"

"Shit, yes," shouted Peter. "Nobody saw anything unusual. Two neighbors gave a description of Tony."

"But Tony arrived *after* the murder."

"Right."

"Let's go to bed. I'm sick of the whole thing. I give up. Did you hear me, Peter? Up, up, up."

"Shhh, calm down. I love you, Norrie."

"Don't just *talk* about love, okay?"

"You bet."

I'll bet dollars to doughnuts that Ken's our M*A*S*Her.

"Thank you, Peter, I feel better now."

"Don't ever thank me for making love to you, Norrie. What we have is not a slam-bam-thank-you-Loot relationship. Rest your face against my shoulder. That's my good girl. You're so lovely, sweetheart. We should turn on the lights and pose together for a Christmas photo-card. Pete and Norrie basking in the afterglow of—"

"Pictures!" She bolted to a sitting position, clipping Peter's chin with the top of her head.

"Ouch. What pictures?"

"Something Magnolia said during my condolence call. She and her husband were shopping for groceries and ran into the 'M*A*S*H' group. Everybody laughed at Harry's resemblance to Frank Burns, and somebody suggested taking a photograph."

"Who?"

"I don't know. Magnolia didn't say. But what if the

killer collects pictures of his victims? Is that logical?"

"What about Natalie? Do you think the murderer lurked around the campus snapping students until he found one who resembled Hot Lips?"

"Before the recital?"

"I assume the killer didn't take a camera to the performance and shoot his victim."

"Maybe he already had one of Natalie." Ellie explained about the newspaper photo. "So you see, the murderer might have a collection."

"That's far-fetched, Norrie, but even if true, we'd need search warrants."

"Get them."

"Do you honestly believe I could ask for warrants to search the homes of a few 'M*A*S*H' club members?"

"I suppose I was thinking about TV, movies. Mel Gibson and Eddie Murphy always search—never mind."

"Get that look out of your eyes, Norrie."

"How can you see a look? It's dark in here."

"Don't play innocent with me, sweetheart. Even in the dark, I can sense the wheels turning. You are *not* to search 'M*A*S*H' club members' houses. It could be dangerous, and if they're not home it's against the law."

"I know that, Peter. I won't go anywhere uninvited."

"Look, I'll run a check on those characters you met tonight. By the way, what was Tony doing here?"

"What makes you think Tony was here?"

"You're not the only sleuth in this bedroom. The toilet seat was up and there's gin on your breath."

"How do you know I wasn't drinking with somebody else?"

"Tony left his shoes under the coffee table. Or have you been entertaining another Gucci addict in my absence?"

"Smarty-pants."

"I'm not wearing pants."

"Tony asked me to marry him again and he dangled Annie as bait."

"You told him to go to hell?"

"He was in the middle of his proposal when I thought about Trask and ran to phone you. I returned to the family room, but Tony had disappeared. I guess he was so pissed, he didn't take time to find his shoes. He rendered a very dramatic proposal. If it had been a movie script, I could swear that Tony committed some crime and proposed because a wife can't be forced to testify against her husband."

"Maybe he wants to get married because he loves you."

"Oh sure. I think he needs a mother for Annie. I think *his* mother is getting on his nerves. In any case, I bruised his ego."

"Do you want to marry *me*, Norrie?"

"I love you, but we don't need a piece of paper to prove it. Speaking of paper, did you check out the note that was pinned to Krafchek?"

Peter settled back against the pillow, his arms crossed behind his head. "Now I give up. Up, up, up. Of course we checked, Norrie. Krafchek's message was on lined paper, the kind you can buy in any stationery store or supermarket. The pin and paste, too. Separate letters were scissored from *TV Guide*. Do you know how many copies of that damn magazine are sold weekly? The lipstick on Natalie's mirror came from her own supply of nonallergenic makeup. No fingerprints," he added, anticipating her next question.

"The dog tag?"

"We thought that would be easy. Certainly an engraver would recall the name Margaret Houlihan. We contacted department stores and jewelry shops. Nothing. We've asked the Denver PD to search, too, but we're talking hundreds of locations."

"What about your mass murder scene?"

"The dolls? Just your average, run-of-the-mill, garden-variety kind. You can buy them at any Kmart."

"Were they used? I mean, played with?"

"Smarty-pants," he mimicked tenderly. "No, the dolls weren't smudged or faded. On the other hand, they weren't recent species like Batman or the Little Mermaid or Belle."

"Belle? Oh, Beauty. How do you know so much about dolls, Peter?"

"I have a niece, my sister Elizabeth's youngest. When in doubt, buy Disney."

"*Were* there any Disney toys?"

"Yup. One. Dumbo. He was perched on a tree branch, watching the whole shebang."

"I wonder if Dumbo was a message, Peter, telling us how dumb we are."

"That's enough, Norrie, go to sleep."

"What about your unsolved cases during the last eleven years? The policeman, cemetery woman, Dumpster killings, Virginia Whit—"

"We're working on it. No, you can't read the files. We're also attempting to see if the same 'M*A*S*H' MO has been used in other states. So far, not a clue." Peter yawned. "Do you have a Weight Winners meeting tomorrow?"

"Nope. I plan to have lunch with Melody Remming. Tony's leaving Annie with me, so I'll take her along."

But first I'll contact "M*A*S*H" club members and set up appointments to visit their homes.

"You know what, honey? I swore in front of Tony tonight." Ellie duplicated Peter's yawn.

"You always cuss, lady."

"I do not. You do, especially when you're pissed. I suppose cussing's contagious—" She paused, remembering Sean's comment. *Insanity's contagious.* What exactly had he meant by that?

"What about tomorrow night?"

"Tomorrow night?"

"Weight Winners, Norrie, we were talking diet clubs."

"We were talking cussing. No, I don't have a meeting."

"Good. I want you to meet me at my office around six-thirty. We're going on a special date."

"Where? Should I dress up, up, up?"

"Nope. Down, down, down. We're visiting a gym."

"What for?"

"What for you ask what for?"

She felt like catching the smile in his voice and placing it under her pillow. "I don't like surprises."

"Could have fooled me. Ain't you a mystery buff, sugar britches?"

"Sugar britches? You sound just like Duke—"

"Snider?"

"Who's Duke Snider?"

"He was an outfielder for the Brooklyn Dodgers. Played on the same team as Jackie Robinson."

"Oh, well, I meant Duke *Wayne*. John Wayne. What's your surprise?"

"I'm gonna teach you the rudiments of self-defense."

"I don't need to learn self-defense."

"Yes you do. I'm serious about this."

She remembered the shadow looming behind her while she fumbled for car keys, the slippery shovel, the pounding of her heart. And the hiccups.

"Good idea, Peter."

"Good night, Norrie."

"If you're going to do something tonight that you'll be sorry for in the morning, sleep late."

"What?"

"Henny Youngman line. I'm sorry I got you out of bed."

"You didn't get me out of bed, you got me into bed. Anybody can make a mistake, Norrie."

Even the great, she thought. Except Jacques Hansen said he didn't make mistakes. Oh yeah? He made one tonight by insisting that he knew the identity of the murderer. If the perp *was* a "M*A*S*H" club member, Hansen's life might not be worth a plugged nickel. But Jacques was bluffing. Even Ellie, who didn't know him very well, could determine that Jacques was a bona fide blowhard. Like tonight's wind. Like Tony.

Snuggling against Peter's warm body, she murmured, "Jackie Robinson and I prefer smelly sneakers to Gucci loafers. Fudge Tony!"

∇

10

Ellie AWOKE TO find Peter's pillow occupied by Jackie Robinson. A piece of paper was propped on her bureau, anchored by an empty mug with the inscription "Cops Shoot the Bull, Pass the Buck, and Make Seven Copies of Everything." From her kitchen came the enticing aroma of fresh-brewed coffee.

Rising, she kicked two pairs of panties under the bureau, scooped up her robe, and retrieved Peter's note.

My Darling Norrie,
I turned off the alarm. Forget your crack-of-dawn jog.
You'll exercise tonight. Which Mutant Ninja Turtle
do you want to play? Dibs on Michelangelo. Give
Annie a kiss for me. Love, Peter.

I do love you, Peter, she thought, and I will give Annie a kiss. Peter was great with kids. Which was another reason why she felt reluctant about accepting his marriage proposal. Because her biological clock had stopped ticking. Hickory dickory dock, the sperm ran up the clock. The clock struck forty-four, the sperm ran down. Hickory dick—

Damn! She had to stop daydreaming. Tony might burst in on her at any moment, especially since he had *not* returned his extra set of keys, the rat!

After a quick shower, she slipped into her full-length yellow bathrobe, set up Annie's portable playpen, and filled Peter's mug with caffeine. Then, sitting on the couch next to her duck, she placed her trusty U.S. West directory between her knees.

There was one listing for a Sean McCarthy. Nobody answered. She didn't bother calling Howie Silverman or Silver and Gold Insurance; she didn't feel like chatting with Howie after last night's episode. She'd check out the others first.

It was sevenish, early for phone calls. On the other hand, she might be lucky enough to catch people at home.

Fred Remming answered on the second ring. In her sweetest tone, using a prepared excuse, Ellie told Fred she wanted to throw a surprise party for Melody. At the Weight Winners meeting, Melody had confessed that she'd turn thirty-two the day after Thanksgiving.

"Could you give me a list of your cousin's friends, Fred? Maybe a few close relatives?"

"Gosh, sure," he replied.

She suggested that they confer at his apartment, then released her pent-up breath when he didn't ask why they couldn't handle it over the phone. Fred gave her a time (five-fifteen) plus his address and apartment number, and she noted that he lived in the same complex as Melody.

"May I speak to your father?" she asked the young voice who answered the phone at Jacques Hansen's home.

"Father? Oh, you must mean my husband. I'm Victoria Hansen."

Using Melody as an excuse again, Ellie said she wanted to get together with Jacques or Victoria to discuss ideas for an article about a local artist's work, inspired by a religious childhood. Victoria, still sounding very young, arranged an appointment for Thursday afternoon.

Ellie tried Kenneth Trask's number, hoping the master of the house wouldn't answer and assume she was accepting his crude invitation. Again, she breathed a sigh of relief when Nancy said hello.

First Ellie thanked Nancy for her hospitality and Ellie's initiation into the "M*A*S*H" group.

"Oh, that's Ken's department. I have nothing to do with the club. By the way, you made quite a hit with Sean—Father Mac—" Nancy paused, then said, "I never *can* get used to that ridiculous name."

"Sean made an impression on me, too. He's very nice." Ellie explained about Melody's surprise party. "You're so organized, I thought we might plan something spectacular."

And maybe I can discover if your husband keeps a hidden photo gallery.

"Ken has errands for me to run today," said Nancy. "Klinger's veterinarian moved to Denver, and Ken insists I drive the dog there for booster shots. How about tomorrow? Is three o'clock convenient?"

"That's fine, Nancy, thank you." Ellie hung up the receiver as her doorbell rang.

Jackie Robinson's fur bristled while his tail poofed to double its size.

"Okay, okay, Tony, I'm coming." Ellie opened the front door. "Please stop ringing my bell. You sound like a Good Humor truck on a hot summer afternoon."

"It's not summer. It's not hot. I'm not in a good humor." He strolled toward the family room while Annie, clothed in miniature Bronco jacket and Oshkosh overalls, rode the crook of his arm. "You were so rude last night, I left without returning these." Tossing keys on top of the fireplace mantel, he added, "I hope insanity doesn't run in your family, Eleanor. I'd hate to think our son might be afflicted someday."

"Stuff it, Tony."

"Stuff it, Tony," parroted Annie.

"Ann Marie, hush! Really, Eleanor!"

"Errie." Annie stretched out her arms. "Mymick?"

"He's at school today, Pumpkin." She retrieved Annie from Tony, removed the little girl's jacket, then placed her in the playpen with her alphabet blocks and a frozen bagel.

Annie held up a *B* block. "Bird. Cheep, cheep."

"Cheep, cheep," repeated Ellie, handing Tony his Gucci

loafers, glancing with amusement at her ex-husband's racquetball sneakers.

"You're such a S-M-A-R-T-A-S-S, Eleanor."

"What are you going to do when Annie learns to spell?" asked Ellie, thinking that Tony was treating her like an undesirable client who couldn't qualify for the loan on a cheap-cheap house. "If I recall, you cussed plenty in front of Mick."

"Michael's male. It's okay for men to swear. My mother's appointment is this morning, so you can return Ann Marie anytime after lunch."

"Would you do *me* a favor, Tony?"

"Well, I suppose I owe you for watching Ann Marie," he said curtly, clutching his status loafers.

"You don't owe me—"

"What do you want, Eleanor?"

"Knock it off, Tony. I'm sorry I disappeared in the middle of your proposal. I'm sorry you had to leave so quickly, you didn't take time to put your stupid shoes on. And the only insanity in my family is a great-grandmother who married an asshole like you."

"Asshore," said Annie.

"What do you *want*, Eleanor?"

"You have a friend who works at the newspaper, uh, Dave Corley. Isn't he a crime reporter?"

"Yes."

"I need to talk to him."

"Why?"

"I'm trying to write an article about unsolved crimes, and I have to, well, research my facts."

"You've always been a poor liar, Eleanor. Why do you really want to see Dave?"

She sighed. "Remember last night when you scared me, and I mentioned the recent murders? You even discovered one of the bodies inside his garage. Franklin Harrison Burns."

"Burns was a suicide."

"I don't think so. Anyway, there have been several un-solved cases, for instance, two lovers who were killed and buried inside a Dumpster. I want to check with Dave and see if the crimes are related."

"Your 'M*A*S*H' nonsense?"

"That's right."

"Boy oh boy, I'm glad I'm not around to watch you play Mrs. Detective."

"*Ms.* Detective. Look, Tony, if you don't want to call Dave for me, just say so."

"As a matter of fact, *I* planned to contact Dave. I want him to meet my new girlfriend, Mary. She works in my office."

"*Woman* friend."

"What?"

"Never mind."

"I meant to tell you about Mary last night, but the whisper martinis made me act, well, amorous. I must confess that I've visited Charley Aaronson's lounge, drank too much, and tried to pick up girls who weren't my type."

"Charley wouldn't let your type inside the Dew Drop, Tony. *Girls* have to be at least twenty-one."

"If that's a joke, it's not funny. By the way, Dave Corley quit the newspaper. He freelances at home, writing nonfiction articles and a book, too, I think. Do you still want to see him?"

"Yes, please."

"Where the H-E-L-L is your phone?"

"On the coffee table."

"That's a *duck*.

Annie glanced up from her bagel. "Quack, quack."

"Very good," said Ellie. "What does a cow say?"

"Mirk. Gimme, Errie."

"You can have some milk later, Pumpkin, okay?"

Tony strolled toward the duck while Ellie ducked into her bedroom and quickly donned navy-blue wool slacks and a bright cranberry V-necked sweater. When she returned to the family room, Tony handed her a slip of paper.

"Dave's address," he said. "Anytime after twelve-thirty. You can take Ann Marie along. Dave has two babies of his own."

"Thanks, Tony."

"You're welcome. Look, Eleanor, last night I lost my cool, but I was sincere when I asked you to marry me."

"Just for grins, let's say I agreed, and we got married again, and I gained weight again."

"Then I'd divorce you again." He grinned. "That *was* a joke."

"I love your loafers, Tony. Are they synthetic or leather?"

"Are you kidding? Leather."

"Holy cow!"

"Moo, moo," said Annie. "Quack, quack. Cheep, cheep."

Once they were seated inside Uncle Vinnie's Gourmet Italian Restaurant, Annie was enchanted with the homemade cheese ravioli, her plastic bib, and the businessman who occupied the adjacent table.

"Mymick?" she asked hopefully. Deciding he was an acceptable substitute, she flirted shamelessly.

Melody was charmed by Annie. She even offered the child her bright red neckerchief, revealing her ugly scar.

"Gordon and I did it last night," confessed Melody, picking apart mussels steamed in a marinara sauce. "Then he asked me to move in with him. That's the reason I wanted to meet you today, Ellie."

"To get my permission?"

"No, your advice. I couldn't talk last night because Gordie was there and we didn't have any clothes on."

"I can't see through the phone wires, sweetpea."

"I know." Melody blushed. "Do you believe it's a sin to live with somebody and not be married?"

"Do you?"

"I did, but I don't anymore. How can something that brings such happiness be considered a sin? If there's a God, I think he must have instigated my meeting Gordon. I've watched the 'M*A*S*H' shows from the very beginning, and I nagged Freddy for a long time before he agreed to introduce me to his group. I think it was meant to be, don't you?"

"I sure do." Ellie chewed her shrimp scampi with enthusiasm. "Melody, what's your opinion of Sean McCarthy?"

"Oh, I adore Father Mac, I'm even remembering my high school Latin."

Annie salted the carpet.

"No, Pumpkin, salt isn't good for people or floors." Ellie smiled at Annie's rebellious glare, then turned toward Melody again. "Annie takes everything I say—"

"*Cum grano salis*," finished Melody.

"Right, with a grain of salt. Wow, I ate too fast. I'm already stuffed."

"Stuff it," said Annie, very proud of herself.

"Speaking of stuffed, Melody, what's your honest opinion of Kenneth Trask?"

"I don't care for him. Gordie promised if—when I move in, we'll share household responsibilities. Cooking, washing dishes, laundry. He'll fix up a room for my artwork, although he wants me to create happy paintings."

"I can't figure out why Nancy's so subservient, why she puts up with Ken's obvious chauvinism."

"Oh, they've known each other forever. He was the boy next door—well, actually across the street—somewhere in Florida. Gordie told me that Nancy and Ken attended the same elementary school and high school and he was friends with Nancy's older brother, who died in some car accident. Her parents died, too. They burned to death in a fire. Nancy was all alone, so Ken married her. Nancy put him through school. On the other hand, Ken took care of Nancy after her family died, and I guess she's always been grateful—" Melody paused to catch her breath.

"I feel sorry for her," said Ellie.

"Well, she puts up with a lot. Ken's a virtual alley cat. He even had a mistress for five years. He built her a small house, his own design. Everybody thought Nancy would divorce Ken, but she didn't."

"What happened to the mistress?"

"She left the Springs. Took everything Ken gave her, except the house of course, and disappeared."

"Did you ever see her, Melody?"

"Sure. Everybody saw her. They attended the theater and ballet together. Ken seemed to be in love with her, but who knows? He didn't divorce Nancy. Once I caught Ken and the girl cuddling together at an art exhibit."

"What did she look like?"

"Tall and leggy. Blond and sexy. She looked a lot like you, except her hair was platinum." Melody's cheeks reddened. "I meant that as a compliment, Ellie. She wasn't, you know, cheap."

"Cheep, cheep," said Annie. "Bird. Shoes."

"No, no," corrected Ellie. "Daddy's shoes are not cheap. When did the mistress leave, Melody?"

"About two years ago."

"Was Ken angry?"

"Furious. Freddy says he closed up shop and took a long vacation in Hawaii. The 'M*A*S*H' club didn't meet for a month. But he's recovered. Ken's had other women since then. Do you think he's handsome?"

"I can see how others might—*no, Annie!*" Ellie retrieved her water glass before the child could drown the salted carpet. "No, Pumpkin, we water flowers, not floors."

"Asshore," cried Annie. Squirming, she tried to stand up in her high chair.

Melody grinned. "Ass whore?"

"She can't say *L*s, and I suggested my ex was an asshole this morning. Hush, Annie. Sit down, baby."

"I'll leave my scarf," said Melody. "It can serve as a distraction. Or maybe a leash."

Ellie glanced at her watch. "Damn, I'm running late for an appointment. I'm happy to hear about Gordon, and I really enjoyed lunch."

"Me, too. Bring Annie to visit again, okay?"

"Of course. Someday you'll have your own kids—"

"No, Ellie, the abortion messed up my insides. After I met

Gordie, I had a full gynecological checkup." She blushed. "I haven't slept around much, but I wanted my blood checked for, well, you know, and the doctor ran every other test under the sun. Gordie says we can adopt. Anyway, my infertility is such a wonderful revenge on my saintly mother."

"But she can't know. You said she's dead."

"She knows."

"Right," said Ellie, thinking that Melody was a very strange atheist indeed.

Driving to Dave Corley's house with Annie dozing beside her in the car seat, Ellie thought about Kenneth Trask. No motive, Peter had insisted. Suppose, instead of vacationing in Hawaii, Trask had tracked down his leggy blond mistress. What if he'd found her shacked up with a man who resembled Frank Burns? Was that as far-fetched as the Howie Silverman ex-wife theory?

Braking for a stoplight, Ellie hummed snatches of an instrumental that played softly from her car radio. What was that melody? It sounded familiar.

Melody! The light turned green and horns honked like New Year's Eve as Ellie sat riveted in her seat.

Melody understood and spoke Latin!

Advocatus diaboli. God will punish you for your sins.

But Melody didn't believe in God.

Oh yeah? Despite her paintings and avowed atheism, a part of Melody still thought it was a sin to live with somebody and not be married. Plus her mother-knows bit.

Could Ellie's new friend be a Dr. Jekyll and Ms. Hyde?"

Toeing the Honda's accelerator pedal, Ellie suddenly remembered the title of the song playing on her car's radio. 1967. The Associations. "Never My Love."

Dave Corley resembled the "Gunsmoke" character Matt Dillon, but only in the clothing he chose to wear. Otherwise, Dave looked like Harry Belafonte. The same chiseled features and soulful eyes.

His diapered son and daughter, one year apart, sat behind the mesh of a sturdy playpen. At Dave's invitation, Ellie placed Annie between the two children, where she nestled happily like the cream inside one of Jackie Robinson's Oreos.

"My wife and I share the kids," explained Dave. "She has a part-time job and keeps them out of my hair all morning. In the afternoon I become house-husband."

How did Tony relate to Corley? Ellie wondered. Then she realized that their male bonding had become solidified before the birth of Dave's children.

"Haven't thought about those unsolved murders for years," said Dave. "I've been writing a novel about Negro cowboys in the Old West. Every morning I transport myself to the nineteenth century, when killing was quick, clean, and sometimes even justified. My wife says I'm beginning to look like a cowboy, but she's dead wrong."

"She is?" Ellie said doubtfully.

"Sure. I've *always* looked like a cowboy."

"Dave, do you remember if any of the female murder victims were blond?"

"Nope. You see, crime reporters tend to write about the whole scene, rather than mutilated bodies. We leave grisly details for the TV reporters. We get reactions from witnesses, rather than close-up photos of dead victims. I'm not sure I'm making myself clear—"

"I have no desire to view corpses, Dave. I thought you might have access to 'before' photos. For instance, Virginia Whitley's article included a graduation picture."

"Virginia Whitley?"

"The young woman who died outside Charley Aaronson's Dew Drop Inn. 1983. Vehicular homicide?"

"You don't want pictures of corpses?"

"Absolutely not. Despite what Tony might have told you, I'm not into dead bodies, and I'm sorry I bothered—"

"I have file folders, if that helps. When I left the newspaper, I made copies of all my articles. Most of the crimes I covered were solved. That's not what you're researching, right?"

"Correct," said Ellie, then realized that Tony must have given Dave her original unsolved homicides fib. Why? What difference did it make? Unless, for some dumb reason, Tony didn't want his ex-wife questioning Dave about the recent murders.

"What's your opinion on the recent murders?" she asked.

"The ballerina?"

"Yes. And the man killed curbside—Leo Krafchek."

"I haven't really formed any opinions yet. Why don't you interview Lieutenant Miller? He's the detective in charge of that investigation."

"Yes . . . well . . . I might do that. Good idea."

Dave opened a black metal cabinet across from his word processor. He sifted through several manila folders, finally extracting three.

The first story involved a missing child, and Ellie put it aside. "Dave, do you remember a policeman shot in his car?"

"Yup, but I didn't cover that case. It happened thirteen years ago, before I joined the paper."

Too early, thought Ellie, but asked, "What did the cop look like?"

"Are you kidding? He was white and wore a uniform."

She opened the second file folder. Peter had mentioned a woman abducted from the Safeway shopping center, later found dead at a cemetery. Corley had reported the crime. Tear sheets included two grainy photographs. The first showed a John Carpenter film set with headstones, grassy plots, and tiny police-blobs prowling amid the graves. It reminded Ellie of a Melody Remming painting.

The other picture was a close-up of the victim before her death. She had short dark hair, glasses, and a gap-toothed smile. No resemblance to anyone.

Ellie made a mental note to dig through her own albums for a flattering photo, one taken after she'd lost weight, just in case her meddling landed her on the obituary page.

The third file was thick with articles about the Dumpster murders, and included several follow-ups. The male victim, separated from his wife, had moved into his girlfriend's apartment. Their bodies were discovered by a woman who had just rented an apartment in the same complex. She'd been discarding empty cartons, wouldn't speak to reporters, and was not identified by name.

"Dave, do you remember the name of the woman who found the Dumpster bodies?"

"No. Why?"

"I just wondered."

"If you interview Lieutenant Miller, he might know."

Ellie glanced down at the tear sheets again. Dave's feature ran for a couple of weeks, reporting the same information over and over, and Ellie recalled Sean's "empty dreams" bit. There were lots of pictures.

"Here, this might help," said Corley, handing her a magnifying glass.

"Yes, that's a lot better."

"Did you find what you needed?"

"Yes . . . I . . . yes . . . thank you very much."

Dave would believe she was nuttier than a fruitcake, thought Ellie, if she were to tell him what she'd discovered. The "before" photo of the man in the Dumpster clearly defined his elfin, Mork-like face. He was the spittin' image of Robin Williams.

But the murdered woman looked like a Calvin Klein model. She had blond hair, and her wide sexy mouth was smiling impishly.

Hot Lips Houlihan!

Why were they killed? Who killed them?

Not the man's estranged wife. She would have been arrested, and the case solved.

Somebody else had trashed the bodies.

Who? Melody? Why? Because they were living in sin?

What about Ken? The Dumpster murders had taken place two years ago, after Ken's mistress had abandoned him and left town. The trashed woman looked like Hot Lips. So did the mistress, sort of. But why would Ken kill the woman's lover? That made no sense. Unless Ken had found them together, then killed the man to throw police off the scent of his Hot Lips trail.

Jesus, maybe she *was* nutty. How could the police connect Ginny, the mistress, the trashed woman, and Hot Lips? Peter hadn't even believed Ellie's "M*A*S*H" theory until Natalie's dog tag and the doll massacre.

All of a sudden, Ellie remembered something Ken had said Monday night, following Hansen's remark about Frank's heroic Purple Heart and the Jehovah's Witness bit—"Let's write our own 'M*A*S*H' show, folks. We'll have Hawkeye shoot Frank's dick off, by mistake of course, and Burns can receive an authentic Purple Heart."

The others had laughed, especially Howie Silverman, but Hansen's eyes had shot daggers.

Okay, thought Ellie, the trashed man looked like Robin Williams, and Leo Krafchek looked like—well, Leo Krafchek. But the trashed woman resembled Hot Lips. So did Natalie. Why would Jacques Hansen kill Hot Lips? Because—holy cow! Hot Lips had *dumped* Frank. She'd even married some other guy and slept with Hawkeye. Could Jacques be that obsessed with Frank? Could *anybody* be that obsessed?

Yes! The Memorial Park "homicides" proved it. And the perp had slaughtered his dolls with *war weapons*.

Peter had said that the killer had a sick mind. And Howie Silverman had said that Jaques had a sick mind.

What about Harry Burns? Why would Jacques kill Harry? Because Harry was doing something that the real Frank Burns—the real imaginary Frank Burns—would never consider. Harry was planning to divorce his wife and marry his whore.

Victoria Hansen's voice had sounded so young over the phone. Did she collect dolls?

$\triangledown$

11

Eℓℓɪᴇ ғᴇʟᴛ ʟɪᴋᴇ Red Riding Hood. Although Ms. Hood didn't drive a Honda, and Ellie didn't tote a goodies basket, both were planning to visit Grandma, and Ellie kept wondering if she'd find a wolfish M*A*S*Her behind every tree. Every shrub. Every stop sign.

Grandma Bernstein's small cottage was located in Manitou Springs, a historic town right next door to Colorado Springs. Manitou had tourist traps, covens, and a truly spectacular view of the mountains. While Annie dozed in her car seat, Ellie's thoughts turned and twisted just like the steep, narrow, winding streets.

Jacques Hansen had become a definite maybe.

On the other hand, Melody had called Kenneth Trask an alley cat. If he became a rejected suitor, would Ken unsheathe his claws?

Rejection. Melody. The Dumpster couple had been committing adultery, living in sin. "I thought about painting a priest blessing a Dumpster, but it seemed too macabre." An unidentified woman had discovered the bodies. Discovered them? Or disposed of them?

Logic, Norrie. The crime occurred two years ago. Dave's newspaper article claimed that the woman had *just* moved into her apartment. Melody said she'd lived there three years. It would be easy to check.

Logic! Fred Remming lived in the same complex. Could Fred have believed himself in love with the blond victim? Or the boyfriend?

Logic! When had Howie Silverman been divorced? More than two years ago? Ken swore that Howie was all bark and no bite, but Ellie had a gut feeling that he bit hard, maybe even drew blood.

Automatically, Ellie downshifted and turned into her ex-mother-in-law's driveway. Annie, still asleep, clutched Melody's scarf. Gently, Ellie woke the little girl and carried her into the house.

Florence D'Amato Bernstein called herself a widow, even though Ellie knew that the woman's CPA husband had slid behind the wheel of his brand-new Imperial after pocketing a grocery list from his wife. Leaving behind a savings account, an education fund for Tony, and real estate investment property—including the cottage—Andrew Bernstein had never returned from the supermarket. Florence reported his "abduction" and waited for kidnappers to call. One week later, Andrew's letter arrived. It said, "Hi Flo, 'bye Flo, have a good life." The letter was postmarked San Diego. Inside the envelope were her grocery coupons. Florence was pissed. The coupons had expired.

During Tony's childhood Florence had ironed her son's wardrobe, from socks to jocks, and she still pressed permanent-press bedsheets. Ellie suspected that Florence sustained shivery orgasms while defrosting her refrigerator.

No wonder Tony had grown up sexist as well as sexy.

"Granma Fro, Granma Fro," chanted Annie, while Florence changed her into clean clothes and handed over Melody's soggy, saliva-stained scarf with distaste.

Ellie swiftly pocketed the red silk material and asked about Grandma's doctor visit.

Florence warmed to the subject. After three cups of herbal tea and three trips to the bathroom, Ellie heard "Grandma Fro's" grandfather clock chime five times.

After kissing Annie good-bye, Ellie drove to Fred and Melody's apartment complex. Damn, she was late.

"Thought you might have changed your mind," said Fred,

ushering Ellie inside and immediately extending a plateful of chocolate chip cookies.

She tried to refuse the cookies and explain her tardiness, but Fred wasn't listening. Instead, he fussily straightened an already spotless living room. Although he had no female companion in residence, the window curtains were ruffled yellow organdy and matched the couch slipcovers. Dried flowers, *dusted,* nodded from ceramic vases. A vacuum hose coiled through an open closet door, looking like an under-nourished python. The kitchen, visible from the living room, smelled like Mr. Clean. Florence Bernstein and Fred Remming were kindred spirits.

Was Ellie the only Colorado housekeeper who hid stained coffee mugs behind rhododendrons? Even Melody's paintings had assumed a tidy structure.

Ohmigod! Atop a polished end table were three G.I. Joe dolls. One wore fatigues while the other two sported scrub uniforms and surgical masks.

Fred followed Ellie's gaze. "Nancy Trask sewed those doctor clothes," he said. "Other people collect unicorns, but my stuff's more original, don't you agree?"

Without waiting for an answer, he strolled into the kitchen, poured green frothy liquid into two salt-rimmed glasses, and washed the blender.

"Drink up," he said, handing one glass to Ellie. "Plenty more where this comes from."

She sipped politely. The salt stuck to her lips.

"*Cum grano salis,*" she murmured.

"Why do you do that? Why does everybody do that?"

"Do what, Fred?"

"Talk like that, so's a person can't understand. You, Father Mac, even Melody. It's not very nice."

"You're right; I'm sorry," said Ellie, then improvised plans for Melody's birthday party.

Fred gulped down two more margaritas, washing the blender each time.

Ellie surreptitiously poured her greenish liquid into a potted ivy, thinking how she'd just killed a living organism. Soon it would become fodder for the vacuum-snake.

"By the way, Fred, do you have any photos of Melody and her friends? I keep a few albums on my bookshelf."

"Albums?"

Ellie realized that she hadn't been exactly subtle. If Fred collected photos of his victims, he wouldn't be dumb enough to paste them inside a scrapbook. Or would he?

"Family pictures—childhood to adulthood," she ad-libbed. "I could enlarge a few, use them as a theme for Melody's party. A growing-up theme. Thirty-two's, well, a threshold. For a woman."

"Really? I thought thirty was the threshold."

"Not anymore. Now it's thirty*something*."

I sound like an idiot, thought Ellie. Thirtysomething? Why not call it the big three-two? Followed by the big four-four. Followed by the loss of one's faculties.

"Oh yeah, that TV show that used to be on ABC, right?" Fred thunked his forehead with his hand. "Darn, Mel has all the family pictures. She says she uses them to paint from. I have that picture there, but she's not in it." He pointed toward a framed enlargement on his wall. It was surrounded by four symmetrically thumbtacked "M*A*S*H" posters—two Radars, one Hawkeye, one Hot Lips.

Ellie stepped closer to the photograph that dominated the middle of Fred's neat arrangement.

"It was taken at the Dew Drop Inn during a M*A*S*H-Bash party," he said proudly. "The last show. March 1983. We were all in costume and I almost won a look-alike contest. That's me on the left."

Ellie studied the photo. She vaguely recalled a group of men seated near the bar. Usually her detailed mind could conjure up clear images, even from years past, but the Dew Drop had been so crowded. She couldn't have found her own mother in that crush of bodies.

The photo refreshed her memory, or maybe it was because

she had recently met the men depicted. There sat Kenneth Trask, costumed as Hawkeye. And Howie Silverman, belly bursting through the buttonholes of his dress. Sean McCarthy wore a straw hat and black turtleneck. Fred Remming clutched a beer-soaked teddy that foamed at the mouth like a rabid dog. Gordon Dorack and Jacques Hansen were missing.

Wait a minute! There were figures in the background, drinking, waving at the camera. One waver was Hansen, his head and upper torso visible between Howie and Sean.

"Did Jacques attend the M*A*S*H-Bash, Fred?"

"Sure did. Funny how he got into the picture, almost as if he knew he'd be joining us. Ken proposed the club that very night."

"Who took the photo? Gordon Dorack?"

"The Dork? No. Golly, I think it was the bartender."

Ellie tried to remember the last time she'd heard a grown man say "golly." "Who brought the camera?"

"Father Mac."

Damn! Another incriminating piece of evidence against Sean. Was he the one who'd suggested taking a picture of Harry Burns?

"Was Gordon at the Dew Drop that night, Fred?"

"Golly, no. Howie found the Dork when he bought his used Chevy. Howie has a company car, a Cadillac that he shares with his partner, but his wife got the family car in their divorce, so Howie bought the Chevy from Dorack, and they started talking about cars, and Howie mentioned my Jeep, and that brought the conversation round to 'M*A*S*H.' Anyway, Dorack said he liked to watch 'M*A*S*H' reruns, so Howie invited him to join our club." Fred wriggled onto the couch and patted the cushion next to him.

"When was Howie divorced?" asked Ellie.

"October 1, 1982."

"Holy cow, you know the exact date?"

"Sure. Howie says it often enough. He says it was the same day that somebody put cyanide inside Tylenol cap-

sules. Seven people died, and the killer was never caught,"
added Fred smugly. "Hey, why don't you sit down? There's
no cyanide in these cushions." He laughed at his own wit.

Ellie suddenly realized that she couldn't search Fred's
apartment unseen. It was too small, too *neat.* Desperate, she
said, "Melody mentioned that you attended the ballet recital
last Saturday night. Did you happen to save a picture of the
murdered ballerina?"

"From the program?"

"No, the newspaper."

"Why would I do that?"

"Because she looked like Hot Lips."

"Really? Golly, I'll have to get my eyes examined."

Ellie finally sat, thinking that her visit was a stupid waste
of time and effort.

Fred unbuttoned his Hawaiian shirt, revealing a plump
chest with sparse body hair. "You didn't have much to drink,
Ellie. Are you relaxed? Ready?"

"Ready for what?"

"Darling." Fred savored the word, then repeated it. "Darling, I know why you really came to my apartment."

"What are you talking about?"

He halted at his waistband, mid-button. "Didn't you
come here to—" His cheeks flushed red, pink, then red
again, like a blinking neon sign. "I th-thought—"

"You thought I came to have a rendezvous? Are you
crazy?"

"But on the phone this morning you talked so sweet and
made up that excuse about Melody's birthday party."

"Excuse?" Ellie felt her own cheeks flush. Guilt.

"You just met her. Why would you give her a party?"

"I love Melody. She's bright and talented."

"You're so elegant, darling, and you look like *her.* I thought
I could—"

"You thought you could what?"

"I was wrong," shouted Fred. "You're just a whore like the
rest of them."

"Who?"

"Everybody. Melody. She fooled around in high school. Did you know that? She used to make fun of me, tease me about not having a girlfriend, about being a virg—"

"Sorry, Fred, misunderstanding," mumbled Ellie, rising from the couch.

Fred stood up. "You'd better be nice to me or I'll pour tequila down your lying throat till you're dead drunk." He stamped his foot. "Take off your clothes!"

"Don't be silly."

"Don't you dare call me silly, bitch. Take your clothes off, or I'll rip them off myself." Fred's cheeks exploded with color, and a forehead vein throbbed.

"I'm leaving," Ellie said calmly.

"No, you're not!" Fred clenched his fists in the classic boxer's pose.

Ellie walked forward.

Fred moved with her, blocking her path. The man was small, almost squishy, but anger had given him a certain strength and power, like a miniature, hairless King Kong. Suddenly he grabbed his margarita glass, knocked it against a table's edge, and held up the jagged rim.

Lord, was she about to become another "M*A*S*H" corpse? Peter would stand over her grave and say, "I told you so." Maybe there wouldn't be a grave. Maybe Fred planned to trash her inside a Dumpster, only this time he'd be smarter, chop her up into teensy pieces first.

Ellie retreated a few steps, slowly maneuvering her hand to her pocket, searching for car keys. Not exactly a lethal weapon, but sharp.

The newspapers would laud her courage and daring. Ms. Bernstein captured the M*A*S*Her with her Honda key.

Wrong pocket. Her hand encountered Melody's scarf.

She fingered the silk material, then thrust it over Fred's head so that it fell, covering his face.

With the roar of a blinded bear, he dropped the glass and reached up to free his eyes.

Ellie zigzagged past while Fred pulled at the clinging fabric. She opened the front door, slipped outside, then sprinted toward her car.

Fred, she thought, would have to go to the top of her suspect list.

Along with Kenneth Trask and Jacques Hansen.

Like an Indy 500 racer, Ellie drove to Peter's office. She had planned to change into sweats, but her whole day was running out of sync.

So she remained seated inside the Honda to compose herself. Because she didn't want a repeat of last night, didn't want Peter suggesting a vacation again. Finally, she took a deep a breath and stepped out of the car onto the sidewalk.

Peter's office was housed in an ancient beige stucco building with a scalloped roof. It had once been an appliance store, then a discount tire outlet. Both had gone out of business. Renovated, the building now included a reception area, individual rooms, and separate cubicles. Just your average, everyday, small-town investigations bureau, thought Ellie, certain that Andy Griffith would soon scold Ronny Howard while Aunt Bea buzzed around the windowpane.

Peter sat at his cluttered desk inside an office off the main corridor. The wall held two framed diplomas from the Law Enforcement Officers Training School, one for general law enforcement and a second for police management. On a side wall, an insurance agency's calendar had pictures of U. S. Presidents squared above date boxes. Toward the back of the room a shelf held trophies for a variety of sports, including equestrian.

I've dated this man for over a year, she thought, and I never knew that he rode horses.

Peter studied Ellie's slacks and sweater. "I thought I told you to dress down, down, down."

"Hello, Norrie. How was your day?"

"Sorry. Hello, Norrie, how was your day?"

"Tony was growly. Annie has a new word, ass-hore. Grandma Bernstein talked for hours; they should market a game called Trivial Medicine. She gave me a headache."

Ellie skipped over the Fred Remming episode; she didn't think she could take Peter's recriminations without bursting into tears. Her headache was real. The phone rang. Peter pushed folders out of his way, reached for a pen, and cradled the receiver between his chin and shoulder.

Ellie glanced down at the folders. The top one had a typed label, "VIRGINIA WHITLEY." So Peter *had* taken her seriously. Sitting on the desk, Ellie pushed the folders toward the edge with her tush. As the top two fell, she knelt and gathered spilled pages.

Peter talked into the phone, fidgeting in his chair as though he rode a carousel horse.

Ellie memorized seven digits while replacing the folders. Virginia's mother's name was Mary.

Finishing his conversation, Peter hung up, then said, "You look very pretty, but why do you always ignore my advice, Norrie?"

"Do I really have to wear clothes, honey? Wouldn't it be more fun without them?"

"More fun, but impractical. You'd get bruised, and I can't throw you on the gym floor naked."

"I thought I was supposed to throw *you*."

"Right." He laughed.

Ellie thought that had a nasty chauvinist ring. "We can go home and you can wait while I change."

"I have a better idea. Follow me." He ducked into a closet storeroom, then emerged nearly hidden by brown mats. "Excess," he said, handing a few to Ellie.

The two struggled through the corridor and out of the building.

"I've always associated foam rubber with pillows," she muttered. "These damn things are heavy. Where's your car?"

"McCoy borrowed it. He and Wanda are celebrating their

six-month wedding anniversary at Uncle Vinnie's, and Will's car is in the shop. We'll use yours."

If Fred Remming had his way, her detective would be stranded without a vehicle, thought Ellie wryly. She released two little hooks, let down the seat, and they stuffed mats into the Honda's hatchback.

"Do you want to drive, Peter?"

"Nope, I need to rest so I can be on my toes later."

He relaxes like a big cat, thought Ellie as she maneuvered through heavy rush-hour traffic.

"Why the hell do they call it *rush* hour, Peter? I'm barely moving. All I can do is clutch. My left leg's cramping. My headache feels worse."

"Grandma Bernstein got to you, Norrie. Calm down."

When the traffic had finally thinned, Ellie drove carefully, unable to see through her rear window, blocked by the brown mats.

She never noticed the BMW playing follow-the-leader.

Jackie Robinson was delighted. While Peter pushed furniture against walls, the cat kneaded vinyl with his front paws, finally settling into a furry black funeral wreath.

"Move your butt or we'll have Persian pancakes for supper," threatened Peter, arranging the mats end-to-end.

"Speaking of supper," said Ellie, "don't you want to eat before we begin?"

"Food is not a good idea when we're flipping each other. You dumb cat, I said *no*." Peter scooped up Jackie Robinson and tossed him outside the front door, narrowly missing a figure who crouched behind the clipped bushes.

Ellie walked slowly into her bedroom. Pulling gray sweatpants and a Mickey Mouse thermal undershirt from a bureau drawer, she stripped to her bra and panties.

"Come here, Peter," she called. "I need your help to unsnap my bra."

"No way, Norrie. If I enter the bedroom, I'm subject to entrapment, and our lesson goes down the drain."

"Damn." She donned her old clothes, then captured strands of auburn hair with a thick rubber band. Returning to the family room, she gazed dubiously at the mats that covered her floor like a second carpet.

Peter had worn black sweatpants under his slacks, and they hugged his slim body while he demonstrated a few simple judo holds.

After a while she said, "I have an idea for a new weight-loss clinic. Twenty-four-hour wrestling. Nobody would ever eat anything again. I feel like the whale who swallowed Pinocchio. Uncle Vinnie's lunch shrimp is swimming inside my chest. Damn, I have to belch." She belched. "How do those Japanese wrestlers stay so heavy?"

Peter lunged, and she fell to the mat with a loud *oomph*.

"Dammit, this is ridiculous," she sputtered. "I can protect myself very well with a silk scarf."

"Scarf? What are you talking about?"

"Nothing. Never mind."

"Concentrate on my hands, Norrie."

"Why can't I just kick you in the balls?"

"If I was holding a weapon, it would be too late," replied Peter seriously. "I could shoot you with a gun or slash you with my knife."

"In a movie you'd drop the weapon, hold your groin, and swear a blue streak."

"This is real life. How many times do I have to tell you that? Kick-the-crotch is okay, but only as a surprise move, and certainly not if the perp has a gun pointed toward you. Let's try again."

Ellie managed to parry Peter's thrust, but he raised his muscled forearm, lifting her off her feet as if his arm were a chinning bar.

"You have to bend my elbow, Norrie," he said.

They worked for another half hour. She bounced like a rubber ball. Sweat poured into her eyes. Hair escaped its band, wisping about her face like angel-hair pasta. Finally Ellie stepped away, rubbing her neck.

"Boy oh boy, I'm going to be sore as hell tomorrow," she said. "At least I can't find my headache anymore in the midst of all this other pain."

"Do you still have a headache?"

"I have an everything ache, but I think I'm getting the hang of it." All of a sudden, she giggled.

"Why are you laughing?"

"Sweatpants. Your erection sticks out a mile. I've been afraid it'll snap off in our scuffles."

"Me, too. C'mere, gorgeous."

"We're finished?"

"We've just started."

"Oh," said Ellie in a small, disappointed voice.

"Don't look like that; you're breaking my heart. We've finished our first self-defense lesson, but we're about to start the next session. A shower together, after which I'll give you a rubdown."

"That sounds great, honey, but what about supper?"

"Are you hungry?"

"Nope."

"You're not? Are you sick, Norrie?"

"Just my dumb headache." She shed her sweatpants. "I'm tired of defense tactics, Peter, tactile though they may be. I prefer to love you to death, smother you into submission." She removed her perspiration-soaked Mickey Mouse. "Unsnap my bra, and I'll race you to the showers."

Instead, he slipped her bra straps down and cupped her breasts.

"I'm all sweaty," she gasped.

"Yeah, me too," he said, tracing her earlobe with his tongue.

"What about that shower and rub—*oh!*"

She shivered uncontrollably as he reached beneath the bra's lace and gently rubbed her nipple with his thumb and first finger. Then he removed his clothes and lowered them both to the mat. Its foam rubber didn't give like her water bed, but Ellie couldn't have cared less. It might be fun to bounce for a change. For a change? She'd already bounced for an eternity. At least.

"Is this in your defense manual, Peter?"

"First page," he murmured, tossing her bra and panties toward the window. "Ohmigod, Norrie, let's hurry or it really will snap off."

"I'm ready. I've never been more ready in my life," she cried, then began to rock like a hobbyhorse.

Outside Ellie's house, a figure walked toward the street, leaving Gucci-soled footprints in the mushy dirt that surrounded thick shrubbery.

Jackie Robinson scratched at the front door, meowing for safety from things that go bump in the night.

$\triangledown$

12

ELLIE'S CRACK-OF-DAWN JOG soon became a wobbly dog-
trot, so she returned home. There were no bruises from last
night's self-defense lesson, but everything hurt. Especially
Jackie Robinson's pushy rub against her legs.

"Okay, okay, I'll feed you in a minute," she muttered, first
stacking, then attacking dishes. "Dammit, look at all these
dirty plates. Peter still believes that breakfast is the most
important meal of the day, bless his heart. Here, puss, finish
my scrambled eggs. Sorry I'm so bitchy."

Jesus, now she was apologizing to a *cat*, a cat who probably
understood three words. Peter. Feed. Puss.

Peter *had* fed the puss—several sausage doohickeys. She'd
chastised him for that, but Peter was Mr. Cheerful this
morning, his grin fragmenting like a sugary breakfast cereal.
Then, ignoring *her* peppery mood, Lieutenant Snapcrackle-
pop had blown her a kiss and hit the road.

"Hit the road, Pete," she sang as she wandered into the
family room, reached for her duck, and Touch-Toned the
number she'd memorized from Ginny's file folder. A woman
answered.

"Whitley residence. I'm Mary Whitley. Who's this?"

"Ellie—" She hesitated. Then, using her maiden name,
Charles, Ellie said that she was a freelance writer researching
an article on Mothers Against Drunk Drivers.

"Oh, I contribute to MADD. How may I help you?"

"Do you have a few minutes available to talk about your
daughter's accident?"

"No, I have to leave for work now. But I could meet you here during my lunch hour. Noon-thirty?"

"That's perfect, thanks." Ellie jotted down the address. Then she scribbled, "Weight Winners lecture nine o'clock, Mary Whitley twelve-thirty, Nancy Trask three P.M."

Damn headache, thought Ellie as she soaked in the tub, trying to soothe muscle spasms. After toweling her sore body she donned a blue-green skirt, beige silk blouse, and heeled boots. Then she arranged her hair into a simple French twist. The sink mirror revealed crimson cheekbones.

"Maybe I'm coming down with the flu," she told Jackie Robinson, who had followed her inside the bathroom. "Hey, do you want to play outdoors today, puss? It's beautiful. You can powder your paws with sunshine."

But when Ellie opened her front door the Persian gave her an enigmatic cat-frown, sauntered to the couch, leaped up, and sat with his paws curled under his fuzzy bosom.

"Guess you didn't appreciate Peter tossing you into the bushes last night, huh? If I get in touch with him, I'll suggest that he apprehend an Oreo. What's cop-speak for apprehend? Collar a cookie? Pinch a cookie?"

Touch. Pinch. Ouch. Ellie ached all over.

Mary Whitley was a small tidy woman.

If she had been a compact car, thought Ellie, she'd probably get a hundred miles to the gallon.

Mary's dark hair, permed and sprayed, framed her round face. A woolly plaid skirt fell exactly below her knees, and a white cotton blouse was tucked neatly into the waistband without a wrinkled pause. Mary's living room was spotless, uncluttered, and smelled like Pledge.

Even the family pooch, who investigated Ellie's arrival with a stubby tail-wag, didn't have those crusty cocker spaniel tears around his eyes. Ellie would be willing to swear under oath that Blackie had never shed one curly wisp of groomed fur.

"Coffee, Miss Charles?"

"No, thanks, I don't want to be a bother."

"It's no bother."

"Really, I'm fine."

Actually, thought Ellie, she wasn't fine. The stupid head-ache clamped her skull like the jaws of a vise.

Mary said she had thirty-seven minutes to spend with her guest, and hoped that Miss Charles didn't mind if she ate a cheese sandwich while they talked. Plopping onto a chair, Mary spread paper napkins across her lap, then chatted about her job. To Ellie's surprise, the woman worked as one of the busy secretaries at Tony's real estate firm.

I want Dave to meet my new girlfriend, Mary. She works in my office.

But Tony fell for women half his age, thought Ellie, unless he was downing martinis. If sober, could an old dog chase new tricks? Mary was what? Early fifties? It didn't add up, unless Tony'd really changed his spots. Maybe Mary was Tony's new type. She probably typed well, too.

"About Virginia, Ms. Whit—"

"Gosh, it's hard to believe she's been gone all these years. Harder with the holidays approaching, especially Thanks-giving. Ginny always tasted the turkey before I brought it to the table. She was a nibbler." Mary sighed. "Next week will be difficult."

"Next week?"

"Thanksgiving."

Holy cow, thought Ellie, next week. I haven't even called Mick. It can't be next week.

"I'm not sure I can help you," said Mary. "They never found the person who hit Ginny, so we don't know if the driver was drunk. We assume he was, but only Ginny would know, and she's with God now. I suppose I could ask her."

"You—you suppose—ask her?"

"Yes. She speaks to me sometimes, but it might be too late for your article on MADD."

"Does Virginia speak often?" Feeling idiotic, Ellie changed her question. "Did Virginia drink very often?"

"Oh no, Ginny hardly ever drank. When she went out with her friends, she ordered Shirley Temples. She adored cherries. I suppose I could ask her about the drunk driver the next time she comes to see me."

Mary Whitley sounded, thought Ellie, as if her daughter was due soon for a holiday visit. Could this woman who consumed her lunch with one careful eye on the clock, who probably never ran out of toilet paper—could this woman believe in ghosts?

"Did—has Ginny ever said anything about that night?" Ellie knew her question was fatuous but felt powerless to resist. "The night she, uh, died?"

"We don't discuss it, Miss Charles. We talk about happy things." Finishing her sandwich, Mary collected the napkins from her lap and dabbed at the corners of her lips.

"How does Ginny talk to you? Does she just appear?"

"No, Miss Charles, she speaks to me through her pictures." Mary pointed toward an album on top of a marble coffee table.

"May I see your photographs, Ms. Whitley?"

"All right, but I have to leave in exactly eight minutes, eleven if I catch all the green lights. But one can't guarantee that one will catch all the lights, can one?"

"I don't think," replied Ellie, "that one can guarantee anything, except death and taxes."

"True." Mary retrieved and opened the thick album, offering page after page of cellophane-protected snapshots. Her daughter as baby, toddler, teen, young woman.

Ellie watched the child's blond hair turn darker as she grew older, and without the wig she didn't resemble Hot Lips. Close, but no cigar.

Trying to hide her disappointment, Ellie said, "How long have you worked for Mr. Bernstein?"

"Eleven years. Well, Mr. B left for a while, but I've been with the company eleven years, twelve in July. I'll tell you a secret." Mary blushed. "I've had a crush on my boss since the very beginning. But he was married to some bitchy blimp. Then, after his divorce, he was trapped into marriage by a slutty cheerleader he believed was pregnant. I don't know why I'm telling you all this. I guess it's because you remind me of—"

"Virginia?"

"No, Barbara Walters."

Ellie's mind raced as she recalled her hunch that Tony had met or found Ginny at the Dew Drop Inn. Logic, Norrie. If Tony had decided to attend the finale, he'd never come costumed as a "M*A*S*H" character, so he'd stick out like a sore thumb. Yup, Tony was much more secure wearing his tailored suits and Gucci shoes. In fact, they had once been invited to a Halloween party. Tony had donned black slacks and jacket over a ruffled shirt and patterned vest, then insisted that he was Bret Maverick.

Driving down lovely tree-lined streets toward the Trask home, Ellie couldn't stop thinking about Tony and cowboys. There had been a cowboy at Charley's M*A*S*H-Bash. She'd noticed him, even from a distance, because he'd *stuck out like a sore thumb*. But that man's outfit—Matt Dillon rather than Bret Maverick—was more Howie Silverman's style.

Still deep in thought, Ellie parked curbside, then walked up the brick path. Damn! There were two cars in the driveway. Their license plates read "TRASK-1" and "WIFE-1."

Nancy Trask, immaculate in lime-colored wool slacks and matching sweater, opened her front door and offered Ellie her patented almost-smile.

If Nancy allowed her short hair to grow and curl about her face, she'd be very pretty, thought Ellie. Nancy could stand to lose a few pounds, but she was tall and carried her extra weight well.

Seated at the kitchen table, the two women sipped coffee flavored with chocolate beans. What a marvelous treat for a chocoholic, thought Ellie, making a mental note to mention the beans at her next diet-club meeting.

"Where's Ken?" she asked.

"He walked Klinger over to Howie's."

"Do you think he'll be gone long?"

"Probably. Ken and Howie are concocting some computer game based on 'M*A*S*H.' I hope you don't mind, Ellie, but I've already started working on Melody's party. I called her cousin Fred and wrote down a list of her close friends."

For a moment Ellie wished she could have seen the expression on Fred's face when he heard that Melody's birthday party wasn't an excuse for a rendezvous. "Wow, Nancy, when did you find the time? I mean, you had to drive Klinger to Denver and—"

"It didn't take much time. I thought we'd hold the celebration here, but Ken vetoed that idea. He doesn't want strangers tramping through the house."

"What about my place? I could handle a party."

"Well, I had a brainstorm. Melody is such a 'M*A*S*H' buff, and I thought we might throw a theme party with costumes. I spoke to Charley Aaronson and he said it's okay to hold our party at the Dew Drop Inn. We could bring Ken's VCR and tapes of the show. Melody would be the guest of honor."

"She'd love it, Nancy, that's absolutely brilliant."

"I'm glad you feel that way. Howie Silverman said you have a boyfriend, and of course he's invited. I've already called Gordon Dorack, and he wants to pay half the expenses. I thought we might take up a secret collection from other club members, assuming Ken gives me permission."

"I'm not sure I can make it for the Monday night meeting." If she was getting close to the murderer, why press her luck? And she shuddered at the thought of facing Fred, Howie, and Trask again. "I'll contribute my share right now, and of course I'll help with the party. Do you want me to keep Melody busy until the big moment?"

"Gordon volunteered. You and I can meet at the Dew Drop a week from Friday, sometime in the afternoon, to prepare. Charley said most of his regulars stay home with their families the day after Thanksgiving, but he'll have to televise football games, so we can show the 'M*A*S*H' tapes afterward. Ken wouldn't miss his football." Nancy hesitated, then asked wistfully, "Would your boyfriend?"

Ellie remembered the Bronco-Jet game when she had questioned Peter about unsolved cases. They had missed a field goal and touchdown. Well, not a *touchdown*, she thought, visualizing their session on the family room couch. Cheeks burning, she excused herself to use the bathroom.

Splashing water on her face, Ellie realized she had accomplished little so far with this visit, except firming plans for Melody's birthday party. And, although she enjoyed Nancy in this less-subservient role, Ellie didn't know how to bring the conversation around to Trask.

She couldn't just come out and question Nancy directly. Did your husband murder his mistress after she took off with a Frank Burns look-alike? Did he kill another mistress and stuff her inside an apartment Dumpster? Did he screw Ginny Whitley, then run her over with his car? Has he ever had an affair with a blond ballerina?

Now there's an idea; maybe that's his connection to Natalie.

Nancy's guest bathroom was on the first floor, not far from the kitchen. Ellie had no excuse to explore. If Trask hid pictures of his victims, they would probably be inside his work area. But Ellie couldn't think of any reason to ask about or visit Ken's drafting room. Would an interest in architecture be too obvious?

"I've always been interested in architecture," she said, returning to the kitchen. "Do you mind if I sneak a peek at your husband's work area? I wouldn't touch anything."

"Oh no, that's Ken department. No, he'd kill me if I let anybody see his sketches. I'm sorry."

"That's okay, Nancy." Ellie sipped her coffee. "You mentioned my boyfriend. He's a police detective, and he's been working on the recent murders—you know, the ballerina and . . . I wonder if I could ask . . . I feel so stupid asking . . ."

"Go ahead."

"Well, as you're probably aware—no, maybe you're not—but, well, some of the murders have involved, uh, 'M*A*S*H.' Well, for instance, a man who resembled Frank Burns was asphyxiated inside his garage. It was supposedly a suicide. I probably shouldn't be talking to you about this. Peter, uh, my boyfriend would kill me, but I wondered—"

"If Ken's club had anything to do with the murders?"

"Yes." Ellie sighed. "I guess I'll have to start at the beginning, and you've got to promise not to tell."

"I promise. Are you feeling all right, Ellie?"

"Do I sound incoherent? I have this dumb headache."

"There's aspirin right here in the kitchen. Maybe we should discuss murders another day."

"Please, Nancy, it's nothing fatal. Last night I overextended myself with some new exercises."

"Oh, I can understand that. I used to exercise, even lifted weights, but I let myself go, and Ken hinted that I might consider working out again. Boy oh boy, can he hint."

Ellie watched Nancy scowl. Then her almost-smile flickered as if she'd discovered the answer to a riddle.

"Last month," Nancy continued, "I joined a health club, the one that opened last year? I could hardly raise my arms the day after I started. That's probably why you're feeling so poorly." She reached into a neatly compartmented pantry shelf filled with carefully labeled medicine bottles.

Ellie gulped down three aspirins. "I think all the 'M*A*S*H' club members, except Gordon Dorack, were at the Dew Drop Inn the night a young woman named Virginia Whitley died. It was the show's finale, and Charley had this contest, and when she wore a blond wig Ginny looked like Hot Lips Houl—"

"I don't mean to interrupt, Ellie, but weren't there dozens of Hot Lips?"

"Yes, but I think Ginny's death is somehow connected to recent events."

"No kidding. Why?"

"I don't know. Intuition, I guess. Nancy, do you recall

running into a man who looked like Frank Burns? At the supermarket?"

"I don't think so. Wait a minute. His wife had a southern accent? Wore a corset?"

"Right. Did anyone suggest taking a photo of Burns?"

"I think the whole conversation lasted maybe five minutes. The men were all joking. I don't remember anything about the photo."

"Nancy, you've known all the club members from the very beginning. Do you believe—"

"That one is a cold-blooded killer?" She laughed. "I think you're barking up the wrong tree, Ellie. Speaking of barking, Ken told me about Howie Silverman. Howie's a jerk sometimes, but he's all bark and no bite. I feel sorry for him. You see, he's never gotten over his divorce, really loved his wife."

"Was she blond?"

"Yes. Bleached."

"Did she resemble Hot Lips?"

"Nope, she looked like that Brady Bunch dipshit."

"The maid?"

"No, the mother."

"Sorry, Nancy, please go on."

"Howie's squeamish, can't stand the sight of blood. He almost fainted once when I cut my hand slicing veggies. He fell to the floor, and this old house shook. Howie's ashamed because it doesn't go with his macho image, but he couldn't kill a fly, much less a person."

Nancy refilled their coffee mugs. "Jacques Hansen's got the guts for killing. The training, too. He's been in the armed services for a long time and must have learned all kinds of combat techniques. But why on earth would Jacques kill Frank Burns? I mean, Jacques adores Frank, thinks he should run for President."

"Well, I'm not sure about killing off Frank Burns look-alikes, Nancy, but, well, you see, Hot Lips dumped Frank, and Jacques could have been pissed."

"Have another aspirin, Ellie."

"You think I'm crazy, right?"

"No."

"Yes, you do. I'm talking about these characters as if they're real. Maybe I've simply imagined the connection. No! The dog—"

"What dog?"

—tag, thought Ellie. Aloud, she said, "Klinger. Where's he hiding?"

"Klinger's with Ken. Didn't I tell—?"

"Yes, I forgot. What about Sean. Could he kill?"

"Not a chance. Sean's kind, considerate, loyal. He has a wife in a sanatorium, a mental hospital. That's why he works so hard for the telephone company. Benefits pay medical bills. Sean could give last rites, but he couldn't kill. Nope, you're definitely barking up the wrong tree."

"Okay, we haven't mentioned—"

"Gordon Dorack's just like his name. I mean, they call him The Dork, and with good reason. He's become less dorky since Melody. You don't suspect Melody, do you?"

"No."

"I can't imagine Gordon as a killer, can you?"

"No, I guess not."

"That leaves Fred Remming. If I had to pick one suspect from the group, I'd choose Fred."

"But he's so whiny, so ineffectual."

"Also virginal and probably sexually repressed. And he's always had this thing for Hot Lips, as long as she stays within her safe television box."

"Okay, he kills Hot Lips because he feels threatened by his sexual urges. Why Frank Burns?"

"Because *he's* getting it on with Hot Lips."

"Oh." Ellie grinned self-consciously. "I can't believe we're doing this, Nancy. Psychology 1-A."

"On second thought, I can't really believe Fred's your murderer, Ellie. I don't know if he's physically strong enough. I think he might fantasize about it, but he'd never follow through. Fred's too wimpy."

Melody had once called Nancy a wimp, thought Ellie. Wrong. The woman's mind processed logical facts and *her* intuition was incredible. Okay, what about Trask?

As if Ellie had spoken aloud, Nancy said, "I've been married to Ken for twenty-seven years. If he was a murderer, I'd know by now." Rising from her chair, she opened the refrigerator and pulled out a roast. "Please excuse me, Ellie, but I have to marinate this while we talk. Ken's invited Sean to supper, and he loves my prime rib." After retrieving a ball of string from a shallow drawer, Nancy efficiently severed the string with a sharp knife.

"I have one other question," said Ellie, "and if I don't ask I'll wonder."

"Ask away."

"Melody said 'M*A*S*H' members attended the ballet recital. Were you ever separated? The group, I mean?"

"We split up during intermission and took some empty seats near the front, closer to the stage, but I'd probably notice somebody leaving. Wasn't the ballerina killed *after* the performance?"

"Yes." Watching Nancy tie the string around her roast, Ellie's stomach lurched at the sight of the lumpy raw beef. "I guess my question is, did anybody disappear after the performance, during the murder?"

"I don't think so. Well, I can't say for sure. Melody and I went to the ladies' room and waited in line. You know how it is, Ellie, three toilets, and fifty women tugging their panty hose up and down. It takes forever. I wish Ken had included a few more bathrooms in his design."

Ellie grinned at the panty-hose image. "You and Melody stood waiting all that time?"

"Melody finally got a stall, then returned to the lobby. I let a woman and little girl go ahead of me, big mistake. Mommy kept begging the child to make poo-poo."

"So you don't know if anybody sneaked backstage."

"Nope. We all left together. Melody and Gordon headed for the parking lot. I drove Jacques and his wife home, then

Sean. Ken, Howie, and Fred piled into Fred's Jeep and took off for the Dew Drop Inn."

"Did anybody seem agitated? Overly stimulated?"

"Yes. Howie. Fred. Ken, too. But they were all geared up to drink themselves silly and swap dirty jokes. At that point nobody knew about the murder."

Except the murderer! thought Ellie. "Nancy, did you see any blood? Natalie was stabbed."

"Uh-uh, no bl—wait a minute. Fred had a bloody nose. But that's not unusual. Fred blows it so often, and he's addicted to nasal spray."

"What if the perp wore a coat?"

"Perp?"

"Perpetrator."

"Are you saying that your *perp* stabbed the ballerina, then hid his bloodstained coat? Where? Didn't the police search the theater?"

"Yes, but they didn't search the audience. It was too confusing, and so many people had already left, and—"

"You want to know if somebody in *my* group wore a wrap to the recital but didn't wear one home, right?"

"Uh-huh."

"When we left the theater, I wore a full-length fake fur," said Nancy, thinking out loud. "Melody wore her blue quilted jacket. Ken wore his fur-lined trench—no, his black cashmere topcoat, the one with those deep pockets. It's at the cleaners right now. The others—Jacques, Victoria, Gordon, Fred—" Nancy shrugged. "I guess I'm not a very good detective."

Neither am I, thought Ellie. I used to believe I was, but I'm not so sure anymore. Everybody had a motive. Nobody had a motive. Opportunity existed for each group member. And the murderer could be a sicko not even remotely connected with the "M*A*S*H" club. Nancy said I'm barking up the wrong tree, and she's probably on the nose.

Unless Fred's bloody nose was a bloody scam.

Or Ken's deep pocket hid a bloody knife.

For some strange reason, Nancy's roast reminded Ellie of the Harry Burns suicide. Well, of course. She'd been cooking a rump roast for dinner that night. Speaking of dinner, she'd better touch base with Peter and find out what time he was due home.

"May I use your phone, Nancy?"

"Sure. It's over there, above that desk. Please excuse me, Ellie, but nature calls. Ken always says that. Howie says he has to take a whizz, Sean urinates, Gordon wee-wees, and Fred has to tinkle. After eleven years, I've got their dialogue down pat."

Laughing, Ellie walked to the wall phone and reached for the receiver. Peter's line was busy. Gazing downward, Ellie saw that Nancy's desk was neat, organized, which didn't surprise her. A Daffy Duck stenciled glass held several pens and pencils, scissors, and a small tube of glue. Near the glass there was a pad for messages. Nancy doodled. No, *Ken* doodled. The pad's first page depicted a detailed sketch of a house, everything drawn to scale. The house was on fire. In fact, the flames had been colored with red, orange, and yellow pencils.

"A sick mind," Peter had said when talking about the doll massacre. And despite Nancy's denial, Ellie was even more convinced that Ken was the M*A*S*Her. But how could she prove it? By eliminating her other suspects?

On a TV movie, she'd get them all together and shout, "You have a sick mind, Kenneth Trask."

"Oh good," he'd say, "that's my defense. I was temporarily insane three times. Four if you count Harry Burns. Five if you count Virginia Whitley. Six if you count Ellie Bernstein."

Then he'd pull out his knife, and Ellie would parry his thrust and easily flip him to the floor.

Music. Credits. This movie is based on a true story.

That night Ellie swallowed three aspirin, fell into a restless sleep, and dreamed.

The Trask Airedale and Mary Whitley's cocker spaniel

stood at the bottom of a tall shade tree, their fangs bared, barking at Ellie while she climbed up through thick branches. On every tree limb sat victims. Harry Burns, Virginia Whitley, the Dumpster couple, Natalie, even the shopping center cemetery lady with her gap-toothed smile. A policeman hunched against the trunk on one branch, his features distorted by bloodstained panty hose. Melody's masturbating priest gave communion to the corpses, then changed into Sean McCarthy. *"Ego te absolvo,"* Sean chanted, prying open dead mouths, avoiding lolling tongues, inserting the communion wafer.

"Give them last rites, Father Mac."

"You betcha, Ellie-Ellie," he said, then crumpled into dust.

On one branch perched a stuffed Dumbo, watching the whole shebang.

At the top of the tree was the murderer, hidden by leaves and foliage. The tree swayed back and forth as the dogs growled. Trapped, Ellie couldn't climb up or down. Suddenly *her* branch was occupied by several cats. Advocatus Diaboli and Agatha Christie and Stephen King's *Pet Sematary* cat. Plus Jackie Robinson, his fur bristling, his eyes slitted, his tail poofed.

"Call the police, you dumb puss. Find Peter."

Instead, Jackie Robinson padded along the branch, which soon began to break apart from the combined weights of Ellie, her fat Persian, and the three other scruffy, maggot-infested felines.

Snap. Crackle. Pop.

"Peter," she screamed. "Help!"

"I'm here, sweetheart." As her eyes opened, he pulled her across the bed and into his arms. "You feel so hot, Norrie. Are you sick? Do you have a fever?"

"No . . . not fever . . . nightmare . . . horrible."

"Shhh, Norrie, shhh." Peter stroked her sweaty tangled hair away from her eyes. "I'll protect you from nasty bugbears."

"Not bears, Peter, bug or otherwise. I dreamed that vicious dogs chased me up a tree, and I think I saw the M*A*S*Her. Damn, I don't rememb—it's too hazy. Ohmigod, is Jackie Robinson okay?"

"Sure. He's asleep at the bottom of the bed. Why?"

"I don't know. I'm scared."

"Good. I'm glad you're finally scared. Don't worry, Norrie, *I'll* catch that damn M*A*S*Her. Just lock all your doors and stay home like a good girl."

It was the wrong thing to say.

▽

13

THE HONDA'S ENGINE sounded louder than usual.

Chug, chug, urp, chug.

Maybe it needs a tune-up, thought Ellie. Maybe she needed a tune-up, as well. Maybe somebody should plug her sparks, rejuvenate her run-down battery, force-feed her high-octane gasoline.

Nope. High-octane anything was out of the question. Because she'd completely lost her appetite after watching Nancy Trask bind a bloody roast with string. Because Nancy's roast had reminded Ellie of Harry Burns. But it also reminded her of Virginia Whitley. Natalie. Krafchek. The couple trashed inside the Dumpster. Because murder wasn't dinner conversation, and corpses weren't pretty. And because no matter what Tony believed, Ellie wasn't into dead bodies.

Chug, urp, pssst.

Jacques and Victoria lived near the Air Force Academy. It was a long drive, and Ellie had seriously considered canceling her appointment. If un-astute Fred Remming had suspected that his cousin's birthday party was (originally) a fabrication, what would happen when she encountered Hansen's sharp military mind and tried to describe Melody's religious pornography? Ordinarily Ellie would enjoy the challenge, but today her brain was unfocused.

She halted for a stoplight. Her black cords rubbed the skin around her waist, so she tucked her lilac sweater inside to absorb chafe. Didn't "chafe" mean to feel irritation? Didn't "irritate" mean to provoke anger? Ellie was irritated, angry, frustrated, and this damn whodunit chafed like hell.

"Whydunit," Ellie murmured. "Not whodunit, whydunit." The *who* was Kenneth Trask. But why? That strange doodle bothered her. Maybe the house on fire was the same house that Ken had designed for his missing mistress.

Arriving at the Hansens', Ellie took a few moments to admire the white picket fence covered by thorny rose vines. Certainly Victoria's handiwork, since Jacques didn't seem the flowery type.

Sunshine pierced the cold air, and several children played War-in-the-Gulf. Or maybe we've declared war against Switzerland, thought Ellie as she noted that distant mountains wore marshmallow stocking caps. Soon Heidi would join her goatherd, Peter—

Peter! Stay home like a good girl and chafe.

Ellie parked, skirted a manicured lawn, and pressed the white button beneath a small brass plaque whose inscription read "Confess Your Sins, Not Your Neighbor's."

Obviously Victoria's handiwork again, since Jacques tended to exploit confessions and felt he was sinless.

I never make mistakes.

The doorbell's resounding ding-dong could be heard in Albuquerque, thought Ellie, but nobody answered her summons.

She turned the knob, peeked inside, and shouted hello. Three curbside children called a truce long enough to stare. Ellie smiled and waved, then entered.

The living room was cluttered but clean as a whistle. Walls were decorated with photographs of the Air Force Academy and presidents. Richard Nixon gazed down at a small table where Tom Clancy shared bookends (and romance) with Danielle Steele. Two framed Reagans smiled from above the chair and sofa. Directly over the TV, Jacques had hung Bush and Quayle. Clinton was missing. So was Gore.

To the right, at the end of a short hallway, Ellie could discern that the—bathroom?—door was decorated with a poster of Kitty Kelley, blown up from a book jacket cover. Although Ellie had devoured Kitty's unauthorized biography of Nancy Reagan, the Hansens probably believed that it lacked moral value—Kitty's eyes, nose, neck, and heart were spiked with feathery darts.

Stereo speakers blasted forth "We Are the World." Apparently the Hansens were into saving hungry children, but not the ozone layer; atop one speaker, an aerosol can of Raid nudged a can of pine-scented Lysol.

Another table next to the front door revealed a piece of lined paper, propped up against an aerosol can of hair spray and anchored by a model helicopter. Hadn't Peter said something about a helicopter at the scene of the doll massacre? But she'd driven here to eliminate Hansen, not condemn him, thought Ellie, staring down at large letters scribbled in a childish print:

JACKIE BEAR, MRS. BERNSTEIN DUE ABT.
NEWSLETTER STORY. I'VE GONE TO THE 7-11
FOR POT. CHIPS AND BEV. BACK SOON.
LOVE & X X X X X X X X, VICKY ANGEL

"Hello?" shouted Ellie. "Jacques? Hello?"

No answer.

Where was Jacques? Missing like Clinton and Gore? Could he have vacated the house after reading Vicky Angel's note? That didn't make any sense. Why leave the door unlocked and the stereo on?

The house wasn't very large. Surely Jacques could hear the doorbell. Perhaps the Hansens had a finished basement.

Yup. She found a door near the kitchen entrance and tentatively toed the first step of a wooden staircase.

"Hi, it's Ellie Bernstein," she called, thinking how the basement smelled like a bunch of dirty diapers covered with an acidic marinade.

Maybe the Hansens had a baby. Maybe there was a bathroom down there. Maybe the toilet had overflowed, and Jacques had left to borrow a neighbor's plunger.

From the top of the steps Ellie could see a tabletop lamp, typewriter, mimeograph machine, and paper cutter. The paper cutter's green-ruled base and blade seemed to be dark with—blood?

Had Jacques cut himself and run for help?

Although her original intent had been to snoop, no, *sleuth*, Ellie felt uncomfortable as she descended the stairs and halted halfway. From her new vantage point, she could distinguish neatly stacked periodicals in different-colored stock—yellow, light green, blue—bound with string. The basement also contained a furnace, water heater, and washer and dryer. Heaped next to both appliances was a bundle of dirty military clothing.

Reaching the basement landing, Ellie turned, blinked, then actually felt her hair stand on end as if she'd spiked it with mousse.

The laundry bundle had a face and looked like a giant G.I. Joe doll.

Not Joe, Jacques. Somebody else had eliminated Jacques Hansen. He lay on his back. Blood covered his body like a blanket, no, more like a sticky bedroll.

Hansen's fingers had been severed by the paper cutter's sharp blade. Then the killer had used newsletter sheets to transport all eight digits. Two fingers covered each eye. Two had been placed across his lips. The remaining four had been glued to his ears by that colorless gunk that stuck to anything.

See no evil, hear no evil, speak no evil.

Ellie stepped closer. The feculent odor was very strong.

"Don't you know what happens when the sphincter muscles relax in death?" she murmured.

Hansen's glasses were missing. A piece of Vicky's lined paper hung like a giant dog tag from his neck, attached with string instead of a chain. The message had been typewritten, probably on the tabletop typewriter:

LET THE EXPERIMENT BE PERFORMED ON A WORTHLESS BODY.

Ellie gagged; she broke out in a cold sweat, feeling as though somebody had punched her in the stomach.

I can't breathe, she thought, while a rush of bile forced its way up her throat. She retched again, then desperately swallowed. Forget it, she was gonna vomit. There was no toilet bowl handy, so she raised the lid of the washer and, as if from inside a tunnel, heard Jacques Hansen's voice: "I know who killed those people."

Then a girlish voice sang, "Jackie, I'm home. There's a car parked outside. Is Mrs. Bernstein here? I'm sorry I took so long, but I ran into Glory Eden, you know, that lady whose grandmother died last year? Glory's Jewish, but she's been acting very strange since her grandmother Esther passed away, and she was ready to talk about subscribing to our newsletter, so I couldn't let the opportunity pass."

"Call the police," screamed Ellie.

"Police? Why?"

"Don't ask questions. Just call them."

"Ohmigod, did something happen to Jackie?"

"Do it, Vicky! Now!"

"I'm coming down."

"Call first. *Please.*"

Resting her hot forehead against the washing machine's cool white enamel, Ellie heard the distant hum of "We are the world, we are the children," then nothing. Vicky had turned off the stereo.

All of a sudden Ellie's eardrums nearly burst from echo after echo of muted thunder as a bullet shattered the lightbulb along with a chunk of ceiling.

"Don't move," said Vicky.

Ears ringing, Ellie looked up. In the dim glow from the drafting table's lamp, she could see skinny legs. Low-heeled shoes descended the stairs. A wraparound khaki skirt appeared, then two hands holding a shotgun.

"This is heavy," said Vicky, "and I'm nervous, so don't you dare move."

Fear replaced nausea. Ellie stood frozen, staring. The

wraparound skirt proudly displayed Vicky's pooching belly. An overblouse rose to a cross on a gold chain, then a face with small features and straight brown hair secured by two clown barrettes.

"Vicky dear, I'm Eleanor Bernstein. Please put the gun down, and be very careful on those steps. You're pregnant, off balance."

"What have you done to Jackie?"

"Vicky, you called the police, didn't you?"

"Yes. I hear them coming now, so don't move."

The uniform division arrived and herded the two women upstairs. They confiscated Vicky's gun. Ellie collapsed at the kitchen table, gasping Peter's name and precinct number. She couldn't have driven home alone if her life depended on it.

Everything blurred, fading in and out like the screen images from a slide projector. Sirens sounded. Flashguns flared. There was the soft thud of a dart striking wood, and a voice shouted, "Bull's-eye." Somebody had pierced Kitty's face. Sick to her stomach again, Ellie wanted to excuse herself and use the bathroom, but she was inexplicably afraid to leave the kitchen. What if the perp lurked behind Kitty's poster? Stupid! If the perp lurked, the police would have found him . . . *hic* . . . her . . . *hic* . . . it.

Somebody else shouted, "You know it's blood and I know it's blood, but let's wait for the ME. It could be ketchup."

"Stumps don't bleed ketchup. Hey, what the fuck do you think you're doing? Don't touch anything!"

"Wish I hadn't eaten those fries and hamburg—oh Jesus—oh shit."

"Hey, don't puke into the washing machine, you stupid fuckup. There might be prints—"

"Fingerprints—fingers—oh God!"

Ellie heard the unmistakable sound of vomiting, then the washer; the stupid fuckup had turned it on. Vicky sounded like the washing machine's agitator. Between convulsive breath sobs she moaned "Jaaa-keee"; Ellie wanted to offer comfort, but couldn't move a muscle.

Peter arrived in time to hear the conclusion of her hiccup-infested statement. After a while he drove the Honda home, stripped Ellie's clothes, and propelled her ice-cold, sweaty body into the water bed.

Her head was bursting, and her eyes hurt like hell.

"Thanksgiving," she said.

"What about Thanksgiving?" asked Peter, sponging her face with a washcloth.

"I can't be sick. I didn't make plans. Mick—Sandra—no turkey."

It was as though she had lit the fuse on a stick of dynamite.

"Fuck turkeys," yelled Peter, throwing the washcloth across the room. "I'm still giving thanks that you're alive. Shit, Ellie, how many times have I told you—"

"Not now," she whimpered, "please."

"All right, I'm sorry. Try to get some sleep."

But when she slept, she dreamed. The same dream. Barking dogs, swaying tree branches, the hidden M*A*S*Her on top. This time Jacques Hansen joined other corpses. He was fingerless, and his bloody mouth opened to receive a communion wafer. Father Mac chanted, *"Dei gratia*, Ellie-Ellie. By the grace of God, it could have been you."

"Peter," she cried.

"I'm here, Norrie."

"Is Jackie Robinson all right?"

"He's fine."

"You'd better leave, I'm gonna throw up."

"That's okay, Norrie, I'll help you to the bathroom, or the wastepaper basket's right by the bed."

"You remind me of Dennis what's-his-name."

"Weaver?"

"No, Quaid. That movie where he played a cop."

"I don't play a cop, Norrie, I *am* a cop."

"I'm so embarrassed."

"Because I'm a cop?"

"No, 'cause I'm gonna throw up. Tony—"

"What about Tony?"

"He used to yell when I had morning sickness. He said it was all in my head. But I can't help it, Peter, honest."

"That's okay, baby, you have a stomach virus. Everybody tends to toss their cookies when—"

"Collar a cookie. Pinch a cookie."

"What?"

"Peter, is Jackie Robinson all right?"

"Norrie, he's fine, I swear."

"Don't let the M*A*S*Her get me," she screamed. "Please, Peter, lock the doors. I'll be a good girl. Don't let him cut off my fingers. Ohmigod, where's the basket?"

"It's right here. I'm here. I've got you. Don't try to be brave. Dammit, Norrie, I'm not Tony!"

For the next three days Peter held her, soothed her, nursed her. When she awoke the fourth morning, she felt weak but recovered. Peter slept on a chair. He wore a black T-shirt, gray sweatpants, and color-coordinated smudges around his eyes.

"You look awful," she said softly. Staring at his smudged eyelids, she fell in love all over again.

He jerked awake. "What is it, Norrie? Another nightmare?"

"No, it's morning. Are you okay, honey?"

"Me? Am I okay?"

"Holy cow, my club meetings."

"I called Weight Winners, spoke to a very nice lady, and explained that you'd be out of commission for a week or two. She said that you deserved a vacation, so don't fret."

"I think I'm hungry, Peter."

"Thank God. Nancy Trask delivered a pot of soup and oatmeal cookies. I pinched a few cookies."

"When did Nancy deliver food? I can't remember the last three days."

"Do you rememb—"

"Jacques Hansen? Yes. I'm not hungry anymore."

* * *

"Thanks for the soup and cookies, Nancy." Ellie cradled the phone's receiver on her shoulder so that she could scratch Jackie Robinson. Except for trips to his litter box and water dish, the cat hadn't left Ellie's side.

"I used to serve my son veggie soup," said Nancy. "It has more vitamins than the traditional chicken broth. How are you really feeling? Physically and mentally?"

"Physically, a lot better. Mentally, I'm not too sure. Did you hear all the gruesome details?"

"Yes. Ken canceled the 'M*A*S*H' club meetings, even though Sean wanted to dedicate it to Jacques. But Ken told Sean he was crazy, so there's no meeting tonight."

"How's Vicky?"

"Maintaining."

"She didn't lose the baby, did she?"

"Uh-uh. Vicky's stronger than she looks, Ellie."

"I know. She wields a gun like Clint Eastwood."

"I guess that destroys your 'M*A*S*H' theory. Jacques didn't resemble Frank Burns."

"Last week Jacques stood in your living room and insisted he knew who the murderer was."

"A bluff, Ellie. Jacques was always doing that. It was part of his job as an OSI officer. He pretended to be aware of details so that people would confess to crimes. Nobody in the group would take him seriously."

Except Sean, thought Ellie. *Don't underestimate Hansen. He may look harmless and sound like a dullard, but he's very sharp.* Like a paper cutter's blade, Father Mac?

Nancy asked how Ellie felt about Melody's birthday party. Nancy thought they should hold the celebration. It would "perk spirits," and several of Melody's friends had already RSVP'd yes.

"I'll be completely recovered by Friday," said Ellie firmly, "and we'll meet at the Dew Drop to decorate, just like we planned."

After replacing the receiver, she turned on a small TV near

her bedside. Theme music, helicopters, a commercial, and then "M*A*S*H" began its rerun—Colonel Blake's last show.

Ellie watched Radar enter the OR, where doctors were operating on the wounded. "I just got a message. The Colonel's plane was shot down over the Sea of Japan. Spun in. No survivors."

Entering the bedroom, Peter carefully carried a steaming bowl of Nancy's vegetable soup. He had showered and now wore faded jeans and a white shirt rolled up above his elbows. Despite the bedside vigil, Peter's forearms were sun-bronzed and corded with muscles.

"What's wrong?" he asked. "Why are you crying?"

"That's my third bowl of soup. Breakfast, lunch, now supper. If I eat any more, I'll turn into a veg—"

"What's really wrong, Norrie?"

" 'M*A*S*H.' Colonel Blake. Death."

Placing the bowl on top of the bureau, Peter rushed across the room and gathered her into his arms. "I've been waiting for this. It's okay to cry, sweetheart. You once told me that it's a sign of strength, not weakness."

When her wild tears had finally slowed to an occasional sob, Ellie said, "I'm g-getting your sh-shirt all wet."

"My shirt's wash-and-wear. Do you feel better?"

"I guess. Peter, can you get immune to death?"

"Never. If you're sick of soup, how about boiled eggs and toast?"

"Could we order Chinese takeout? Szechuan? Very spicy?"

"After a stomach virus? Over my dead body."

"That's not funny."

"Sorry, Norrie, I didn't think."

"No, Peter, *I'm* sorry. I don't want you to have to choose your words before you speak to me. That would be some strain on a relationship. Ohmigod, look at your face. I've opened Pandora's box."

"If I don't have to choose my words, we have things to discuss, Ellie."

"Please don't call me Ellie. I'll come clean, at least I will if you promise to make my sentence lighter. Second-degree disobedience rather than first-degree mutiny."

"Okay, Norrie, second-degree insubordination."

Launching into a nonstop recitation, bringing Peter up to date on all her activities and discoveries, Ellie told him about photos of victims she had viewed at the Corley and Whitley homes. She related her conversation with Nancy and revealed her encounters with Ken, Howie, and Fred.

"Melody learned Latin in school, but if you hung around Sean long enough you'd absorb some of the language, just like Mick did with me when he was growing up. The whole 'M*A*S*H' club probably knows certain expressions, especially Ken, who's closest to Sean. Well, everybody but Fred Remming. He just chafes, or pretends to."

Peter listened carefully. Except for the tearstained shirt, thought Ellie, he looked thoroughly professional. When she'd finished, he referred only to the carside hustle by Howie Silverman.

"Did he hurt you, Norrie? Threaten you?"

"Not really," she replied. "Howie couldn't have killed Jacques Hansen, Peter. Or Natalie. Nancy said he faints at the sight of blood, and there was certainly plenty of . . . of . . . I still think it's Trask. Melody's story about his disappearing mistress—you don't seem surprised."

"We're way ahead of you. I investigated when we ran a check on your 'M*A*S*H' club members. Trask not only flew to Hawaii but he took his wife with him. The Dumpster murders happened two years ago, on August 13. But we can't question your suspects about where they were and what they were doing. It's not like the bombing of Pearl Harbor or Kennedy's assassination. Do you remember where *you* were?"

"During Kennedy's assassination?"

"No, you nut, the Dumpster thing."

"I went to the movies and danced with wolves."

"You're kidding."

"Yes, honey, couldn't resist. Sorry."

"Don't do that, Norrie, or I'll force-feed you veggie soup."
Peter discarded his professional pose. "I'll tie your arms to
the bedposts—"

"That sounds like fun. The second part. Damn, I don't
have bedposts."

"Seriously, I could swear our perp's an amateur, but so far
he hasn't made one mistake. The closest he came was
footprints backstage at the theater, but those were obliter-
ated by Mick and Belinda."

"He?"

"Generic he, sweetheart, although I can't imagine a
woman severing—"

"Hey, wait a minute! Outside Hansen's house, the block
was crawling with children."

We are the world, we are the children.

"Very good, Norrie," said Peter. "The kids described you
as 'a pretty lady with red hair.' "

"*Me?* Why don't you arrest Tony and me for the murders
of Burns and Hansen?"

"Don't get angry. Damn, you're flushed again."

"Dear God, Peter, it's so frustrating. If they noticed me
and the color of my hair, they would have seen the killer.
Didn't he leave before I arrived? How could they see me and
not him?"

"Because there's an alley behind all the houses. Kids have
been warned to stay away, since there's a deep culvert. Our
killer could have parked in back, then entered."

"Is there a back entrance?"

"Through the kitchen."

"Unlocked?"

"Victoria Hansen says no. Claimed she kept the front door
open, since she expected her husband to return shortly. He'd
gone over to a neighbor's house to borrow milk, just in case
you wanted coffee and didn't drink it black. That's when
Victoria left her note. She says they usually kept the back
door locked."

"Which means—"

"That our perp was known to Hansen if he entered through the kitchen. But Hansen had lots of enemies, Norrie. In his job, you make enemies."

Plumping pillows behind her back, she sat up straighter. "How come the neighbors didn't hear a shot?"

"The killer used a muffler, what you civilians call a silencer."

"I thought a silencer wasn't silent."

"It's not, except possibly on a very small gun. We figure he used a goat's nipple to cover the muzzle."

"What's a goat's nipple?"

"It's rubber nipple stretched over a baby animal's feeding bottle. It can be used for calves, horses, any newborn. Works much better than a muffler, and it still traps the gases. Sounds like a cough or pop."

"Snap, crackle, pop," murmured Ellie. "How do you know our perp used that nipple thing?"

"We found tiny shards of rubber on the floor."

"Of course. Rubber! Footprints!"

"Rubber footprints?"

"You said the killer slipped up at the theater and left footprints. What about rubber tire prints? Was the alley paved?"

"Nope, dirt. You have such a fine mind, Norrie. If you'd only keep it safely indoors and stay away from—"

"The police already checked for tire prints, right?"

"Correct. That day, the day of the murder, a truck delivered a cord of cut wood to the house next door. Delivered and stacked it. Parked between Hansen and the neighbor. Can you imagine the mess in dry dirt? Uh-uh, Norrie, it was *before* our killer arrived, and the driver didn't see anything," said Peter, anticipating.

"*Fata viam invenient,*" muttered Ellie. "That's from Virgil."

"And means?"

"The Fates will find a way. Our killer was lucky, Peter. Desperate, too. If he believed Hansen's statement about knowing the identity—" She paused, yawning. "When you checked out the 'M*A*S*H' club members, did you find anything illegal?"

"Sure. Fred Remming was arrested for dealing cocaine. Five years in the Fed pen, Norrie."

"Please, I'm serious."

"Okay, Fred Remming has fifteen unpaid parking tickets, Kenneth Trask has a bunch of speeding tickets—his insurance bill must be a doozy—and Howie Silverman has a DUI."

"Tell me about serial killers, Peter."

"Why?"

"The doll massacre."

"Where should I start, Norrie? For one thing, he usually takes a souvenir from the scene, a trophy, so to speak. He might have a power-control fantasy that started with his childhood. For instance, he could have tortured his sister's dolls."

"Power . . . control . . . Trask." Ellie yawned again.

"Serial killers love to read about their crimes in the newspaper," said Peter, warming to the subject. "If caught, they love to talk. When they talk about their murders, they talk in third person, and they feel no guilt. They like to drive. Sometimes they'll drive for hours, just cruising, looking for the right victim. They always search for a specific type of victim, and sometimes they'll even drive around with dead bodies in their car sea—"

"That's enough, Peter, I get the picture. You forgot to tell me that he's always described by neighbors as a 'nice guy.' "

"Yup. Always."

"Aren't there any nice *gals?*"

"Probably, but I've never heard of any. Serial murders are usually sex-related."

"Nice gals don't have sexual hang-ups?" She yawned for the third time.

"Take a nap, Norrie, and I'll wok some Chinese food, okay? I don't think," he added, "that our M*A*S*Her could be considered a serial killer. We've only had three murders. Natalie, Krafchek, and Hansen. Four if you count Burns."

"Five," murmured Ellie, closing her eyes. "Seven if you count the Dumpster couple."

She dozed, but a part of her mind kept working.

Why did Vicky drive to the 7-Eleven when Jacques was borrowing milk at a neighbor's? Why not also borrow pot. chips and bev?

Dumb, Norrie, dumb. Why would Vicky Angel kill her Jackie Bear?

Ellie recalled a game she'd played as a kid: What Is Wrong with This Picture? Usually the dog was missing a tail, or the tree was upside down, or the woman in an apron had a missing finger.

Burrowing deeper into her pillow, Ellie shuddered, then forced herself to replay the scene inside Hansen's basement.

What the hell's wrong with this picture? Jacques wasn't really *missing* fingers, even though they'd been severed. He was covered with blood. Blood had even begun to soak the crude message tied around his neck with string.

String bound the newsletter stacks. Vicky's lined paper was the same kind of paper that had been pinned to Krafchek's chest. But Jacques's paper simulated a dog tag.

Dog tag. Natalie.

Natalie. Mirror-message in Latin.

Latin. Father Mac.

Father Mac. Why would Sean murder "M*A*S*H"·look-alikes? What would be his motive?

Motive: insanity.

Insanity. Nancy said Sean's wife was mentally impaired.

Be careful, Ellie-Ellie, insanity's contagious.

Contagious. Jackie Robinson was behaving quirky, uncommonly attentive. Had he caught Ellie's fevered fear? Or did the cat know something she didn't?

Dammit, something was definitely wrong with the picture inside Jacques and Vicky's basement. But for the life of her Ellie couldn't figure out what was missing.

Something to do with string, she thought, just before she fell into a deep, dreamless sleep.

▽

14

Mick ARRIVED HOME two days before Thanksgiving, and Peter returned to his duties at the precinct.

"I'm glad Mick's here to protect you, Norrie."

"Mick's a kid."

"Mick's a man."

"Men have been murdered, too."

"Weak men."

"Jacques wasn't weak, Peter."

"Okay, but he was taken by surprise."

"You always have to have the last word, don't you?"

"Yup."

Nevertheless, Ellie felt a lump in her recently healed throat as her son presented her with Susan Isaacs and a giant Nestlés' Crunch. Then he arranged for Grandma Bernstein to "cater" their Thanksgiving meal.

"Tony and Annie will be here, too," warned Ellie as she reclined on the couch with Susan.

"I'll survive. Muffin has agreed to play hostess, so you don't have to lift a finger. Too bad Peter can't sample Grandma's toasted ravioli stuffed with chopped liver."

"Peter has a familial gathering in Denver," said Ellie. "Isn't it funny how all this came about *after* Grandma Flo accepted your invitation?"

" 'Over the river and through the wood, now Grandmother's cap I spy!' " Mick reddened, then muttered, "Lydia M. Child, born 1802, died 1880. English Lit."

"You're amazing, kiddo."

"Like mother, like son. Sandra once said you had more quotes than Keebler has chips."

"True, but I tend to quote Spielberg, Erma Bombeck, and pelicans with bellicans."

"Peter should be back in time for your friend's birthday party, right?"

"Sure. He wouldn't miss it, and he'll finally get a chance to hear your band play."

"And Belinda sing. I wish I could use Sandra, but my drummer insists on Belly." Mick's face brightened. "It was swell of Mrs. Trask to hire Rocky Mountain High."

"A man named Gordon Dorack is footing half the bill. He's Melody's . . . the birthday girl's . . . uh . . ."

"Lover? Mom, are you blushing?"

"I'm not embarrassed over the word lover, Mick. It's just that, well, you have to know Melody Remming. I'd call Gordon her soul mate."

"Soul mate. Right. Anyway, the band is practicing songs from the fifties. Belly sounds great. In fact, we're thinking of using some golden oldies for other gigs." Mick hesitated, then blurted, "How old do you think a man should be before he considers getting married?"

"Depends on the man. Are you serious?"

"I knew for sure during the ballet. Afterward—when Natalie—I thought to myself, what if it had been Muffin? I'm afraid of losing her."

"Michael Anthony Bernstein! Sandra's been in love with you for years."

"People change. You did. You and Dad."

"That's different."

"Why is it different?"

"Your father and I didn't establish ground rules. A lot of it was my fault. He's so handsome, just like you." Ellie smiled. "And he wasn't so stuffy when we met. He viewed the world through rose-colored glasses. Then he switched to Ray-Bans. What I'm trying to say is that there has to be mutual respect and shared responsibilities, honey, from the very beginning. I don't mean that a marriage has to be so structured it's inflexible, but you need to give each other room to stretch. Do you understand?"

"No."

"Yes, you do. What happens if Sandra's a bigger success than you are? Videos, movies, the whole enchilada?"

"Great. We'll make more money, buy expensive cars, and live in Aspen with all the other celebs."

"Ouch. Do you really mean that? No jealousy?"

Mick crossed his heart with his first finger. "I swear. She'd have to quit when we had kids, of course, but I don't plan on children right away."

"What? Quit with kids?"

"Well, sure, the wife-and-mother bit. Dad says—"

"Holy bull, Mick, you've still got a lot of growing up to do."

"You, too." Mick's grin was a carbon copy of his father's. "You look like my kid sister, Mom."

It might have started with his childhood, thought Ellie. He might have tortured his sister's dolls.

After Thanksgiving she'd snoop, sleuth, *check out* childhoods, especially Ken Trask's. Didn't Melody say that Nancy had known him forever?

Thanksgiving Day. Florence Bernstein arrived early, her plastic shopping bags overflowing with Tupperware containers. She switched on Ellie's oven, and turkey, cornbread stuffing, and pumpkin pie filled the house with holiday fragrances.

Then "Grandma Fro" watched the Macy's Parade, waiting for what Annie called "Santy Claws in his led suit."

Jackie Robinson, a black-furred Pilgrim, swayed from kitchen to family room, anticipating food scraps.

In her bedroom, Ellie belted a white wool shirtwaist decorated with a splash of embroidered red poppies. She left her hair loose, and it swirled past her shoulders to become part of the dress pattern.

"A woman your age should cut her hair short or wear it pinned up," sniffed Grandma, removing her gaze from the giant ballooned Snoopy that floated above Broadway.

"Errie pretty," said Annie. Blissfully reclining on her stepbrother's lap, she wore an orange party dress, miniature white tights, and patent-leather Mary-Janes.

"Annie," said Mick, "where do sheep go for haircuts?"

"To the baa-baa shop."

Ellie laughed and excused herself.

During her illness and recovery, she had resurrected her mystery manuscript. Now she edited pages while Florence bustled about inside the kitchen and Annie watched a Bugs Bunny special with her beloved "Mymick."

Damn, my plot still has a beginning that never stops beginning, thought Ellie, just like the "M*A*S*H" homicides. I wish I could come up with a middle and end. Maybe I should join the kids. Yes. Cartoons make more sense.

Tony and Sandra arrived together, then consolidated with the TV watchers. Bugs Bunny's carrot became a football as Oilers drilled and Cowboys branded tight ends with congratulatory handprints. "Footbore," said Annie.

"A realtor," stated Tony, "is just like a doctor."

"Somebody wasn't feeling up to par, and you had to examine—" She paused, glancing toward the kids. "Make a house call?"

"No, Eleanor, I had to show one of our listings on a holiday." Tony loosened his tie's Windsor knot. "In fact, it was your suicide's house."

"He's not *my* suicide, Tony. Was Magnolia there?"

"His wife? No, she's flown south for the winter. You look very nice."

"Florence says I look too young," Ellie said smugly. Then she beckoned to Sandra, who was sitting at Mick's feet, one pretty cheek resting against a bony, denim-clad knee.

They walked outside into the crisp air. Up above, clouds resembled fluffy biscuits buttered by the sun.

Sandra wore a pink angora skirt and matching sweater.

She had captured her hair away from her face and it fell below her shoulder blades in one thick, ropy braid.

"I meant to visit when you were sick, Ellie," she said. "I really did."

"That's okay, I wasn't very seeable."

"I had exams, midterms."

"I know. How are *you* feeling, Muffin?"

"*Me?* Fine."

"You're not still blaming yourself for Natalie?"

"No, it wasn't my fault, any more than it was Mick's fault about the trapdoor footprints. It just happened."

"*Fata viam invenient,*" said Ellie. "The Fates will find a way."

"Right. I wish I knew Latin. There seems to be a saying for everything."

"Muffin, do you mind if I ask you some questions about Natalie?"

"I can handle it," she replied, a puzzled expression merging her freckles.

"First of all, did she buy a used car recently?"

"No way, Ellie. Natalie was saving her money, every cent. She wanted to move to New York or San Francisco and join a ballet corps. That's all she talked about."

"Did she date often?"

"Uh-uh. She didn't want to form attachments, since she planned to leave Colorado. I told all that to Peter."

"So Natalie wasn't seeing anybody special?"

"Nope. Wait a sec! She was! It had to be an older man, because she called him Daddy Longlegs, like Fred Astaire."

"Did you ever see Natalie's, er, Daddy?"

"Never. I don't think anybody did. He wouldn't come to the dorm, so Nat met him other places. I'm sure she was sleeping with him, Ellie, or at least he was sleeping with her. Nat said sex made her legs weak and hurt her dancing."

"Did Natalie ever describe her lover?"

"Uh-uh, except for the nickname. Rats! How could I forget to tell Peter?"

"That's okay, you remembered just now. When I retire, I'll pass my crown to you."

"Give me a break. When you retire? No way!"

Porch boards reverberated from the *whap-whap* of Mick's oversized Reeboks.

"Is this a private discussion," he said, "or can a lowly son and soul mate join you?"

Sandra's cheeks turned a heavenly shade of mauve. "Shut up, Dopey, you promised not to kiss and tell."

Mick kissed both women. "Dinner is served," he announced with a flourish.

Tony carved the bird, handing one drumstick to his son and the other to a delighted Annie.

Ellie shivered when her ex-husband's sharp knife severed turkey limbs, especially the wings. It was too close to recent images.

Carefully placing the knife and pronged fork on the serving platter's scalloped edge, Tony said, "I guess now's as good a time as ever to make my announcement."

"What announcement?" Florence fastened a bib around Annie's neck.

"I've decided to move to California," said Tony, "and patch things up with . . . um . . . my wife."

His hesitation, Ellie knew, was brought on by Flo's refusal to call the young woman by her name. "That girl" or "Tony's second wife," she always said.

And Natalie called her lover Daddy, not Kenneth Trask. Damn!

Tony's timing, as always, was impeccable. After he had dropped his bomb Florence ate in stony silence, dabbing her lips after every small bite. She sipped apple cider as though it would cool her burning tongue and prevent the recriminations that were sure to come later.

Ellie excused herself to check out Jackie Robinson. The cat had escaped from Annie's painful attention to consume his share of turkey giblets on the front porch.

Tony trailed behind, loosening his belt a notch. "Good meal. I'm stuffed."

Damn stuffed shirt, thought Ellie, watching her cat hiss, then creep beneath dense shrubbery.

"So you're escaping to California," she said conversationally.

"Escaping? That's a funny way to put it."

"Sorry. I'm not sure why I said it that way, Tony. I guess it just slipped out."

"I have to leave Colorado, Eleanor."

"Why? Are you in some kind of trouble?"

"Of course not. Well, sort of. One of my secretaries, Mary Whitley, thinks we . . . I've never encouraged her, but she believes . . ." Tony swallowed, then blurted, "Once, a long time ago, I slept with Mary's daughter."

"I knew it," shouted Ellie. "I knew you balled Virginia Whitley."

"Eleanor, please, walls have ears."

"So do asses! Was it a one-night stand or an affair?"

"Define affair," said Tony uncomfortably.

"Tryst. *Affaire d'amour.* Business transaction."

"It was more than a tryst, and it wasn't business. Look, I'm not very proud of myself. We were still married. I suppose I was going through some midlife crisis."

"If you slept with Ginny before she died, you were thirty-five. *Now* you're over the hill, almost fifty. *Now's* the time for a midlife crisis." If she hadn't been so angry, she would have laughed at his pained expression. "Tony, did you attend Charley Aaronson's M*A*S*H-Bash?"

He mulled over her question as if it were a riddle. Then he simply said, "Yes."

"Costumed as a cowboy?"

"No."

"What, then?"

"A doctor." He grinned wolfishly. "You know how Jewish mothers always want their sons to become doctors."

"Your mother's not Jewish, Tony, your father's Jewish. Did you see me that night? Sitting at the bar?"

"Yes. I'm not very proud of mysel—"

"Did you talk to Ginny?"

"Of course. We planned to meet there."

"And?"

"Eleanor, she was falling-down drunk, half naked, and looked like she was about to puke her guts out."

"So you left the Dew Drop?"

"Not exactly. I thought I'd rent a motel room, sober Virginia up a little. Why are you ask—"

"What happened in the parking lot, Tony?"

"We never got there. Virginia was hot to trot, if you know what I mean, but then she bolted for the rest room."

"And?"

"She staggered out with somebody else, shouted something about losing her cherry and drinking gin. Anyway, I'd seen you at the bar and my conscience—"

"Bullshit! What did the somebody else look like?"

"I don't remember. It happened ten years ago."

"Eleven. Was he tall? Short? Fat? Thin? Did he wear a hat? Glasses? Did he have a mustache?"

"Yes. No. Maybe glasses. I don't rememb—"

"Did he wear a goddamn costume?"

"Yes. Fatigues."

"Could you be a tad more specific?"

"Okay, if you insist. He looked like Hawkeye."

"Oh, great. There were dozens of Hawkeyes."

"Eleanor, why are you grill—"

"Tony, did you run over Ginny with your car? Did you?"

"No! Why would I do that?"

"Ego."

Tony's eyes slitted. "Virginia was no big deal."

"Really? I thought she was hot to trot."

"What?"

"Forget it." Ellie sighed. "We were talking about California."

"Yes. I have contacts on the coast and even if things don't work out with . . . um . . . my wife, I still need a change of scenery. Could we make arrangements for Mick to visit this summer?"

"That's between you and your son. I'll miss Annie."

"But not me, huh?" Tony cleared his throat. "I have a confession to make, Eleanor."

"*Another* confession? Ginny's not enough?"

"One night last week I was downtown, and I saw you with your cop, so I, well, followed you home."

"Ohmigod, the night Peter and I . . . the wrestling mats. No wonder Jackie Robinson's been acting so paranoid."

"I watched at the window for a long time, and I saw you right there in our family room, so I decided that I can't deal with your slutty attitude."

"Slutty attitude? How dare you!"

"I'm ashamed I spied. It was stupid and not like me at all. But it proved that I could never take you back."

"Take me *what?*"

"Back. I can't forgive and forget, so we could never start all over again. But I wanted to let you know about playing James Bond, apologize for the peeping."

"James Bond never peeped; he didn't have to."

"Low blow, Eleanor. I shouldn't have confessed. I shouldn't have told you about Virginia, either."

"Well, Tony, we all have our lapses in perfection."

"I guess that's true," he replied seriously. "I'd better go inside and soothe my mother. I'll give you ten to one she follows me to the coast." Tony shrugged, then entered the house.

I won't take that bet, thought Ellie. Florence'll set up housekeeping in California and make Tony's life hell, the rat.

Rat. Perfection. Kenneth Trask. The perfect husband and father, community sponsor, the perfect architect. Except he collected women like other people collected baseball cards, including one half his age.

Wait a minute. Sandra said an older man. How old is old to a college sophomore? Howie was Trask's age. Sean, too.

Fred Remming was younger, mid-thirties—but that might seem old to a twentyish ballerina.

"Are you okay, Mom?" Mick's mop of blond-streaked hair dominated the doorway entrance. "I thought you might be brooding over Annie."

"I'll miss watching her grow, but you can tell me all about her after you visit your father."

"Aw, Mom, it's not the same."

Mick folded Ellie in his arms, and she noted with amazement that she barely reached his chin.

"Can I join the party?" Sandra carried a silver platter cluttered with dessert plates, forks, and napkins. She set the tray on porch steps when Mick extended one arm.

The three stood peacefully together while the sun set in a burst of Technicolor brilliance and Jackie Robinson licked Cool Whip off the tops of pumpkin pie slices.

Ellie's mind raced. Why did the perp *slice* off Jacques Hansen's fingers? Why not just shoot Jacques and leave? Why was the murderer so furious that he'd sever a dead man's fingers with a paper cutter?

And why was she so positive that Kenneth Trask was the M*A*S*Her? Because Ken drew sick doodles? Because Ken had a son who'd played with dolls? Because Ken drove a luxurious car with a license plate that read "TRASK-1," and according to Peter serial killers enjoyed driving? Because Ken had designed the theater passageway? Because Ken wore a black topcoat to the recital? A coat with pockets deep enough to hide a knife? A coat that Nancy had subsequently taken to the cleaners. Holy cow, she'd missed that particular clue when her mind was fevered, unfocused.

Okay, Norrie, focus. Had Ginny really been escorted from the Dew Drop rest room by Hawkeye? Or did Tony make that up?

Ellie recalled the photo on Fred's apartment wall. Reigning over the seated group was a cocksure Kenneth Trask, clothed in fatigues and Hawkeye's Hawaiian shirt.

What's wrong with this picture?

Ken's cocky smile? Howie's cockeyed dress? Fred's cocka-
mamie bear? Sean's cross?

If you crossed Father Mac, would he retaliate?

"No," said Ellie, "I don't believe it."

"Believe what, Mom?"

"That your father compared himself to James Bond," she
improvised.

"Sean Connery, Roger Moore, or Timothy Dalton?"

Ellie pictured Tony with Ginny. "Woody Allen."

▽

15

ELLIE SHIFTED HER body and felt the water-bed mattress ripple. Before Weight Winners it had sloshed like amplified womb music.

"Hey," she said, "I forgot to ask about *your* Thanksgiving meal, honey."

"It was traditional," replied Peter. "We talked turkey. My sister Elizabeth was disappointed that I didn't bring you along. I think she wanted to regale you with confessions of our misspent youth, mine in particular."

"Speaking of confessions," said Ellie, then told him about Tony watching them through the window.

Peter's eyebrows Groucho'd, and he said, "What a turn-on. Wish I'd known at the time."

"You're kidding. You're not kidding. I was disgusted. Is it a turn-on to picture Kenneth Trask with Natalie?"

"How many times do I have to tell you, Norrie? You can't prove that Trask was Natalie's lover."

Upon his return from Denver, Ellie had greeted Peter with the information about Natalie's affair. Tony, Annie, and Florence had already left for Manitou Springs, while Mick eagerly escorted Sandra to her dorm. As Ellie had guessed, Peter responded with his no-proof allegation, and she'd wanted to snap his neck like a turkey's wishbone.

Now she said, "I told Tony we all have lapses in perfection. I used the most acrimonious voice I could muster, but he took me seriously. Perfection, hah! Suddenly, out of the blue, *you* expose—admit that voyeurism's stimulating. Christ,

I'm gonna become a nun. By the way, did I ever mention the nuns dancing bare-assed across Melody's canvas? Or her masturbating priest?"

"Yes. What's your point?"

"If that's a joke, it's not funny. Tony's conception of perfection isn't funny, either."

"I can understand Tony's attitude." The bedside lamp illuminated Peter's grin. "I think I'm perfect."

"Me, too," replied Ellie lightly.

Forget mysteries, she thought, forget murder. Peter looked unbelievably sexy, and if his point had been less anatomically blunted it would have pierced the mattress.

She kissed him, then repeated, "Me, too."

"You think I'm perfect?"

"I was talking about me."

"You? Perfect? Good Lord!"

"So I get in trouble once a week with your 'fercockteh murder cases,' as my friend Charley Aaronson would say. So I leave the house messy, unlike Grandma Flo or Fred Remming or Mary Whitley or Nancy Trask. So I don't know the difference between judo and Judah. So you've got to admit, Loot, that I'm kind of terrific between the water-bed sheets."

"Perfect," agreed Peter as Ellie straddled his waist. Then, in one quick motion, he flipped her over and pinned her elbows to the rippling, sloshing mattress. "Norrie, didn't you learn anything during our self-defense lesson?"

"Do you honestly expect me to perform self-defense while we're getting ready to make love? On a *water bed?*" She tried to flip his body, but couldn't. "I give up, up, up," she muttered, "and I've been practicing."

"With whom?" Peter's tongue circled her inner ear.

"Jackie Robinson," she gasped. "I flip him easily, and he surrenders. Waves his paws toward the ceiling and begs to have his tummy rubbed."

"Wave your paws, Norrie."

"I surrender, Peter, I surrend—"

*   *   *

The next afternoon Ellie joined Nancy at the Dew Drop Inn.
Gordon Dorack was there, too, attaching red, white, and
blue crepe streamers above the party tables.

Nancy had made place cards with cutouts of the "M*A*S*H"
cast for the table where club members could congregate—
Ken as Hawkeye, Howie as Klinger, Fred as Radar, Sean as
Father Mulcahy, Dorack as Trapper John, and Melody as a
nurse. Ellie's scissored and pasted magazine figure depicted
Hot Lips Houlihan.

"Where did you find all those 'M*A*S*H' photos, Nancy?"

"Ken's got a collection of articles from *TV Guide* and other
magazines." Nancy put down the last two cards, straightening
their folds. "See, Ellie? I made your boyfriend that doctor with
a mustache. Lieutenant Miller has a mustache, doesn't he?"

"How did you know that?"

"I've been reading the newspapers. Even Denver and
Boulder wrote about the ballerina's murder."

"Nancy, why didn't you make a place card for yourself?"

"Are you serious, Ellie? Who could I be?"

"Another nurse."

"Nope, I'll just be plain old Nancy."

"You're not plain. Old, either. In fact, you look great. Still
working out at the health club?"

"Yes, it makes Ken happy."

"It's probably none of my business," said Ellie, "but
shouldn't you do things to please yourself?"

Nancy almost-smiled. "I do things to please myself."

"Okay. Sorry. Should I buy a birthday cake?"

"I've already made a low-cal frozen yogurt cake, shaped
like Radar's teddy bear. Yogurt's on your diet, isn't it?"

"Wow, you're unbelievably considerate. I'm really proud
to call you my friend."

Nancy actually blushed. "Melody's cake is stashed inside
the Dew Drop's freezer. I didn't even know there was a freezer
until Charley Aaronson told me. He said it was a 'strolling
ice chest.' "

Ellie laughed. "He means a walk-in. Charley's lounge used to be a restaurant called Costilla de Adam, and the kitchen still exists. Charley always swears he's going to knock out walls, make the Dew Drop larger. Meanwhile, he uses the freezer for ice cream so that he can whip up froufrou drinks like Toasted Almonds."

"Toasted what?"

"Almonds. It's vanilla ice cream laced with Kahlua and amaretto. I used to drink them."

"Charley has a freezer big enough to be a walk-in closet and he uses it for ice cream? What a waste."

"He also stores bodies."

"*Bodies?*"

"Rabbits. Venison. I don't know what else." Ellie shuddered. "During hunting season it's a good way to stock his tavern with celebrants. They freeze their kill and stick around to drink."

Ellie was tempted to ask Nancy about Ken's childhood, but she couldn't say, "Speaking of hunting seasons, did Ken ever mangle his sister's dolls?" and, unfortunately, the right opportunity never really presented itself.

The three conspirators finished decorating. Gordon said he hadn't figured out how to get Melody in costume, but since she was the guest of honor it didn't matter. The plan, he suggested, was to meet Ellie and Peter at the Dew Drop for drinks before they supposedly hit the movies. Wouldn't Melody be surprised?

Ellie and Nancy agreed.

"Nothing's gonna spoil our fun," concluded Dorack.

Peter and Ellie bathed together, then dried each other off.

"If we were protagonists in a romance novel," she said, "we'd maneuver our nude bodies to the bedroom."

"If we were romance novel protagonists, we'd never leave the bathtub. Hours, days, months would pass, and we'd become stewed prunes."

"I despise prunes, stewed or otherwise. Anyway, what do

you know about romance novels? You read thrillers."

"I used to sneak peeks at my sister Elizabeth's paperbacks. *Sweet Savage Sex* was my favorite."

"*Sweet Savage Love.*"

"Get dressed or I'll sweetly savage you, and we'll never make the party on time."

Ellie donned khaki shorts and a "M*A*S*H" T-shirt.

"Where'd you get that shirt?" asked Peter.

"Mick. There was a time when his standard uniform was shredded jeans and T-shirts. Is this one too tight?"

"Nope, perfect." Peter had opted to clothe himself in tan chinos and a loose Hawaiian-style shirt that hid his holstered gun. His thick black hair was partially covered by a Yankees baseball cap.

"Holy cow, Peter, you look like Thomas—"

"Edison?"

"No. Why Thomas Edison?"

"Wasn't he played by Don Ameche? My sister Elizabeth says I look like Ameche."

"Don Ameche played Alexander—"

"The Great?"

"No, Graham Bell."

"Okay, I was only kidding. I look like Thomas Magnum, right? The baseball cap's a dead giveaway."

Ellie stared at Peter's cap. "Why New York?"

"Didn't Hawkeye come from the East Coast?"

"Maine, I think. Sure he did. Crabapple Cove. The closest baseball team would be—ummm—the Boston Red Sox." She suddenly recalled Magnolia's mama and murmured, "You're awfully nice for a Yankee."

"*Awfully* nice? Add that one to authentic reproductions and professional amateur."

"Speaking of professional amateurs, Peter, what if Ken pissed off Natalie, and she threatened—"

"You're going to freeze in those shorts, Norrie. Never mind. Since I don't intend to let you out of my sight, I'll keep you sweetly savagely warm."

"Then you finally agree that our murderer might be a 'M*A*S*H' club member?"

"At this point I suspect everybody."

"Peter, let's be realistic. Melody and Gordon couldn't kill. Jacques Hansen's dead. Howie Silverman faints at the sight of blood. Fred Remming's an impotent fuddy-duddy. Sean doesn't have a motive. That leaves Kenneth Tra—"

"You have beautiful legs, sweetheart."

Ellie sighed. "Belinda drove the van. Did Mick use your car to drive Sandra?"

"Yup. Looked me straight in the eye and said, 'Can I borrow the keys to your Scamp, Pete?' I felt very fatherish. When are you going to marry me, Norrie?"

"It's *may* I borrow the keys."

"When?"

"I don't know." She had a mental image of a subservient Nancy. But Melody and Gordon seemed to balance the scales. "I love you, Peter. Isn't that enough?"

"For now. Just remember that I expect our romance novel to end happily ever after."

"Don't they all?"

The Dew Drop Inn had a kind of gimcrack beauty; a sleazy ambience, thought Ellie. Charley's buzzing-bee personnel served cocktails, but Peter didn't drink. Neither did two members of his squad who had volunteered their services on an informal stakeout. Both straddled bar stools, pretending to be customers, glancing every now and then at the televised fourth quarter of a college football game. Detective William McCoy, Ellie's friend from the diet-club murders, sat next to Kenneth Trask.

Trask wore pressed fatigue pants and a Hawaiian shirt. He had refused to join the party until the game ended.

Following Charley's suggestion, Peter downed a glass of bubbly Dr. Brown's Cel-Ray Tonic.

"It'll never take the place of Scotch," he muttered.

"You're not on duty, honey. Have a sip of my wine."

"Nope, I'm playing Norrie Charles tonight." He chuckled at his pun. "All I need is a dog named—"

"Asta?"

"No, Klinger. Didn't you tell me that the Trasks have a pooch named Klinger?" Peter surveyed the room. "I plan to study your 'M*A*S*H' club members very carefully. If I could get away with it, I'd speak with a Jewish accent and fool all the *pipples.*"

"Did you catch that too, Peter? I'd be willing to bet on a stack of bibles that Charley's vocabulary's perfect."

Perfect, she thought. Tony's perfect, Peter's perfect, I'm perfect. What about Kenneth "P-for-Perfection" Trask?

Melody arrived. Surprised and delighted, she let out her throaty screech, then hugged everybody in sight. Most of her friends were fellow artists, and she shyly conceded that she'd begun a new series of paintings. Still swirling colors with a palette knife, her tiny figures were now Aspen celebs.

"I've painted Kurt and Goldie," Melody whispered to Ellie, "but I couldn't resist adding one naked woman riding a ski lift. She looks like you. Hope you don't mind."

"Not at all. Is the canvas for sale? Title it 'Sweet Savage Ski Jump' and auction it off to Peter."

The football game ended. Mick's band played "Shimmy Shimmy Ko-Ko Bop" and "Big Girls Don't Cry."

They sounded professional, very fifties, thought Ellie, although an amplified rock beat wound through their music like colorful thread woven through a black-and-white tapestry. Belinda carried the songs with a certain flair, her husky voice less polished than, oh, say Linda Ronstadt, but more sultry.

"I'm not jealous of Belinda anymore," said Sandra, joining Ellie and Peter, "or her voice. Just her legs."

"You have very nice legs, Muffin, and a better voice."

"Listen to Belly's throaty technique. I couldn't do that in a million years."

Belinda sang the Patti Page hit "How Much Is That Doggie in the Window," slowing the tempo and hesitating before the word "doggie." Ellie had visions of streetwalkers and brothels.

During a break Mick strolled over and said that his band planned to record the doggie arrangement on a demo tape. "If our star singer can remain sober," he added, pointing toward the bar.

Gulping shots of tequila, Belinda sucked limes and licked salt from her knuckles. She wore a short white strapless sheath à la Marilyn Monroe. It molded her breasts and emphasized long legs shod in four-inch heels. Ellie saw Trask hand Belinda a business card.

Damn alley cat!

"Trask just gave Belly one of his business cards," she whispered to Peter.

"I can't arrest a man for that, Norrie," he replied, leaning back in his chair.

They sat on the curve, where tables had been placed together to form a U-shape. Melody and Gordon shared the table's middle with Nancy, Ken's empty seat, and Sean. Then, spreading out, came the rest of the "M*A*S*H" club members and Melody's friends.

Mick returned to the stage and tuned his guitar.

Several pitchers had been placed at intervals on top of the party table. Clothed as Radar, clutching a teddy bear, Fred drained and refilled his mug while sending poison-dart glances in Ellie's direction.

"Mick and Sandra are right on target," said Peter, picking up Ellie's place card. "All you need is a blond wig. Or a good bleach job."

"What do you know about bleach jobs?"

"I once solved a horse-theft case by proving that the mare's color had been altered."

"Are you comparing me to a horse?"

"No, I'm comparing you to Hot Lips."

"That's ridiculous. I don't really look like her."

"Yes, you do, Norrie."

"Hey, get a load of Howie Silverman."

Howie's stomach burst through the buttonholes of his dress. He had cornered three of Melody's friends at the bar. In front of the women were rum drinks. Like the odometer on a dashboard, straws indicated full, half, and empty. One glass was full. One girl was working on half. The other girl's head lay on the bar's surface, cradled within her arms.

Remembering Ginny, Ellie started to rise.

"Where," said Peter, "do you think you're going?"

"Look at that young woman slumped next to Howie. I plan to walk her around outside or hold her head."

"I'll come with you."

"Don't be silly. I'll simply escort her to the powder roo—"

"No."

"Peter, I realize you're being protective, and I appreciate it, but—"

"No."

"Holy cow, if we decide to get married are you going to lock me inside the house every day when you leave for work?"

"Only if *this* particular murder case remains unsolved."

Turning her back on his words, Ellie surveyed the center of the table.

Ken's seat was still empty.

Nancy sipped a martini. She was clothed in the traditional olive-green T-shirt and a pair of fatigue pants. Around her neck was a gold chain. At the end of the chain was a ballerina charm. Ellie had worn a similar charm when she was Small-Indian. Hadn't Natalie sported a ballerina necklace, too? Yup. Sandra once said that she and Natalie had exchanged charms for Christmas, and—

"Jesus, I'm blind as a bat."

Startled, Ellie glanced toward the bar and saw Ken on his knees. He was spreading Belinda's legs.

"I di'n' lose my contac' *there*," continued Belinda in a loud, drunken voice. "It's on the floor near my stool."

Ken said something Ellie couldn't hear.

"Yeah, sure," said Belinda. "Everybody promises, but nobody delivers, 'cept the pizza guy. Hey, get your hand off

my you-know-what, Mr. Trash. Aw, what the fuck. Buy me
'nother shot an' I'll sing jus' for you."

Mr. Trash! Ellie shook her head. Hadn't Nancy heard
Belinda? Or did Nancy, like Magnolia, choose to ignore her
husband's affairs? Probably the latter, thought Ellie, remembering Melody's comments about Ken's mistress.

Holy cow, the missing mistress. Could Nancy actually be
angry enough to kill? But this was the nineties. Today jealous
wives didn't do murder; they did divorce.

Could that sick doodle be Nancy's? No, the house was
too perfect, drawn to scale, the sketch of an architect.

Ellie watched Sean whisper into Nancy's ear, then head
toward the rest rooms.

Mick's band returned and began their next set, but
Belinda soon staggered down from the platform. Mick
caught Ellie's eye and winked. Then he helped Sandra climb
up onto the stage. Garland, Streisand, and Whitney Houston merged into a style distinctly Sandra Connors. The
fifties kaleidoscoped into the sixties, seventies, eighties,
nineties—and Melody asked Peter to dance.

"Stay put, Norrie," he said before letting Melody lead him
onto the dance floor.

Ellie gave Peter what she felt was her best screw-you
glower. Then, glancing toward the center of the table
again, she saw that Sean had returned, but Nancy had
vanished. Concerned, Ellie considered searching. Instead,
she waited, feeling goose-bumpy, wishing she'd worn
longer pants. Focusing on Charley's Budweiser clock, she
tried to tell herself that she was goose-bumpy from the cold,
not because she was ignoring some obvious clue. What
clue? The charm necklace? Which brought to mind Jacques
Hansen's "necklace." The string—something about the
string—

"Hoo-hah," said Charley, leaning over Ellie's chair. "You're
in costume this time, Miss Hot Mouth. Having fun?"

"You bet." She sneaked a peek at the clock. Ten minutes
had passed since Nancy's disappearance.

"The cowboy's here, too," said Charley.

"What cowboy? Do you mean the man who stuck out like a sore thumb at your M*A*S*H-Bash?"

"Yup. He comes all the time now, for years. His name's Dan-something and he's a regular. S'cuse me, Eleanor, Dan wants me. He looks mad."

Twelve minutes.

Howie's third girl slid from her stool on the floor. A small group gathered.

Charley pushed his way through onlookers. "I'll let her sleep it off in my office, then call a taxicab. Don't want no trouble." Beckoning toward the cowboy, Charley called, "Hoo-hah, Dan, help me carry Miss Rum Punch to my office couch. And you, yes you, Mr. Man-in-a-Dress, stop getting ladies drunk in my tavern."

Howie had the grace to blush while Fred slurred, "Silverrr-man wantsa get laid in the men's, dontcha, Howdy Doody? Get it? Howie Doo-doo."

Fred giggled, while others turned away, embarrassed.

Nancy finally returned to her seat. For the first time since Ellie'd met her, Nancy's hair was mussed, sticking out like the short, thin straws that decorated the Dew Drop's rock glasses. Even from a short distance, Nancy's eyes looked red. Was she weeping over that bastard of a husband who had followed Belinda from the lounge? Sean patted Nancy's hand, and Ellie determined to mind her own business.

Was Belinda in any danger? No, Belly didn't resemble Hot Lips, not with her brown curly hair and heavy makeup.

Peter danced with one of Melody's friends.

Should I tell Peter about Belinda and Trask?

Undecided, Ellie realized that she had to go to the bathroom. Badly. Catching Peter's eye, she gestured toward the rest rooms and mimed a pained expression. Peter shook his head no. He held up his hand. Five fingers. Five minutes. She had to wait five minutes.

We forgot about the birthday cake, thought Ellie.

"We forgot the cake," she called to Nancy.

"What did you say? Are you having a good time?" Nancy withdrew her hand from Sean's and waved.

"No, no," Ellie shouted, "the frozen birthday cake."

Nancy pointed to her ears, smiled, shrugged.

Ellie left her chair and knelt by Nancy's knees. "We forgot to defrost the cake. It must be hard as a rock. Do you want me to get it?"

"I'll go."

"I have to use the ladies' room anyway. Sit, drink your martini, enjoy the party."

Peter danced with Melody again, dipping her toward Mick's guitar. Melody's scarf brushed the floor, and she screeched with delight.

I'm not going to pull him off the dance floor, thought Ellie. She walked forward.

"Wait, I'll go with you," said Nancy.

"That's not necessary. Didn't you go before?"

A bulky figure wended his way around the table. "Mrs. Trask, could I talk to you, please?"

"Of course, Charley."

"You've got that game set up, your pin-the-tail picture."

"What about it, Charley?"

Ellie glanced toward a huge "M*A*S*H" poster mounted on the wall. Nancy had scheduled a game of Pin the Tail on Hawkeye, to take place after the dancing. Near the poster were pillows, just in case people wanted to sit or kneel while watching the game. Pillow *heads*, thought Ellie, admiring the truly remarkable caricatures of Hawkeye, Hot Lips, Radar, and Frank. Radar even had a pair of real wire-rimmed glasses sewn above his nose.

"My arrows are missing," said Charley.

Nancy's brow furrowed. "What arrows?"

"For the Dew Drop target contest. Every night. My regulars are kvetching, especially Dan-something." Charley pointed toward a regulation-size dartboard across the room. "I thought maybe you borrowed my arrows."

"*Darts*, Charley."

"Darts, arrows, my regulars are mad."

"Nancy," said Ellie, "did Ken design those pillows?"

"No, me. They were easy to sew, just seams. Why?"

"The faces. You're quite an artist."

"Not really. I cheated and traced the faces. Drove to a print shop and had them blow up Ken's magazine pictures."

"By the way, Nancy, I've been admiring your necklace. I had a charm just like that when I was a kid."

"Did you? I didn't. My parents wouldn't let me take ballet lessons." Scowling, she fingered the necklace. "Ken gave this to me as a reward."

"Reward?"

"Yes. I finally lost ten pounds." Glancing toward the bar, she added, "The health club promised and delivered."

Aha, so Nancy *did* hear Belinda!

"Mrs. Trask, my arrows," said Charley.

The serial killer always takes a souvenir, thought Ellie. Ken must have stolen Natalie's necklace and Hansen's glasses. What had that rotten bastard taken from Harry Burns? And Krafchek? And the Dumpster couple?

Should she tell Peter? Absolutely. First the bathroom—she couldn't wait any longer. Smiling at Nancy, Ellie nodded toward the rest rooms, then walked swiftly in that direction.

Afterward, washing her hands, Ellie wondered if Peter needed a warrant to search Ken's house. And, if he did, could he get one quickly? She was convinced that Peter would find Harry's surgical tape, plus—what? Krafchek's watch or ring? Which, of course, Ken wouldn't simply hand over to his wife.

Should she forget about the birthday cake? No. Retrieving the cake wouldn't take more than two, three minutes tops, and she wanted everything to look normal while Peter left to get his warrant.

The kitchen was halfway down the hall. Ellie entered, heading toward the walk-in. Damn, the yogurt would never defrost in time unless Charley had a microwave.

The freezer's door swung open. Shelves were filled with brown-wrapped slabs of beef. All sizes. All shapes. One large see-through plastic bag contained a furry bunny. Long ears. Marble eyes. Unskinned. Ungutted. Mopsy? Flopsy? Cottontail? Thumper? Brer Rabbit?

Ellie screamed.

It wasn't a loud scream, her recently healed throat had clogged up again.

Forget the dead bunny. On the freezer's floor was a dead body. Kenneth Trask. He had a bullet hole in his chest, but he'd also been used as a target. Darts decorated his shirt.

Ken reminded Ellie of the poster on the bathroom door inside the Hansen home. But Jacques couldn't throw darts, she thought incoherently, because his fingers had been severed. And Vicky Angel wasn't here tonight.

Icy freezer temperatures had coagulated Ken's blood after the first initial gush. So the killer probably didn't get any blood on his costume and could return to the party without somebody screaming, "Ohmigod, look at the blood!"

Ellie saw Trask move, or was it her imagination? No. Mesmerized, she watched his head sway back and forth like a cobra.

"Brother," he whispered, "mother—father."

"Father?" Ellie willed herself to kneel and lean over the body. There was another ugly wound at Ken's crotch. "Did Father Mac do this to you?"

"My wife—please—Nancy—"

"I'll get Nancy, don't die," begged Ellie, then realized that her plea came too late.

Staring at Ken's open, expressionless eyes, she suddenly wondered if he'd meant that Nancy had killed him.

She replayed the last few weeks like a VCR on fast-forward. Every clue that pointed to Ken could also implicate Nancy, right? Wrong. What about the doodle? Okay, Ken had sketched the house, and Nancy had added flames. What about the secret passageway? Maybe Nancy had studied Ken's blueprints. How'd she hide Natalie's blood? Maybe her fake-fur coat was black, and the blood didn't show. Why kill Harry Burns and Leo Krafchek and the Dumpster couple? Maybe Nancy had meant to kill the Dumpster *man*, not the woman. Okay, but *why?*

"I don't know, dammit! I'm not a psychic!"

The doll massacre. Peter had said the dolls looked like new. They weren't faded or smudged. Wouldn't that be a Nancy trait? Wouldn't Nancy clean them, patch them, keep them in perfect condition after her son had outgrown them? Sure she would. And she'd have stitched up costumes for the Raggedy dolls, just like she'd stitched up costumes for Fred's collection.

Okay, but what about the Latin on Natalie's mirror and Krafchek's piece of paper? Not much Latin when you really thought about it. Two words. *Advocatus diaboli.* Maybe Nancy had learned Latin in school. Maybe she'd learned it from Sean. Maybe she'd bought a record from Berlitz.

Did Nancy have the traits of a serial killer? She liked to drive, had even driven Klinger to Denver for his booster shots. And then there was the most damaging evidence of all—Natalie's charm necklace and Jacques Hansen's glasses. If *Ken* hadn't stolen them—

Why was she just sitting here, thought Ellie, frozen to the spot? She had to tell Peter.

Bolting from the freezer and kitchen, she skidded to a halt when she heard approaching footsteps. Peter? But Peter would shout "hello" or "who's there?" Anybody friendly would do the same. It had to be the killer.

"Help," she whispered, running toward the back of the building. It ended in a T, and she turned right. Recessed overhead lighting suddenly blinked off, on, off. The perp was fiddling with the wall switch.

Feeling her way along the wall, she found a door. The footsteps sounded closer. Desperate, she slipped inside the room. Groping through darkness, her hand encountered boxed shapes, and she smelled liquor. Somebody had recently opened a gin bottle. The odor lingered, like one of Tony's whisper martinis.

Striving to maintain calm, Ellie crouched behind the first

stack of cartons. The string, she thought, something about the string. She pictured the Hansens' basement. The string was . . . was different from . . . from the string tied around Vicky's stack of newsletters.

Thinner! God, a diet-club leader should notice thinner right off the bat. The string was . . . was the same . . . the same string that Nancy Trask had used to bind her roast. There! She'd finally remembered! What a relief!

The storeroom door opened, then closed. An overhead lightbulb flickered into life. Ellie tried to stifle her gasp, while her Nancy theories crumbled to dust faster than the priest in her nightmare.

Somebody else had access to Ken's blueprints and the Trask dolls—even the damn string.

"I heard you." The man turned toward her hiding place, but Ellie didn't move a muscle. "Stand up and walk forward," he ordered. "I can smell your perfume."

She stood and circled the cartons, caressing rough cardboard for support.

"Sean." Ellie felt tears sting her eyes. "Dammit, Father Mac, I didn't want it to be you. Why did you kill all those people? *Why?*"

∇

16

S EAN MCCARTHY REMOVED the straw hat from his head, revealing flattened strands of tinselly hair.

"Ellie-Ellie," he said, surprised. "I didn't know it was you. I thought—oh well, it doesn't really matter. *Qui facit per alium facit per se.*"

"Not now, dammit! Don't give me Latin, you bastard. I'm too upset to translate—"

"He who does something through another shares the responsibility."

Tears streamed down her face. "Ken invited you to dinner the night before Jacques Hansen's murder. You saw the roast, made your plan, probably on the spot, and pilfered the ball of string from Nancy's kitchen drawer. You studied Ken's theater blueprints and somehow managed to heist those war toys and dolls. Ken gave you the run of the house because you're his best friend, and this—*this* is how you paid him back."

"Are you nuts, Ellie-Ellie? What string? What dolls? What are you talking about?"

"Earlier tonight I told Peter that you had no motive because, oh God, how I prayed it wasn't you."

"It wasn't. It's not. It's me." Nancy Trask stepped out from behind another stack of cartons. "You knew all the time, didn't you, Sean? That's why you just said that thing about shared responsibility."

"I figured it out after Hansen's murder." Sean tossed his hat toward the lightbulb and the bulb began to swing.

Ellie watched brief blobs of illumination create dancing

shadows across liquor boxes. Shadow boxes, she thought. She felt the urge to shadowbox Nancy, but merely stood there, waiting for an explanation, answers, an *ending*.

"I paid Vicky a condolence call," said Sean. "She told me that the killer had ripped pages from her pad and practiced writing on her typewriter. It's hard to type Latin unless you know the language well, so the killer gave up. Police confiscated the scraps, but Vicky remembered two words. *Fiat,* because of the car, and *experimentum,* because it sounded like experiment."

"*Fiat experimentum in corpore vili,*" said Ellie.

"Let the experiment be performed on a worthless body." Sean winced, as though he'd rubbed a lemon slice across an open sore. "I was talking about my sick wife, Nancy."

"Jacques Hansen," she said. "Stupid, stupid man. Swore he'd discovered the killer's identity. Jacques couldn't have seen me go backstage. But when Melody returned from the bathroom without me, I thought Jacques had put two and two together. He called and said he wanted to discuss the ballerina's murder. I knew he was bluffing, yet he sounded so sly, so positive. *Asshole!* Want to hear something funny? He thought it was Ken. If Jacques had kept his mouth shut, he'd be alive today."

"Why—" Ellie swallowed and rubbed her eyes, erasing tears. "Why did you cut off his fingers?"

"I was so angry, I couldn't think straight. You see, I had to plan an airtight alibi. Checked into my health club, sneaked out wearing leotard and tights, then returned later to shower and throw away the bloody workout clothes. It was such a hassle. I'm sorry you found Hansen's body, Ellie. It must have been a real shock."

"Vicky might have lost her baby, Nancy. Did you think about that?"

"Yes, but I couldn't take a chance. Jacques had a way of getting people to confess. So Nancy shot him with Ken's gun. Ken bought that gun years ago when we lived in New York. We were robbed twice," she added indignantly.

"After the ballet," said Ellie, "you didn't wait in line for the bathroom?"

"Melody waited. I bid her godspeed and hightailed it backstage."

"You said you wore a fur coat. Natalie's blood—"

"Fuck fake fur! I wore a black satin cape and hung it between other costumes on a rack inside the wardrobe room. The Star Bar Players had performed *Dracula* on Halloween. My cape looked like part of Drac's ensemble."

"What did *you* wear home?"

"Dracula's cape. Nobody noticed. Nobody ever looks at *me*. Except Sean, bless his heart."

"You went through the passageway to Natalie's dressing room?" It was a rhetorical question, and Ellie didn't expect an answer. But she got one—a doozy.

"The trapdoor was my idea," said Nancy. "I designed the recital hall, not Ken. I designed all his buildings." She turned toward Sean. "You knew I was the murderer and kept silent even when we made love?"

"I share the responsibility." Gazing down at the floor, he whispered, "And the guilt."

"I don't have any guilt, darling." She laughed. "Poor Sean. Insane wife. Psychopathic lover."

"You're not psychopathic, Nancy."

"Oh yes, I am. I don't sit in the corner and suck my thumb like your wife does, Sean. I prefer to be actively crazy. Dammit, I couldn't get free from Ken, couldn't find a way to kill him, because if it wasn't done right I'd be the first one the police suspected."

"Why didn't you simply divorce Ken?"

Ignoring Ellie's question, Nancy said, "Twelve wonderful years with Sean, and Ken never guessed. Why would he? I was his damn *musame*, his American moose. Nancy told Ken about Sean just before she killed him. Pricked his pride while she shot his prick. Let him take her confession to hell. You believe in hell, don't you, Father Mac?"

Ellie watched Sean trace the contours of a liquor carton

with his first finger. For a moment she thought he'd genu-
flect. Instead, he slumped over several carbonated drink
capsules, their coiled hoses a nest of metal vipers.

"*Ego te absolvo,*" he murmured.

"Forgiven?" Nancy laughed again. "Not a chance. Sit
down, Ellie, it's a long story."

Serial killers love to talk, thought Ellie. When they talk
about their murders, they talk about themselves in third
person and they feel no guilt.

"Peter will be searching for me," she said aloud.

"I don't think so, my dear. I saw you two arguing earlier.
Even if he does investigate, I told Charley that I'd taken his
missing darts home this afternoon and forgotten to bring them
back. I said that you and I were going to retrieve his arrows.
We can be gone quite a while before anybody gets suspicious."

"Peter's not stupid, Nancy. He'll check the parking lot and
see that your car's still here."

"I didn't come to the party in 'TRASK-1' or 'WIFE-1.' We
carpooled. Howie volunteered his company Cadillac."

Ellie sat on top of an open crate of champagne bottles.
Cheap-cheap, she thought, as foil-covered plastic corks poked
at the exposed skin on her thighs. But she was too emotionally
exhausted to move from her uncomfortable perch.

"I guess the best way to explain is to start at the
beginning," said Nancy. "I was born one cold, gray winter
morning in December."

"Don't editorialize," muttered Sean.

"Yes, editorialize," said Ellie.

Nancy's almost-smile flickered. " 'You were a goddamn
accident,' my father used to say. I heard his words. I never
saw his face, his mouth, only the back of the hand he used
to bounce me around the room. 'I almost died giving birth
to you,' whined my mother. I saw her face clearly. *She* slapped
with words."

"Are you trying to make Ellie feel sorry for you?"

"No, Sean. I've had enough 'Poor Nancy's to last a
lifetime. I'm not looking for sympathy."

"Then why the disquisition? What's the point?"

"Please, Sean, don't. Ellie has to understand. You've got to understand, too. I told you about Todd." Her mouth quivered. "My older brother Todd was the apple of my parents' eye. Todd got new clothes while I inherited his hand-me-downs. Todd took guitar and drum lessons while I *begged* for ballet lessons. Todd needed two rooms, one for his instruments, so I slept in the basement where it was always dark and musty. I dreamed about rats. One night I woke up and there was this big ol' rat sitting on my chest."

"Oh God, you poor thing," blurted Ellie, shuddering.

"We became friends. I named him Matt. Matt the rat. You see, I had this big crush on 'Gunsmoke' 's Matt Dill—"

"Nancy, please!"

"Am I editorializing again? Sorry, Sean. Even you've never heard all the details, and Ellie has to understand why I must kill her." Reaching into her deep pants pocket, Nancy retrieved a small gun with a rubber-nippled silencer. "My parents presented Todd with his first car at age fifteen. Another new car at eighteen. I had never even owned a *bike*. Mother discovered Matt, and Father set traps. Is there a heaven for rats, Sean?"

"*Dei gratia.*"

"What?"

"By the grace of God," said Ellie.

"Nancy planned Todd's death very carefully. She bought him a bottle of Boodles gin with her babysitting money. Isn't that a funny name? Boodles? She told him she wanted to have sex with him, that she'd read books and wanted to practice. Her brother thought it was a great idea, but said that he was too drunk and needed her help. So he let her tie his arms and legs to his car's steering wheel, the bondage bit. 'Go down on me, Nan,' he said. She poured the rest of the gin down his throat, stuffed rags under the garage door, then turned on the ignition. Todd choked and whoopsed. Ugh! I can't tolerate the sight of vomit or snot. Puke and buggers are so disgusting."

The lightbulb wasn't swinging anymore, thought Ellie, so why did the shadows still seem to dance? Now they were waltzing toward haphazardly stacked zinfandel cartons.

"Nancy walked across the street and began to bounce her ball. One potato, two potato, three potato, four. No, dammit, that's jump rope, I must be losing my mind. Anyway, it occurred to Nancy that she might be blamed for Todd's death. She went back inside the garage. Todd had passed out. She retrieved the rags, untied Todd, pulled a pack of cigarettes and a silver lighter from his pocket. The cigarettes were Lucky Strikes. Todd's lighter was engraved with his initials. Nancy wanted people to think that Todd, stinko, had tried to light his cigarette, and they did. Her brother blistered and oozed like a Stephen King character. Have you ever read King, Ellie? Of course you have. Everybody has. The house burned, too. Nancy's parents were inside, asleep. They went to bed early. A horrible accident, just like her birth."

"You were young, abused, confused," said Sean.

"I was sixteen. But Nancy didn't mean to kill her parents, just Todd. The fire engines came. They watered the lawn, the flowers, the house. Flames lit up the night. The fire engines were red. They had a dalmatian. Poor dog was hit by a piece of flaming debris and burned, just like a Stephen King dog. King loves to kill dogs. And cats. And kids. Stephen King's my hero. Remember that old riddle, Ellie? What's black and white and red all over? A newspaper. An embarrassed zebra. A dalmatian on fire.

"*Whoosh*. Smoke, flames, it was a goddamn silent movie. Everybody moved their lips, but there was no sound, just *whoosh*. Nancy watched from across the street while her parents burned. Ken watched, too. He saw the whole thing from the very start. She was hysterical because of her mother and father, because of the accident. Why bother killing Todd with her parents dead? They wouldn't love her better. She told Ken to drive her to the police station. She wanted to confess. Ken said that was stupid and it wouldn't bring her parents back, and he promised that he'd always protect her."

"Men were created to protect their women," said Ellie, remembering the carside hustle.

"Ken didn't love me, either. He needed a slave. I worked to put him through school and learned more than he did. Finished his assignments, waited on him hand and foot, so grateful. When he became an architect, I drafted his buildings. I designed your home, Ellie, and the house for Ken's mistress. Nancy killed her, then cremated her body and buried the ashes. Ladybug, ladybitch, fly away home. Fire, fire everywhere. Ashes to ashes, dust to dus—"

"Please," cried Sean, "no more."

Would he make it through Nancy's confession with his stomach intact? wondered Ellie. She was immune after Jacques and Ken. Perhaps the mind could only consume so much horror before it became insulted. She'd probably react later. If there was a later.

Walking toward the back of the storeroom, Nancy retrieved an open bottle of gin—Beefeaters. Then she tilted the bottle to her lips with her left hand and drank. Her right hand held the gun.

"My throat's dry as dust," she said. "Okay, where was I? The mistress. After she vanished, Ken and I flew to Hawaii and we had a goddamn second honeymoon while I dreamt up the recital hall. I should have left Ken a long time ago, but he knew too much about me."

"Isn't there a statute of limitations?" asked Sean.

Ellie thought the question bizarre under the circumstances. In any case, there was no statute of limitations on murder.

"I was trapped," Nancy said bitterly. "Ken kept mentioning the fire. Pull the strings and watch Nance dance. I think Ken guessed about the 'M*A*S*H' murders, but he kept on *protecting* me. Why wouldn't he? He had a good thing going. Kenneth Trask couldn't design a fuckin' doghouse for Klinger, not without *my* expertise."

"Please stop swearing," muttered Sean.

"But I don't understand why you killed those other

people," said Ellie, then realized that she still felt sorry for
Nancy. Matt the rat had done it.

"The whole thing started with Virginia Whitley, my dear.
One potato. Then Ken's mistress. Two potatoes. Everybody
knew about her. I was such an object of ridicule. Ken just
laughed when I asked him to be more discreet. He said Frank
Burns wasn't discreet. She—Ken's mistress looked like—he
called her Hot Lips. Same blond hair, sexy. I could bleach my
hair and join your diet club, Ellie, but I'd never look like Hot
Lips. She was the type who attracted Ken. I merely raised his
son and drafted his blueprints. Blue. The perfect color. Blue.
Sad."

The perfect color. The perfect murder. The perfect lapse
in perfection.

Aloud, Ellie asked, "Why did you kill Natalie?"

"What makes you think—"

"The charm. That's her necklace, right?"

Nancy nodded. "I took it as a souvenir. Ken promised to
finance Natalie's dancing career. But he procrastinated. He
preferred keeping her here, showing her off to Howie. Funny,
isn't it? Jacques figured that part out."

So did I, thought Ellie. Natalie and Daddy Ken.

"The dog tag," said Ellie. "Margaret Houl—"

"I picked it up in Denver after Klinger's vet moved there.
I bought it for me. I wanted to play Hot Lips in bed, but I
never got the chance. Ken had already found his dancer. I
knew the dog tag couldn't be traced; the shop's gone out of
business."

"Why," said Ellie, "did you kill Frank Burns?"

"You killed Frank Burns?" Sean shook his head. "I don't
understand. Frank's not real. He's imaginary."

"Not Frank, darling, Harry. Franklin Harrison Burns.
Sanctimonious prick! He was screwing around on his wife."

"But we were having our own affair."

"It's not the same. I didn't flaunt you like Frank Burns
flaunted Hot Lips, like Harry flaunted his Mex whore, like
Ken flaunted his mistress. All my life people have flaunted

things. Todd, Ken, even you, Sean, with your sick wife Juliet and your sense of honor. I couldn't even have *you* all to myself."

"Did you steal something from Harry's house, Nancy?"

"I took a Daffy Duck glass, Ellie. How did you know?"

"I . . . serial . . . lucky guess."

"Anyhow, we met Harry at the supermarket, and his wife looked so pathetic. Ken wrote down their address, and I copied it. Then I bugged Harry's phone while his pathetic wife was home alone. I pretended to check the equipment, just like Sean does; it helps to have a lover who works for the telephone company. One morning I caught Burns calling for an appraisal. He planned to sell his house and live with his whore. Well, I couldn't let that happen, could I? So Nancy pretended she was a real estate agent and killed him the same way she killed Todd. Well, not really. She didn't burn Burns. And she used Chivas, not Boodles."

"Did you commit the Dumpster murders?" asked Ellie.

"What Dumpster murders?"

"The couple killed and trashed at the apart—"

"Killed and trashed? What fun."

Okay, so I barked up the wrong tree, thought Ellie. But then, *I'm* not perfect.

"What about Leo Krafchek?" she asked.

"He had a wife, three kids, and a lover. Howie sold him insurance, and Krafchek made his whore the beneficiary. Can you believe that shit? Howie and Ken laughed about it. Then Nancy saw Krafchek and his wife at the ballet. After she dropped off Jacques and Vicky and Sean, she drove aimlessly, no special direction, and there he was, Krafchek, in a bar. Nancy saw him through the window. The knife was in her purse—"

"Wait a minute! What about that piece of paper with words cut from *TV Guide*? If you just happened to see Krafchek, how could you have a note handy?"

"I didn't. I drove home, cut and pasted, then drove back and waited till he left the bar. Nancy likes to drive, Ellie."

"What did you do with the murder weapon?"

"You saw it when you came to visit, my dear. I used it on my roast."

How very Hitchcockian, my dear, thought Ellie.

Sean gagged. "You sliced our dinner roast with a knife that had stabbed two people?"

"I cleaned it first."

"Nancy," said Ellie, "why'd you kill Virginia Whitley?"

"Virginia." She sipped from the Beefeaters bottle. "The M*A*S*H-Bash. Ken and Ginny."

"She had nothing to do with Ken," said Sean. "Howie was trying to palm her off on Fred."

"You're such an innocent, my darling. Ken followed her inside the rest room—"

"Hold it, you weren't there," said Sean.

"Of course I was there. I blended in fine. So many people, and I sat in the corner, away from lights. It was like sitting behind a one-way mirror. I followed Ken and waited outside the bathroom. Somebody else was waiting, too, but he took one look at Ginny and bolted. Ken led Ginny down the hall, past the kitchen, into this very room. He toted a pitcher of beer, and she chugged it all and then went out of her mind. Ripped off her clothes. 'Eat pussy, drink Gin,' she screamed. They began to fu—"

"Don't swear," cried Sean. "Please don't swear."

"Okay, humped. It's really a better word because that's exactly what they did. Humped. The door was open a crack, and I watched. Afterward, Ginny cried, and Ken dressed her like you'd dress a rag doll, like my son used to dress Klinger. I finally got rid of those fuckin' toys."

"Memorial Park," said Ellie.

"Yup. I thought I'd read about it in the newspaper—what fun—but your detective took the dolls away so quickly. That was mean, Ellie."

"Peter has a mean streak. You should have been there when he told me about the bodies."

"Where was I? Oh yes. Ginny was hysterical, so Ken

buggered off, the bastard. He didn't see me. I ran down the hall and ducked into the kitchen. When I returned to the storeroom, Ginny said she didn't feel good. I helped her outside. There's a back door. Fresh air, I said, might make her feel better. She took one deep breath, fell to the ground, and tossed her cookies. Disgusting! She was in such pain, kept moaning 'I want to die, I want to die,' so Nancy killed her with Ken's car."

"Ken's car," repeated Sean, his voice a gurgle.

"Well, Nancy wasn't stupid enough to drive her own car, darling. She took a bus."

Ellie gasped. "You planned to kill Ginny?"

"No, Nancy planned to kill Ken, but Ginny was so easy. It was like running over those tittie-bumps at the parking-lot entrance. Except Ginny was squishy."

"Blood," said Ellie, dazed. "The tires must have been covered with—"

"Nancy drove to a car wash, the one where you plunk quarters down a slot. Then she drove back; she likes to—"

"Drive. Yes, I know. How did *you* get home?"

"Dan."

"Dan? Oh, the cowboy."

"It was scary. I thought he might crash his truck. He was stinko. Called me Melanie."

"Melody."

"What?"

"Dan brought Melody one double martini."

"Really? Lucky strike for me she didn't fancy him. Anyhow, he kept singing something about happy trails while he fingered my boobs."

"You slept with a *cowboy?*" asked Sean.

"No, I made him let me off a few blocks from home and I walked. Walking's good exercise. Don't you preach that at your diet club, Ellie? Nancy burned lots of calories while killing Ginny. There's a rush, you know, like good sex."

Now Ellie *did* feel sick to her stomach. Sean, too. Retching, he leaned over the soda capsules.

Nancy maneuvered around cartons. "Sean darling, I promise I won't talk any more. I thought you knew."

"I figured the mistress and Hansen. Gin—I believed Fred was involved with Ginny's death. He was so nervous. I thought he started to take her home, and she fell from his Jeep, and he ran her over. I'm sick, Nancy."

"Sean, no, please. Here, drink."

"I can't."

"It will settle your tummy, darling."

Sean tilted the Beefeaters bottle and drank. When he'd finished, large beads of sweat pebbled his forehead, and his shoulders spasmed.

"Listen, darling, we'll leave the Dew Drop soon, and then I'll cook some veggie medicine. Oatmeal cookies, too."

"Please . . . do . . . not . . . mention . . . food."

"Sorry. You can't be sick, Sean. Nancy needs you."

"Can't . . . uh . . . help it . . . uh . . . uh . . ."

"No, Sean, no, don't throw up. I've never been able to tolerate sick people. Oh, very well, if you really must."

Ellie watched with disbelief. Here was a woman who had cold-bloodedly snuffed her brother, burned her parents, squished one woman with a car, cremated another, knifed two people, shot her husband's penis, severed a man's fingers. Now she couldn't bear the sight of *vomit?*

I must be dreaming, thought Ellie. Soon she'd see barking dogs, corpses, maggot-infested cats, and Nancy Trask on top of the tree.

Turning away from Sean, Nancy placed both hands across her ears and closed her eyes, shutting out the sight and sound of Sean's pitiful performance. The gun rested against her hair, pointed toward the ceiling.

It's now or never, thought Ellie. I won't get another opportunity.

Her hand dipped between her legs and closed around the neck of a champagne bottle. Stripping the foil with her fingernails, she was relieved to find no twisted wire.

I knew it. Cheap stuff. Shame on you, Charley.

Aiming at Nancy's gun, Ellie thumbed the champagne bottle's plastic cork. It flew through the air and struck Nancy's left shoulder. In reflex, she dropped the gun and clutched her shoulder with her right hand.

Ellie followed the cork's flight. Her body hit Nancy's, and they fell together. Although Nancy was strong as an ox, Ellie used the moves Peter had demonstrated and finally secured Nancy's arms behind her back.

"Let her go," said Sean, picking up the gun.

"Goodie, goodie. After you kill her, we're free. We'll put her body in the freezer with Ken. My husband was screwing that slutty singer in this very room, just like Ginny. But the singer passed out before Ken could finish. She's in the parking lot. Nancy dragged her there. Too bad Nancy didn't have Ken's car handy."

"Ken's in the freezer?" Sean's face was very green.

"Oh dear, I promised not to mention dead bodies."

"Put down the gun," said Ellie calmly.

"Let us go, Ellie-Ellie. I won't shoot if you keep your mouth shut and give us a head start."

"Are you crazy, Sean?" Nancy's eyes glittered. "How far do you think we'd get? She'd scream her head off."

"Would you, Ellie-Ellie?"

"No."

"Let Nancy kill her, Sean."

"Give me the gun, Father Mac."

"I can't," he cried. "I'll lock you up inside the freezer, okay?"

"But she'll freeze to death," said Nancy. "That's not very considerate, darling."

"I'll take my chances," said Ellie. "Let's go," she urged before Sean could change his mind.

All three entered the hallway.

And ran smack-dab into Peter. He aimed his revolver toward Sean, who'd instinctively pulled Ellie against his body. Leveling Nancy's gun at Ellie's forehead, Sean said, "Drop it, Lieutenant."

"No, Peter, he won't shoot. *Nancy's* our kill—"

"Father Mac, Nance, Ellie, I've been lookin' all over for you." Fred Remming strolled down the hallway, clutching his teddy bear. "Melody's gettin' ready to open her birthday presents, but she won't start without Nance and Ellie, and I wanna leave soon. Howie Doo-doo gave me one of his girls, the one in Charley's office. She's better now, and looks like *her*—hey, what's goin' on?"

Ellie had felt Sean release his tight hold at the sight of Fred. Wrenching free, she stepped forward, grabbed Fred's bear, then turned and batted the gun away. Even after she heard the clatter of metal skidding, she kept slamming the bear against Sean's chest.

"Whoa, uncle, I give up," he yelped. Turning toward Nancy, he said softly, "*Ego te amo.* I love you."

Ellie dropped the bear and trembled while Peter whistled loudly several times. William McCoy and the other detective came running. They handcuffed Nancy and Sean, then escorted them toward the back exit.

As Peter led Ellie into the Dew Drop's lounge, she was struck by the normalcy of the scene. Mick strummed his guitar, Sandra sang, Melody danced with Gordon, Hawkeye smiled from his poster. On Charley's overhead TV a taped "M*A*S*H" show flickered. Hot Lips could rerun through eternity.

Was there another nut out there watching "Star Trek" repeats, planning to kill Mr. Spock look-alikes? That would be more difficult. How many men had pointy ears? Ellie began to laugh at the thought.

Peter swiftly propelled her onto a stool, hurdled the bar, reached for a bottle, poured, then handed her a snifter of brandy.

"Drink it all down," he said.

"Spock, Peter, *hic.*" Ignoring the snifter, she separated her first two fingers from the last two, and gestured with a Leonard Nimoy benediction.

Peter leaned across the bar, grasped her shoulders, and

stared into her eyes. *"Ego te amo.* Did I say that right?"

"Perfect. I, *hic,* love you, too." She took a deep breath and counted to ten. "Peter, how did you know I was in the, *hic,* storeroom?"

"Well, at first I believed you'd gone with Nancy to retrieve Charley's darts. When Trask didn't return, I began to fret, but Howie Silverman kept me occupied. He wanted to escort Melody's rum-drinking girlfriends home, and he kept bitching about how his Cadillac couldn't tote Ken, Nancy, Father Mac, Fred, and Melody's friends. 'Fudge carpooling,' he said, then hinted that I might consider chauffeuring the gaggle of guests. Christ, I must have consumed too much celery tonic, Norrie, because it took a few minutes to realize that Nancy had driven to the party with Silverman. Anyway, I checked the parking lot for your Honda—"

"Mein Gott!" Charley joined Peter behind the bar. "Mrs. Trask was meshuga. A dead body inside my strolling ice chest. The priest tossed his cookies all over my soda pop. *Oy vey,* does Eleanor have the hiccups? Move your tush, Lieutenant, and let me pour. Vodka and Kahlua are good for spastics."

"Spasms, Charley, not spastics, *hic."*

"Drink my free Russian, Eleanor."

"Don't worry, she'll be fine," said Peter. "In one week she'll be searching for a new mystery to unravel."

Ellie drowned her hiccups with Charley's Russian. "I don't have to wait a week," she said between sips. "During the football game, we talked about a policeman shot in his car and a woman discarded at a cemetery, not to mention those damn Dumpster homicides. If you let me peruse the files, Lieutenant, I'll solve your unsolvable crimes."

"Over my dead body, Norrie."

"I prefer your body alive," she replied, then leaned across the bar for Peter's kiss.

In his youth, thought Charley, people kissed in private, under the table. Like that couple over there.

"Hey you," shouted Charley. "Yes you, Mr. Bird-of-Prey. Stop eating Miss Hot Mouth under my table. It ain't kosher."